THE
SECOND
GLASS

OF
ABSINTHE

THE SECOND GLASS OF ABSINTHE

A Mystery of the Victorian West

MICHELLE BLACK

FORGE®

A TOM DOHERTY ASSOCIATES BOOK
NEW YORK

THE SECOND GLASS OF ABSINTHE

Copyright © 2003 by Michelle Black

This book is printed on acid-free paper.

A Forge Book
Published by Tom Doherty Associates, LLC
175 Fifth Avenue
New York, NY 10010

www.tor.com

Forge® is a registered trademark of Tom Doherty Associates, LLC.

ISBN 0-765-30854-1

First Edition: September 2003

Printed in the United States of America

0 9 8 7 6 5 4 3 2 1

This book is dedicated to all the usual suspects
who reside in my heart:
Doug, Ross, Brendan, and Krystle

ACKNOWLEDGMENTS

I wish to thank my editor, Dale Walker, for his tireless assistance, guidance, and friendship. Thanks also to my agent, Nat Sobel, whose counsel and critique are always impeccable.

The writings and theories of Jonathan Ned Katz were priceless to me in developing the characters for this book, particularly his groundbreaking study, *Love Stories: Sex Between Men Before Homosexuality.*

A special thanks also to Dr. James Harding, for his technical advice on nineteenth-century dentistry, and to Robert Gleason, for his knowledge and expertise on tarot cards.

Prologue

*After the first glass [of absinthe] you see things as
you wish they were. After the second, you see
things as they are not. Finally, you see things as
they really are, and that is the most horrible thing
in the world.*

—Oscar Wilde

A cold, black wave washes over him and he picks up the
scent of cloves. He can hear the ocean, yet he lives more
than a thousand miles from the nearest coast.

When the black water recedes, a splinter of moonlight
parts the draperies and casts a luminous wedge of silver-
gray light into her darkened bedroom.

Images, feelings, memories all blur into a confusing
mosaic. He feels a light kiss upon his lips.

Kiss him again. You know you want to.

The soft lips return and linger passionately. The large bed
floats upon the waves in an undulating, seesaw fashion that
makes him feel dizzy.

Where are the bedsheets? The room is so cold. May is a
cold month at ten thousand feet. He is used to hot summers
with nights as shiny and black as beetles' wings. The shift in
climate worries him. He senses a chill upon the naked skin

of his belly. His hands and feet feel enshrouded in ice like the buds of the aspen trees on frosty alpine mornings.

See how he wants this? she whispers. *Just look at him.*

A caressing hand wanders down his torso and strokes him . . . strong, rhythmic strokes. He wants to speak, but cannot locate any words.

"What?" he finally manages to say. Or has he merely thought he said it?

The hungry mouth kisses his neck, his chest, his belly. A warm tongue invades his navel, then travels farther south. She's never kissed him there before. He flinches at the novel sensation.

The ocean roars in his ears and he picks up the scent of cloves again.

Another crash of breakers and he stands on a hot, sunny beach. He is nine years old and all his family is around him: his mother, his grandmother, his aunt, and his twenty-four-year-old uncle, Brad.

They all wear bathing costumes, all except his grandmother, who is so old-fashioned as to believe such garments to be indecent.

Uncle Brad has brought with him his fiancée, Miss Markham, who looks so stunning in her bathing ensemble she could be mistaken for an angel, a goddess. The other bathers gape openly at her and she soaks up their admiring gazes along with the broiling rays of the sun. His uncle dips his head beneath her dainty blue parasol and steals a kiss from her, as though to proclaim to the world, *She's mine.*

Then Uncle Brad turns to him and says, *Let's go!*

Miss Markham smiles and waves as they run off into the rush of the oncoming waters. The sun has warmed the shallow depths but the sea grows colder as they head deeper. When the water reaches waist high, he stops, unable to go on. He sees a huge wave heading straight for his uncle. The sun glances off the crest of the water to blind him for an instant. He clenches his hands into fists and pinches coarse sand between his toes. Is Miss Markham still watching them? He worries that she will notice how scared he is.

He sees his uncle dive into the mouth of the breaker. The wall of water swallows him whole. He feels a moment of terror until Brad re-emerges on the other side, laughing as he pushes his dripping hair back from his face.

Come on, Kit, don't be scared!

He trembles as he braces himself for the looming monster to strike. The massive wave envelops him in its shadow before the force of it knocks him off his feet. He barrel-rolls out of control. Water shoots up his nostrils. He panics and chokes as he thrashes helplessly, not knowing which way is up.

Then a strong arm encircles his skinny chest and locks him in a tight grasp below his armpits. His face comes out of the water just inches from that of his laughing young uncle. He is so happy, he wants to cry. He coughs and sneezes at the same time, which makes Uncle Brad laugh harder.

Going to be all right?

He swallows hard, but manages to smile. He wraps his arms and legs around his uncle and kisses his cheek.

He opens his eyes again, but sees only darkness. Are his eyes open or not? The sandy beach has vanished, but there is the reassuring wedge of moonlight and he knows he is still in her bedroom.

"What? I . . ."

Are you mad? Someone will see us.
There's nobody around for miles. Come on.

He feels that luscious mouth at work on him, slow and sensuous at first, then faster.

"Time flies, time flies," squawks the parrot in the corner.

"Stop," he says with a growing sense of alarm. Will another wave hit him? Why are his arms and legs useless? Why does the bed float upon the ocean? Yet the wedge of moonlight does not waver. His thoughts collide and make no sense. The room is so cold, yet his loins are on fire, stealing all the blood from the rest of his body.

Waves of pleasure flood through him, stronger in force than the wall of water. He does not understand where he is or what is happening. He wants the mouth to stop its tantalizing motion. And he also wants it never to stop. He swells larger and harder in response, a slave to the exquisite sensations bearing him aloft.

"No," he says in confusion, but the word sounds more like a plea than a command. The delicious feelings build to an intolerable peak. He longs for release, but he is afraid. Another wild breaker is headed straight for him. He braces himself for it to hit. Will the water feel cold or hot? Where is his uncle? Will no one rescue him?

He cannot hold back any longer. With an unstoppable moan, he spends it all, the blessed relief pulses out of him. He gasps for breath, then relaxes, undone and exhausted.

The scent of cloves fills his nostrils as wet lips press his cheek for one last kiss.

"Time flies, time flies."

The black wave silently engulfs him once again, drowning him in the blissful refuge of sleep.

One

MAY 1880

A second glass of absinthe is usually a mistake. Kit Randall had learned that much since his arrival in Leadville. He had come to this town in the clouds looking for the kind of fun that gives fun a bad name and absinthe never failed him on that score.

"Green" dreams were frequently strange and sometimes frightening, but could they produce a vision never imagined, much less experienced, by its dreamer? Was that why Lucinda limited their adventures over the slotted spoon to once a week?

"We must be prudent, darling," she would say. But she was prudent about so little else.

Waking up alone in the big bed, Kit yawned and stretched himself. How many hours had he slept? The sun shone through the sparkling, leaded panes of the bay window with such intensity and at so high an angle it must have been nearly noon. That the curtains were drawn open was Lucinda's not-so-subtle hint that he had slept too late.

He massaged his temples to try to soothe the brutal pounding in his head. He felt like an ice pick had been

13

forced into his brain. The pain radiated out in all directions, starlike, but gritty.

His mouth was dry as parchment. He looked for the bedside pitcher, but found it empty. He felt as though he did not have enough energy to fetch some water, though his thirst tormented him.

Lucinda poked her head in the room. "Oh, you're awake."

She walked briskly to the bedside, saw that the water pitcher was empty, and picked it up to refill it. She looked so beautiful in her lace dressing gown, which allowed a generous view of her bosom. She did not own a single dress that did not advertise those round, perfect breasts. Gazing down that enticing décolletage had aroused him through a hundred dinners and caused him to lose interest in the food before him. And Lucinda's coy smile always told him she knew precisely the effect she was having, though she often slid a wanton hand into his lap, just to check.

She even did this sometimes when they were dining with her son. This embarrassed Kit. If Christopher Ridenour raised his eyes from his plate at just the wrong moment, he would surely see what his mother was up to. Kit suspected she enjoyed the challenge of keeping a straight face while indecently fondling her young lover under the tablecloth. No wonder she had made a good living on the stage prior to her marriage.

Scandalous behavior carried few consequences for Lucinda. As the widowed heiress to the Eye Dazzler Mining fortune, she could pretty well do as she pleased and everybody knew it. Leadville, Colorado, was the richest mining district on earth and the richest mine there by far was the Eye Dazzler.

Twenty-year-old Christopher would not dare to object. He was the shyest human being Kit had ever met, a turtle of a boy, almost impossible to coax from his shell. He rarely spoke above a whisper and virtually never made eye contact with anyone. Kit barely knew the color of his eyes, they were so seldom visible, hidden beneath his downcast red-gold lashes.

He served as his mother's accountant for the various Ridenour ventures which, in addition to the mine, included a casino on State Street called the High Life Club. Though the atmosphere of the High Life was a constant riot of high-rolling mirth, Christopher seldom emerged from his tiny office in the back. He apparently found better company in his endless columns of figures and stacks of account books and his collection of carefully sharpened pencils all laid out in a row.

Kit could tell that the quiet boy was intelligent. In an unexpected moment he could offer a remark or opinion of surprising wit or insight. That Christopher did not mind Kit moving into their home and into his mother's bed gave Kit pause. But only a moment's pause.

His eyes now fell upon the ebonized surface of the bed's footboard. The elaborate carvings reminded him of ocean waves. He had not seen the ocean in more than a year.

Lucinda returned with the pitcher filled and he eagerly gulped water straight from it without bothering to pour it into a glass. This small breach of decorum made her frown.

His terrible thirst slaked at last, he wiped his wet chin on the bed sheet. "Lucy, tell the maid to make up the fire. This room is chilly."

Lucinda made yet another sour face. "I'll have to start it

up myself. You know Sadie won't come in here when you're not dressed."

"I'll put a robe on," he said, then muttered under his breath, "like she's never seen a man in his drawers before," in contemptuous reference to Sadie Branch's previous profession in the State Street brothels. The Ridenour house did not seem able to attract servants with very nice reputations. He had wondered about this more than once.

"Never mind, Lucy."

He watched her fuss about the room, preparing for her day. Her long hair hanging loose upon her shoulders gave her a girlish look, despite her thirty-six years. He glanced up at the oil portrait of her above the mantel of her bedroom fireplace. In it, she reclined upon her favorite chair and held her parrot, Mr. Sparks. Even playing with a pet, she looked sensuous, with her cascade of reddish brown hair hanging down the chair back.

He had naively thought her hair was naturally red. After all, her son had red-tinged hair, though it tended toward strawberry blond.

He learned the truth one day when he watched her maid apply the henna. So much of Lucinda was artifice; would he ever know the balance of what was real and what was carefully contrived illusion?

"What's wrong, darling boy? Why such a long face? Don't you know I live to see those dimples each morning?"

Her round Southern vowels bloomed and dripped. He loved the lilting music of her voice so much he ignored the possibility that one of her Rebel relatives might have shot his father dead in '62. That savage conflict was fast becoming an old man's war. He had no memories of it, just as he had no memories of the father who died at the age of twenty-one, just the age he was now. Whenever Kit looked ahead in his life, he now thought of all the things his father had been cheated of. That somehow made the future all the more precious.

"I have a headache," he said with a slight pout.

"Poor baby. A hangover?"

"I didn't drink enough last night to cause a hangover."

"At this altitude, who knows? Do you want to take something? Let me go see what I have."

"You and your pills and powders. Sure, of course."

She brought him an envelope containing white powder. She had all sorts of concoctions at her disposal. Her dressing room was better stocked than most pharmacies.

They indulged in a wide variety of drugs during their many decadent nights together. Opium from the Orient, hashish from Morocco, absinthe from France—no sordid diversion fell beyond the reach of the Eye Dazzler money. Some of the drugs made Kit feel giddy, some sleepy, others made him think he was flying or that he possessed extraordinary strength. One memorable powder had the ability to prolong the sexual act ten times beyond the norm. He and Lucinda both woke up quite sore the morning after that one.

"What do you plan to do with your day?" she asked as she poured him a glass of water to mix the powder in.

"If I can get rid of this headache, I thought I would go down and work with that new gelding you bought. He's crazy, you know."

"He's just green. That's why we got such a good price on him."

"He's more than green. We might have to hire a professional trainer for him."

She was in her dressing room and might not have heard him. He could see her pulling out and then discarding a number of frocks. She went through this ritual every morning. He grinned and shook his head. With a perverse snicker, he added, "You like geldings, don't you, Lucy?"

"Of course I do. It's the stallions and the mares who give you no peace."

He chuckled that she had missed his point. "Looks like a nice day. Why don't you come down to the stables with me?"

"I'd love to, darling," she said from the recesses of her enormous closet. "Unfortunately, I have to go up to the mine today. Christopher insists that we meet with Jacob. He's certain he's found evidence of wrongdoing on him. He's done something unforgivable and we're going to have to sack him. George Hauser says we have no choice. It's going to be a dreadful day. I'll need some of your very special cheering up tonight."

"That's what I'm good at. I live to amuse." He offered this lightly, but inwardly he sulked. He had originally hoped Lucinda would give him a position in one of the Ridenour companies. He was a college graduate after all, more than qualified to serve in any number of capacities. But three months had passed and he remained merely Lucinda's lover, her companion, her—he knew that others in town had far more creative names for his current situation, but he did not want to think about them. His official title of "houseguest" did not fool many.

"What's the story on you and old Jake?" he said, smirking with mischief. "Sadie Branch told me you took up with me just to spite him because he wouldn't leave his wife for you."

She poked her head out of the dressing room. "Malicious gossip. Stop talking to the servants."

He could only guess at her past relationship with Jacob Landry, but the man was far from friendly on the few occasions Kit had crossed his path.

The first time he had been introduced to the Eye Dazzler's superintendent, Lucinda had behaved in a curious manner and he quickly realized that more was going on than a simple business meeting. They had all sat around a table in the anteroom of the late Orson Ridenour's office. While Lucinda spoke of the renegotiation of smelting contracts, she placed her hand around Kit's neck and delicately stroked the skin above his collar as though he were a pet cat.

Landry's remarks had been formal and businesslike, but his dark eyes never left her slender fingers as they caressed her young lover's throat. Kit felt a cold heat radiate from the man's disturbing gaze. He discreetly removed himself from her toying embrace, resentful she had used him so. The damage was already done, however, the point decisively made.

Landry's parting smile at the end of that meeting had been the worst moment of all. The man had extended his hand and Kit took it, but for an instant, as their hands and eyes met, Landry's icy smile put Kit in mind of a line from *Macbeth*. The nervous sons of the murdered Macduff had worried about the "daggers in men's smiles," and Kit had never sought a moment alone with the Eye Dazzler superintendent after that. In fact, he had been more than happy just to get his hand back.

His thoughts returned to that bizarre absinthe dream. Why did it refuse to leave him? What had really happened here last night? In his only solid memory he had "watched the clouds come out." That was his euphemism for gazing at the slow, tantalizing process by which one prepares to drink the liqueur the French called *la fée verte*, the green fairy.

The light emerald liquid was dripped through a sugar cube that sat perched atop a slotted spoon. Icy water was then added which rendered a spectacular transformation. The clear green absinthe blossomed into a milky opalescence and was ready to sip.

He recalled settling back deep into the sea of sofa cushions in Lucinda's bohemian-inspired second parlor and staring up at the famous Eye Dazzler rug hanging on the wall. He loved to watch the bright zigzagging pattern come alive. A thousand triangles danced before his eyes in a carefully terraced lockstep, vibrating red-black-white, red-white-black, hypnotizing him as it always did.

And then . . . just a nonsense kaleidoscope of images and feelings, some very erotic, yet all strangely ominous.

He tried to muster the energy to get out of bed, but instead collapsed back down into the bedclothes and stared at the painted clouds on the high ceiling of the room. He remembered seeing those clouds in his dream, only they had floated over a raging seascape.

Then he caught the whiff of a familiar scent. He grabbed the pillow next to him and sniffed it. *Cloves*, no doubt of it.

No, no, no. Panic gripped him. His breath came in short, ragged spasms. *"Lucinda?"*

"Yes, darling?" she said from her dressing room.

"What happened here last night?"

She peered at him from around the edge of the door frame. A shadow crossed her face that seemed to age her ten years.

Two

"Imagine the irony," Lucinda said with a bitter smile.

After two hours of searching, Kit finally located a boarding house on Oak Street that did not require advance payment. The elderly widow who owned the house apparently judged him creditworthy by his well-groomed appearance and his finely cut pin-striped frock coat. Shamelessly employing the Randall family dimples did not hurt either. He had her giggling like a schoolgirl with his elaborate compliments.

She led him to his room on the second floor and announced the house rules: No alcohol, no chewing tobacco, and no immorality would be tolerated on the premises.

He collapsed onto the small bed the moment she left him alone. The angry words of his last argument with Lucinda still burned in his brain, playing over and over. He stared at the brown water stains on the ceiling.

"Did you dose me up with something last night?" he said, in horror at his own suspicions. "I don't even remember leaving the back parlor."

"Where do you get such notions?" Lucinda said, now recovering her usual blithe temper. "You ought to stay away from the absinthe. You simply can't handle it."

"Something happened last night. Something . . . unspeakable."

She smiled nervously. "Don't be silly, pet."

"I'm your pet? To use as you please?"

"Lower your voice, darling. Do you want half the neighborhood to hear this discussion?"

No, he did not want anyone to know this, ever.

"Just leave and let me get dressed."

"An excellent idea. I'll go have some breakfast made, although it must be nearly noon. I suppose we shall have to call it lunch."

"Don't bother. I'll be gone by then."

She smirked at this threat. "And where will you go? And with what money? Remember the night Christopher brought you home? You had nowhere else to stay. You'd gambled away your inheritance and your hotel had evicted you for nonpayment."

"I'd rather live in hell than with the pair of you!"

He would have to stay here in Leadville until the end of the month when his trust fund check usually showed up. He was not so destitute as Lucinda thought. He had kept his trust fund a secret from her so that she would not be tempted curb her lavish generosity to him.

The end of May seemed like an eternity away, so anxious was he to leave this accursed place, but he needed that check. One hundred and twenty-five dollars. Not a fortune, but enough for a twenty-one-year-old bachelor to live comfortably without a job.

He was feeling pretty destitute until he remembered there was a pawnbroker located over the bookstore he and

Christopher Ridenour used to frequent on a weekly basis, one of their favorite outings.

"Good day, Mrs. Lieninger," he said to the bookstore owner's wife as he entered the shop.

"Where's your shadow today, Mr. Randall?" she said, referring to Christopher.

"I'm visiting your neighbor. Business, not pleasure, I'm afraid." He gestured to the pawnshop upstairs.

Mrs. Lieninger had often remarked that he and Chris were her best customers—Leadville was not an intellectual town—since the passing of old Orson Ridenour, whose memory the woman never failed to praise.

"Too bad for me," she said and continued her dusting of the front window display.

He managed to hock one of the fine suits Lucinda had ordered custom-made for him. The tightfisted pawnbroker gave him only five dollars for it though the suit was worth fifty. Still it meant he would eat for a week.

He had next attempted to sell one of the horses Lucinda bought for him until the stableman informed him that any horse wearing the zigzagging Eye Dazzler brand could not be sold "without the personal say-so of the missus." Lucinda was no fool.

He was jerked out of his reverie when a heavy fist pounded on his door. He sat up, confused and still groggy.

"Open up, this is the police," came a voice from the hall.

Kit stumbled to the door.

"Are you Christopher Randall?"

"Yeah. So?"

"Someone swore out a complaint against you."

"What the hell?"

"Let's talk." The police sergeant ushered himself in without an invitation, but Kit did not protest.

The sergeant was an older man, late forties perhaps. He was fond of poker and roulette and was a regular at the High Life Club where Kit sometimes dealt faro when Lucinda was shorthanded. Kit knew his name was Sorel Weston—"Westy" to his friends, a select circle which did not include the Ridenours despite the many hours the man spent at their gaming tables.

"Lucinda Ridenour swore out a complaint that you stole some items from her house."

"That's a damned lie, sergeant. What does she say I stole?"

"Clothing, for one thing. Her son's clothes." He squinted at the piece of paper in his hand and read out, " 'Three suits, tailor-made of the finest wool; handmade shirts of imported cotton—' "

Kit stomped angrily over to his valise and opened it up. He pulled a shirt from it and displayed the embroidery on the inside of the collar. "Look at this, 'C.R.'—my initials."

"Could stand for 'Chris Ridenour.' "

"Chris is a whole head taller than me. A shirt like this would show three inches of his wrist, for christsake." He held the shirt against his body to show it fit him precisely.

"Also, a gold and silver watch," said the sheriff.

Kit pulled the watch in question from his pocket. A beautiful carving of a wolf's head embellished its cover. Lucinda picked it out because she was fond of calling him her "wolf cub." Lucinda adored everything pertaining to wolves. She even had a tattoo of a howling wolf framed by a full moon adorning her hip. He had never heard of a woman with a tattoo before—outside of the circus, that is—until he met

Lucinda. But he didn't know a lot of things until he met Lucinda.

He wished now he had thought to pawn the watch. He snapped open its cover to display the engraving, "*To my darling Christopher, love eternal.*"

Love eternal. Kit frowned and shook his head. With Lucinda, eternity had lasted three months. He said to the officer, "I suppose you're going to say she calls her son, 'my darling Christopher.' "

The older man shrugged. "Could be. The pair of them are little *too* close if you ask me. Most who've met 'em would agree."

"You don't know the half of it," Kit said under his breath.

The wolf's head watch reminded Kit of his matching wolf's head pocketknife. He slid his hands over all his pockets—trousers, vest, jacket. Where was it? He could pawn that, too, if only he could find it.

When was the last time he saw it? He recalled using it to peel an apple a few mornings ago while sitting in Lucinda's first parlor. She had scolded him for eating in there. That was her formal room for receiving guests, which was odd, since virtually no one ever called on her. He had been tempted to point this out, but had instead thrown the apple and the knife on the floor. Though Lucinda Ridenour was nobody's idea of a mother figure, she always seemed to inspire him to act like a petulant child around her.

Weston walked over to the window and gazed out into the street as he fiddled with the brass buttons on the front of his double-breasted, navy blue policeman's uniform. The muddy road was clogged with midday traffic—horses, mules, oxen pulling every type of freight wagon and carriage. Leadville boomed and burgeoned with the daily gold and silver strikes. With a population approaching twenty thousand, the young town now rivaled Denver as the largest city in Colorado.

"You've been living up at that funny-colored house for quite a while."

"Only three months."

"What made you leave? Lovers' quarrel?"

Kit burned with the thought of discussing such personal matters with a total stranger. "Something like that. I suppose she's mad that I left her and she's trying to make trouble for me. That's all, Sergeant. You know what Shakespeare says about 'a woman scorned.' "

"I don't suppose that I do."

" 'Hell hath no fury . . . '? "

"Well, all right, if you say so." The sergeant turned back to him with a sly smile. "Is it true what they say about her?"

Kit felt a cold sweat breaking out. He did not know how to answer.

"You know," Weston coaxed, "that she's *insatiable*."

Kit instantly relaxed. The man was simply fishing for a bit of salacious gossip. A saucy tale, something to entertain the boys at the local barbershop. Kit placed his hand over his heart with mock insult. "Sergeant Weston, you're asking me to be less than a gentleman."

The man's grin broadened and he arched one brow. "Everybody says that's why she likes 'em so young. Fellows her own age can't keep up with her. You know that's the sad fact of getting older, don't you, son? Everything slows down." Weston studied Kit's sudden change of expression. "Come on, now. You surely didn't think you were her first."

27

"Lord, no," Kit said. "Probably won't be her last, either. Well, the stories you've heard about her are all true and then some!"

"Damn, I knew it!" He laughed out loud and slapped his knee.

"That woman nearly wore me out. She demanded my attentions morning, noon, and night."

"Sweet Jesus—in broad daylight, you say?"

"Lucinda Ridenour is not a woman to let a little daylight get between her and a good, hard ride." Normally, he would never talk so crudely, but Leadville, Colorado, in 1880, was a town with more money than manners. Bella Valentine, a girl he met on his first day in Leadville, had told him this and it proved more true every day. He had never seen a place with more wealth and less refinement.

The policeman wistfully shook his head with a chuckle. "If only my wife liked 'riding' a little more."

"That sort of thing—like anything else—can be over-done."

"Well, I'd sure like to see for myself one day. You're a clever sort, Randall. I like you."

"Trust me, sergeant. By week's end, she'll have found my replacement and these charges will all be forgotten."

"If I had to guess, I'd say you're right. You'll stay around town for a while, won't you? I'll just let this matter get a little cold and we'll see."

The two men shook hands and Weston departed. Kit breathed a sigh of relief. The audacity of that woman, charging him with theft! He sat down on the hard little bed and tried to sort out what he knew for certain about Lucinda and Christopher Ridenour.

He knew damned little, he realized. Just sketchy bits and pieces. Christopher had only opened up and spoken about his past on one of their rare snowshoe treks to the hot springs. As they steeped in the steaming pool, surrounded by the surreal landscape of endless snow, Christopher seemed to relax and talk freely for the only time in their friendship.

He confided to him that he had thought Lucinda was his sister until he reached the age of nine. She had given birth to him at sixteen, out of wedlock. To avoid the stigma of illegitimacy, she had passed Chris off as her little brother whom she was forced to raise after the death of their parents. She was so young, she easily managed the deception, until they met a cousin by chance who innocently let slip the truth.

Lucinda supported them by singing in bars and coffee houses and occasionally acting in plays. Kit could only guess at how else she picked up money.

With her looks, an admiring, older gentleman of means was sure to come her way. No doubt several had already by the time she met Orson Ridenour six years ago when he was a freshly minted millionaire on Carbonate Hill, courtesy of the Eye Dazzler Mine.

He was an educated man, a lawyer from St. Louis, but was called to Leadville when his younger brother, whom he had grubstaked to a mining claim, lay dying of pneumonia. Ridenour arrived the day after his brother's death and thought it only proper he should be buried on his claim.

The men hired to dig the grave had not even reached the prescribed six feet when one of their shovels hit a black rock that turned out to be an exposed vein of silver. The brother's grave was to become the glory hole of the Eye Dazzler Mine.

Ridenour immediately decided his brother could lie just as comfortably in the local graveyard. He left the practice of law for the mining world and within two years his bank account had swollen by four million dollars.

They say he named it the Eye Dazzler in honor of the rug an old Navajo woman had sold to the ill-fated brother, telling him it would bring him luck. It hadn't saved him from pneumonia, but Orson Ridenour was not a superstitious sort. He named his new mine for it and hung the rug in his office to honor his departed sibling. After Orson's death, his wife rehung it in the second parlor as a remembrance.

Lucinda was singing in a nearby music hall when Ridenour asked her to pose for a commissioned painting to hang over the bar in his new gambling house, the High Life Club. They say he opened the casino after being snubbed for admission into Leadville's ultra-exclusive Argot Club.

Lucinda posed nude on the mysterious Eye Dazzler rug and the painting created a scandalous sensation. The millionaire married his beautiful model a week later and even adopted her son. She and fourteen-year-old Christopher had moved into the Ridenour mansion on Third Street, three floors of gabled, turreted, nouveau riche glory iced with an unholy degree of black trim. The dark, elaborate fretwork embellishing every eave and railing inspired the locals to call it the "Black Lace House."

Kit had learned most of this from Sadie Branch, Lucinda's personal maid. Lucinda seldom spoke about her late husband or her early life.

"Every family has its secrets," she would say if he asked.

"Family boundaries are defined by the secrets they keep. You are not inside that circle."

Kit now realized there was so much about the Ridenours he did not know, it scared him.

He hugged a pillow to his chest and buried his face in it. He could no longer hold back the tears of humiliation and despair. He rocked back and forth as the pillow absorbed his shuddering sobs.

"Oh, darling, don't cry." She walked over and sat by his side. She placed her hand on his bare shoulder, but he jerked away.

"How could you? I trusted you! I thought you were my friends."

She began to lose patience with his belligerent self-pity. "Are you upset about what happened last night . . . or that you enjoyed it?"

Jacob and Ellen Landry sat down to their supper in silence. Their small but well-appointed home on Sixth Street was the quietest on the block. Ten years of marriage had not managed to fill the nursery on the second floor of the little blue house so now it was used as Ellen's sewing room.

Jacob waited until Ellen poured his after-dinner coffee before breaking the hollow quiet of the dining room, a room darkened by heavy curtains at the window perpetually drawn to shut out the view of the house next door, which sat only five feet from the Landry home.

"I lost my job today," he announced without emotion.

"What?" his wife cried, setting the coffeepot down with a rattle.

He threw his napkin on the table with an annoyed sigh. "I knew you'd go to pieces. That's why I didn't tell you until after we'd finished eating."

"Is there some reason why I shouldn't go to pieces?" she said. "What happened? How could you lose your job? You run that place. The Eye Dazzler couldn't function without—"

"The Ridenours fired me. In front of everyone. It was mortifying." He stared at the center of the table as he spoke. He did not seem to address his wife.

"The *Ridenours*." Her thin lips twisted as she uttered the most hated word in her vocabulary. "Why, oh why, does the good Lord allow the wicked to prosper—"

"No preaching at the table, Nell. Have you forgotten our agreement?"

Ellen Landry folded her hands in her lap as she tried to control her seething and contradictory emotions. She nervously fingered the silver filigreed scissors case that she wore on a chain at her waist. The shears had belonged to her late father, a barber. Her father had trained her in the barbering arts. She used them to trim the hair of the children at the Presbyterian Orphan Asylum where she worked on a volunteer basis.

Jacob was not half the man her father had been. Her father would never have . . . no use rehashing all the miserable events of the last six years.

Perhaps she could become a dressmaker. Dressmaking was an honorable profession for a lady, though as a married woman she never thought she would be forced into the degrading situation of having to support herself. She squeezed the scissor case again until the filigree pattern impressed marks upon her fingers.

"I suppose I will be forced to seek employment," she said.

"Damn it, woman! As usual, you have no faith in me at all." He pulled out a small cigar from his vest pocket and made preparations to light it.

"I don't think we can afford luxuries like tobacco, if you are unemployed." She sighed loudly, not caring if she angered him.

He lit the cigar, drew deeply, and exhaled. "Just you rest easy. I have plans. The winds will blow a new direction before I'm done."

Three

"You did what?" Christopher Ridenour stared at his mother in outraged disbelief as they sat down in their enormous and very empty dining room.

Lucinda shrugged. "Just a little mischief. Don't worry about it."

"You filed bogus criminal charges against my best friend and I'm not supposed to worry about it?"

"Calm down, dear." She frowned in a threatening way because her maid, Sadie Branch, who was now doubling as the cook, had entered the room bearing a large, steaming tureen. "I'll retract them tomorrow and say I was mistaken."

The servant set the china bowl down on the table so hard its contents sloshed overboard onto the white linen tablecloth.

"Sadie, good grief!" said her mistress.

Christopher tried to mop up some of the mess with his napkin before it ran over onto the carpet.

"I ain't no cook," said the maid. "Wasn't hired for it, never said I was good at it."

"We'll get someone hired soon," said Lucinda. "I've placed an advertisement in the paper."

The sullen, middle-aged woman served them and abruptly left the dining room.

Christopher stared at his unusually humble dinner. "This is the third time we've had beef stew this week. Doesn't the woman know how to make anything else?"

"Be a good sport," his mother said, though she, too, grimaced at the unappetizing dish before her.

"Soon you'll have fired or driven off everyone and we shall have to do it *all* ourselves. What do you plan for us next? Do we go down into the Dazzler and start mining the silver, too?"

"Don't be so melodramatic. And Kit will come back. They always do. People who love luxury as much as he does won't stay mad forever."

"I don't see why he should after the rotten trick you pulled with these false charges."

"I'm not the reason he left, dearest. Let's lay the blame at the proper doorstep."

The son threw his spoon into his bowl with a clatter. "I didn't do anything wrong. Why do you keep implying—?" He stopped and stared at this mother. "What did you tell him? What did you two quarrel about anyway?"

Lucinda continued to eat as though her son had not spoken. This was her habit. If she did not wish to converse, she simply pretended the other person in the room did not exist. This custom drove those who loved her, and especially those who didn't, to distraction.

Christopher's tone turned self-pitying. "Kit was my best friend. My only friend. Now I'll never see him again. How could you be so cruel?"

She remained silent, so he continued. "We were never so happy as when Kit lived with us. This house is dark as a tomb without him. I'll never forgive you for this. He was the only good thing to happen to us since Orson's passing. You were just getting bored with him, weren't you? What's wrong with you? Why can't you fall in love and stay in love like a normal woman?"

She issued a long sigh of annoyance and finally spoke. "The world is filled with a thousand Kit Randalls. We'll find another."

"No, we won't." He blinked back a tear.

———

With a disgusted sigh, Kit rose from the little boarding house bed, having drifted unwillingly into an opium-laced nap. The room was growing dark, so he realized he had missed the house supper hour. He decided to walk down to the far end of State Street and find a place to get drunk. Maybe then he could shut off the thoughts of Lucinda and Christopher and all that had transpired in the Black Lace House.

"Jesus, you're a monster."

Lucinda gazed at herself in the mirror and she looked at his reflection as well. "I'll thank you not to judge me, if you please. You—the biggest whore of all."

He folded his arms across his chest and glared at her.

"Oh, stop pouting," she said. "Everyone's a whore at some price."

———

Kit bypassed the regular stops like the Ruby and Hatten-back's. He crossed the street to avoid the High Life. The last thing he wanted to do was run into someone he knew.

He had walked for nearly half an hour and was debating whether to simply go back to his room when he caught sight of three men from the Eye Dazzler Mine. They were all shift bosses, important Ridenour employees.

What caught his attention was not the three men walking together—the employees often fraternized after their shifts—but their manner. They whispered among themselves and glanced over their shoulders frequently. Whenever they did this, Kit ducked back into the darkness. The crescent moon lent precious little light to the walkways; it was easy to slip into the shadows of the gaslights.

The men turned into an alley, one that led to the large smelter at the end of Fourth Street. There was a vacant lot at the far side of the alleyway, but it was not vacant this chilly May night.

A group of a hundred men or more had gathered beneath torchlights as a tall stranger took his place atop a large crate and began to speak to the assemblage.

"Good evening and welcome, gentlemen," said the man in a deep and resonant voice. "My name is Mike McCoy and I and Mr. Bender here represent the Knights of Labor. I am glad you all could make this meeting on such short notice. As you may know, the chief superintendent of the Eye Dazzler Mine—Jake Landry—was fired today. We all know why he was fired."

A man in the torch-lit crowd yelled out, "He wouldn't give her ladyship what she wanted in bed!"

Raucous laughter greeted this remark, and even the serious-voiced man on the podium had to chuckle. He raised his hand for silence. "Now Mr. Landry's personal affairs are his business. What I refer to are his union activities. His employers discovered his connection to my organization, the Knights of Labor, and they promptly sacked him for it."

A good deal of grumbling churned through the crowd in response to this announcement.

The information stunned Kit. Jake Landry was involved with the unions? He was in management. He should be siding with his employers, shouldn't he? Did his falling-out with Lucinda run so deep he was willing to sabotage her mine employees, just to get back at her?

Though Kit had only recently begun to fully appreciate his own role in the ongoing spiral of retribution and recrimination between the former lovers, that Jake would try and usurp the Eye Dazzler power structure by organizing its employees was a bold gambit indeed, he thought.

"You all know," the man continued, "that hard rock Leadville miners are making only three dollars per day when all the surrounding mining districts are paying four. Summit and Teller Counties make that wage, and work an eight-hour day to boot! Union scale in other parts of the country is five to eight dollars."

Another wave of outrage rolled through the crowd like an ominous rumbling of summer thunder.

"Are Eye Dazzler miners worth *less* than Summit County miners?" shouted the labor organizer.

"No!" responded the crowd en masse.

"Is the Eye Dazzler Mine *less dangerous* than the mines on the other side of the pass?"

"No!" The cry grew louder.

"Are we going to stand for such ill treatment?"

"No!" came the angry chorus.

"Have you ever wondered why the owners of the Eye Dazzler and the other mines can't pay you more?" said McCoy, suddenly switching into a surprisingly seductive tone.

The crowd grew silent.

"Oh, they have a very good reason, gentlemen," the man continued.

This remark was met with grumbling disbelief.

On cue, McCoy was handed a large brown ledger book. "If Mrs. Ridenour raised your wages, she might not be able to pay . . ." He opened the book and scanned the page. "Eight hundred and fifty-seven dollars to a dressmaker!"

An outraged murmur rose from the crowd. Kit recognized the ledger book as belonging to Lucinda and Christopher. He had seen both write countless personal drafts for their household expenses. Had Jake Landry stolen this account ledger and given it to the union men? No wonder they fired him.

"On April second of this year, she spent two hundred and twenty-five dollars on *flowers*," continued McCoy with malicious glee. "Hope those buds smelled sweet."

The men roared with an even mix of laughter and anger.

"On April twelfth," continued the union organizer, "she bought her young paramour—a boy hardly older than her own son—a gold and silver watch for the princely sum of three hundred and ten dollars—"

Kit felt like he had been punched in the stomach. He dashed from his hiding place and did not stop running until he was safely back in the noise and bustle of State Street. He had heard many rumors about the so-called Elephant Club, the secret society of union organizers who sought to forge the labor force of the district into a unified bargaining group. He had not known until this night, however, that they were indisputably real and active in Leadville.

Chris had spoken often of their alleged existence. He and every mine owner and manager in the county worried about the threat of labor unrest. Lucinda had even suggested that Christopher start arming himself whenever he visited the workings. She worried about her son, fretted over his safety. At least she was that much a normal mother.

He tried to calm himself as he traversed the entire mile-long strip of merriment that was State Street looking for a cozy dive he could call home for an hour or two. He finally settled for a humble, though rowdy, den called Hansen's. He entered the poorly lit, smoky bar and sat down at an empty table in the corner. He promptly spent half his food budget on a bottle of fine, aged Scotch. Three months of living on the high end with Lucinda Ridenour had given him a taste for quality.

He did not care for the atmosphere of the place. It catered to a rougher clientele than the High Life Club. Miners still filthy from their shift filled most of its rough-hewn interior. He needed to be alone and he certainly found no friends here, yet he felt their critical eyes upon him. Did they know something? What if Lucinda's servants knew and talked?

And Lucinda—what if *she* said something? She wouldn't do that, surely. Yet she had taunted him with her knowledge: *Don't worry, darling, your little secret will always be safe with me.*

The longer he sat at the beer-stained table, the more anxiety he felt. He feared every man in the place was laughing at him or scorning him.

He turned once more to glance about, using the large, smoky mirror hanging over the bar to survey the room. Reflected in its dark glass, he thought he saw a boy he had gone to school with at Georgetown. His name was Ian Greene. He wore his school blazer and his long blond hair hung past his collar. He gazed at Kit with pale, colorless eyes.

The sight of him startled Kit so badly he knocked over his little shot glass. The whiskey ran in all directions.

The bartender saw his mishap and tossed him a towel from the bar. Kit did not see it coming and it hit him in the side of the head, causing several men at nearby tables to laugh.

Kit made a feeble attempt to smile back at them and quickly mopped up the spilled whiskey. Then he turned to look at Greene again. His eyes searched the room, but the boy was gone. Vanished. Another man who looked nothing like the smooth-faced, blond-haired schoolboy sat in his place.

His hands felt icy cold and began to tremble. The din of the surrounding conversation dulled into a low roar in his ears. He knew he could not have seen Greene. Ian Greene was long dead.

He had not thought of his unfortunate classmate since coming west, though during his four years of college, not a day had passed without some reminder of him.

Kit had moved out of the dormitory before the end of his first term because of what had happened, though he never told anyone the true reason. He started living with his aunt Jennetta and her young family while he continued his education.

The noise of the crowded bar filled him with a sense of panic. He could not silence the whispers he heard in his mind. They were all talking about him, at least speculating about him, he could tell. The whiskey had not given him any respite at all.

He bought a small, green bottle of absinthe and decided to host a private party for himself, back in his rented room. The accommodating bartender even gave him a handful of sugar cubes to complete the treat.

He returned to the boarding house on Oak and sometime before dawn, he slipped into a spiraling, absinthe-soaked oblivion.

Four

The morning paper reported that Lucinda Ridenour had filed theft charges against her former houseguest, Christopher Randall, though no arrest had yet been made. Neither of the Ridenours could be reached for comment.

The second bit of Ridenour news on the front page of the *Leadville Herald* involved the firing of the long-time Eye Dazzler superintendent, Jacob Landry. The paper speculated that the brewing labor troubles were at the heart of the matter, though, once again, none of the principals was willing to make any public statements.

Hmmm, Lucy Ridenour had a busy day yesterday, Bella Valentine mused as she finished her morning coffee. The Eye Dazzler heiress was feuding with all the men she'd bedded recently. How interesting.

Now was the time for decisive action. Bella had been waiting for this moment for three months. She had lost Kit Randall to that Eye Dazzler slut, but not gracefully. She was going to get him back at last. She would leave nothing to chance this time.

She tossed a quarter on the table and left the café without finishing her breakfast. She hurried back to her rooming house on Chestnut Street and upon entering her crowded little bedroom, opened the window to clear the stale air.

The bedclothes needed washing, but it was so hard to find time for mundane housekeeping chores and the local laundries overcharged shamelessly.

She frowned at the brilliant morning sun streaming in. She did not like casting glamours in the scalding light of day, but she had no choice.

She pulled the heavy leather-bound book from under her bed. The tome bore no title, but grimoires seldom did. They did not need to advertise themselves.

Did she need a love spell to bring him back? Or did she want to send out something negative to vanquish her rival for good? Lucy Ridenour's power over men was the stuff of legend here in this town above the clouds. It was common knowledge the woman had kept the very married Jacob Landry on her string, bouncing him like a bandalore over the bumpy course of their six-year-long affair, which they brazenly conducted under the noses of both her husband and his wife, as well as half the town. No wonder the Ridenours were never received in polite homes, despite their astounding wealth.

The fire that raged between Lucinda and Landry had mysteriously burnt itself out right after old Ridenour's death, just when the whole town expected them to get together at last in some kind of legal, if not moral, union. But there remained the nettling problem of Jacob's wife. Had a sudden attack of decency sent him back into her arms? Possible, however unlikely.

Lucinda Ridenour was hardly one to take such a rejection lightly. She had subtly declared war on the Eye Dazzler superintendent. They said her son was the only reason he had remained employed there. Christopher refused to fire him, standing up to his imperious mother for once in his young life.

The heiress had been forced to seek other ways to punish Jacob for daring to reject her. Kit Randall had then conveniently arrived on the scene. A handsome young lover, barely older than her own son, was the perfect antidote to so public a jilting.

What had changed? Why had the Ridenours now found an excuse to terminate Landry from their employ, when previously they had not? The newspaper had raised all manner of speculation, none of it very convincing.

That was not Bella's concern. Her interest was Kit Randall and how to insure that he would come back to her humble door after spending three months in the hideous splendor of the Black Lace House.

She set to work, first shoving her bed up against the far wall to clear a reasonable space on the floor. She smiled at the sight of the bare floor with not a single insect in evidence. There were benefits to living in this harsh environment. Most such pests could not survive the long winters and brief summers. Though she had grown up coping with all manner of vermin—cockroaches, bedbugs, spiders, and the like—they were all just a bad memory now. No homeowners worried after termites at this altitude, no dogs or cats were bothered by fleas. Even the horses were blessed by the absence of flies in Leadville, this frigid wilderness made home by man and greed.

She pulled her deck of tarot cards from the leather bag she carried with her everywhere and began to draw them one by one and lay them out on the floor in a large circle.

She finished casting the circle by taking out her long,

pointed ritual knife, touching its tip in the little bowl of salt on the dresser, then slowly drawing it around the circle of cards.

She set her red candle on the western edge of the circle, her blue candle on the eastern perimeter, then the incense bowl on the north. She lit the sandalwood cone in the bowl and inhaled the delightful fragrance. Finally, she removed the glittering crystal pendant she wore around her neck, kissed it, and placed it on the south side of the magical circle.

Holding a pine bough she had previously cut and used to adorn her room to celebrate Beltane on May 1, she sat herself in the middle of her circle, closed her eyes, and vividly imagined Kit Randall's sweet face before her. She saw his curly black hair, his dark, merry eyes with their long lashes, the finely cut nose with flaring nostrils, and best of all, his amazing smile bracketed by those deep dimples.

She began to chant:

"Holy Mother Isis, queen of the night, hear my prayer. In this season of Beltane, the celebration of the life spirit when the young God, born of the Goddess at Yuletime, reaches the fullness of his manhood and desires the Goddess and mates with her to create in her womb the God of the coming year, let my plea for perfect love be answered.

"God of the Day, who is both son and lover, strike down all that might stand in my path to this perfect love, foretold to me by the cards and the spirits on the day I met him."

She drew in a deep breath, filling her lungs with the scent of the sandalwood, then opened her eyes and smiled.

All would be resolved by the summer solstice.

A banging on her door broke the sweet, sleepy calm induced by the ritual.

"Hey, Bella? Want to go shopping with me?" came the voice of Etta, a girl who lived down the hall.

"I'm busy. Maybe later."

"Oh, honey, did I interrupt you? I'm sorry. I swear I'm sorry."

"It's all right, I was done."

"You're not mad at me, are you?"

Bella sighed. "For the love of Jesus, go shopping!"

———

Jacob Landry approached the Mineral Bank with apprehension. He did not want to talk to reporters and had had to sneak out of his own house through the bedroom window to avoid them that morning.

He entered the bank and mounted the stairs in the rear, trying to show an air of confidence as though he belonged there, as though he had been summoned to the offices of the bank's officers.

"I need to see Mr. Hauser," he said to the clerk outside the office of George Hauser, the bank's chief operating officer.

"Is Mr. Hauser expecting you, Mr.—?"

Landry swallowed. Hauser should be expecting him, that was for damned sure. "Landry. And, yes."

"One moment," said the young man. He rose from his desk and entered his supervisor's office. He returned almost immediately.

"Mr. Hauser said he does not have an appointment with you, sir, and that he does not have time to see you."

Landry drew an angry breath. "Tell him to *make* time."

"I'm afraid you'll have to leave."

"I'm not leaving until I see Mr. Hauser."

"If you do not leave immediately, I shall summon the guard from downstairs."

Landry glared at the closed mahogany door of George Hauser's office with its rich carving and high polish. He tried to compose himself. He did not wish to make an embarrassing scene that would no doubt find its way into the *Herald* as had his termination from the Eye Dazzler. When his wife read that story in the newspaper, she had burst into tears and refused to leave the house. She told him she would likely die of the shame.

Then they quarreled, then she cried some more. The same scene that had repeated itself a thousand times in the last six years. The six years since he had gone to work at the Eye Dazzler and had met Lucinda Ridenour, the owner's new wife.

He could remember that day in every detail, how the sun had glinted off her earrings, how she smelled of roses thanks to the rose petal milk baths she favored to keep her exquisite skin soft and purest white. She had not said a word to him as she was introduced by old Ridenour. She had simply smiled and just barely a smile it was. She had not even parted her lips.

She did not need to say a word, once she had fixed him in her gaze. She looked into his eyes and she did not blink.

He could not speak from that moment on. All his words vanished. He forced himself to shake her gloved hand and that of her awkward, quiet, too-tall fourteen-year-old son— how could she possibly have a son that old?—but every other person in the room became a shadow to him. Her blazing presence annihilated them.

The Eye Dazzler was not a mine to him after that day. No precious metal could shine brighter than Lucinda. Perhaps the mystical Eye Dazzler rug, which hung above them on the wall like a window into a supernatural otherworld, was lucky after all. His whole world changed the day he walked into old Ridenour's office and under the vibrating aura of the Navajo rug, his existence entered a new dimension of heightened senses and limitless possibilities.

But all that magical brilliance lay in the past now. Merely the dust of memory or a half-forgotten dream. He stood in the offices of the Mineral Bank and clenched his fists in impotent rage.

"Tell Mr. Hauser that if he will not meet with me, I cannot be responsible for what happens next."

"I don't understand."

"Don't worry, Mr. Hauser will understand."

Landry returned home to find his wife waiting for him. He stiffened as he silently entered his house.

"Well," she said, "what did he say?"

"He said nothing. He refused to see me, the son of a bitch." He added this last in a growl under this breath. Ellen did not like him swearing in the house. She hated that even worse than his smoking. As though mere words could bruise her delicate sensibilities.

"I've got to find McCoy and Bender. They're my only hope now."

"No, please don't," said his wife. "You don't want to get mixed up with those union men."

"I don't need you to tell me my business, Nell."

He paced around the room, unable to decide whether to stay or go. He did not feel at home in his own house. He had never felt at home there since the day he met Lucinda. Not that he cared to take up residence in the Black Lace House. Far from it. Yet he knew that the moment he had broken his marriage vows to Ellen he could no longer think of the house he shared with her as his own, despite the mortgage payments he made to the Mineral Bank each month.

Ellen could hardly bear to say the words, but they needed to be said. "You know what you must do now. You need to talk to *her*."

"Never. I would slit my own throat before I would humble myself before her now. Her or that stupid son of hers who thinks he's running things."

"But you need your job, Jacob. If your name is linked to these union men, no mine in Colorado will hire you. Then where will we be?"

He sighed bitterly. Every word she said was true. He could not refute her logic. She was surprisingly clever for a woman. Her insight and intelligence were what had first attracted him to her when they started courting all those years ago.

What a fool he had been. So young and innocent. Blind to the reality that the choices he made during that youthful innocence would have consequences that would haunt him throughout his adult life.

He had never wanted to hurt Nell. She was a good

woman, annoying at times, too preachy and self-righteous, but he probably deserved it. If only they had had children together. She would be a different person if she had the children she dreamed of. Being a mother was all she ever wanted out of life. Maybe if their union had been so blessed, they would have had a real marriage and he would never have been tempted to stray. . . .

What horseshit. He knew better. No power on earth could have prevented him from being slammed by the speeding, erotic freight train that was Lucinda Ridenour. Nor would he have wished it otherwise.

"Jacob, are you even listening to me?"

Her voice intruded upon the unholy seclusion of his thoughts. He wanted to slap her. Anything to stop her braying voice.

"Leave me alone, Nell. I need to sort things out."

"You need to go ask her for your job back."

"No." He said the word quietly to try and collect himself.

"Demean yourself if you have to. You need that job. *We* need it! What is the cost of your pride? Will you sacrifice everything on its altar?"

He raised his hand to strike her. She braced herself, but did not back away. He relaxed his arm. He could not bring himself to do it.

She reconsidered her tactics. She turned and reached for her Bible on the sideboard. "Sit down and rest yourself. Read this. It will calm you."

"No. That book gives *you* comfort, not me."

"No sinner is past redemption, my dearest. Please, do it for me. Just sit a while and read it."

He had nothing else to do with his day. He did not know

how to get in touch with the out-of-town union leaders until after dark. They stayed carefully hidden in the light of day. If he went out again, he might be accosted by more reporters.

He tried to smile at Ellen, but his attempt proved so feeble it resembled a grimace. He took her beloved Bible and sat in the small chair by the front window. The chair was uncomfortable, but its placement afforded the best light in the dark little house.

Ellen closed her eyes in a silent prayer of thanks that his mood had begun to quiet. Once he was himself again, she would start trying to talk sense into him. Before the day was out, he would have his job back at the Eye Dazzler. She felt certain of it.

She watched him sitting in the front window, but he did not seem to be reading any helpful, restorative Bible verses. He remained agitated and distracted. He had picked up a pencil and was scratching something on the morning's newspaper, the one which contained that horrible story about his dismissal.

Half an hour passed, then Jacob Landry abruptly rose to leave.

"Where are you going?" she asked.

"Out."

"Out where?"

"Just out!"

He slammed the front door so hard the little portrait of the Savior which hung above it on the purple ribbon rattled against the wall plaster.

When he got in those dark moods, he frightened her. She picked up her Bible where he had casually tossed it on the floor, then she glanced at the newspaper he had used for his frantic scribbling.

Her face twisted with the blasphemy she saw there. Crude drawings of a nude woman with some sort of mark on her hip. Were these pictures of Lucinda Ridenour? His artwork was not skillful enough to create a recognizable portrait, but she had heard the rumors that a shocking painting of the woman hung in her late husband's casino on State Street and that the likeness revealed a tattoo on her hip. It was said to be a wolf. She was probably involved in some kind of sinful, degenerate, occult activities.

No doubt Lucinda employed the black arts to ensnare good men like her husband. The tattoo was probably the devil's mark upon her. She had surely corrupted that young man she had living with her as well. He had the same name as her son, didn't he? What an odd coincidence. Sinister, almost. Maybe not a coincidence at all.

The boy seemed to be the friend of the son, yet the rumors in town held that he shared Lucinda's wanton bed. Ellen had met him once. He had been coming out of the Eye Dazzler offices with Christopher Ridenour. She had stopped by to find Jacob to tell him he had received a letter from his sister. He so loved receiving mail from his family in the East.

Young Mr. Ridenour had introduced them. The curly-haired young man displayed deep dimples when he smiled. He had said something charming to her that made her blush. She had left the brief encounter feeling sorry that he had fallen victim to such a wicked woman. To see inno-cence defiled was a painful thing. Yet at least it meant the notorious Lucinda was leaving Jacob Landry alone.

She gathered up the newspaper with the obscene drawings and hurried to the kitchen to toss it into the remnants of the oven fire from breakfast.

Before the embers ignited the paper, she noticed more scribbling. Words, thankfully, not more embarrassing, disgraceful drawings, but they made little sense: *A new Noah's flood.*

Her lip trembled and she bit back tears. Was her husband losing his mind?

———

Sadie Branch, Lucinda's maid, returned from her marketing chores at just past three. She had spent most of the time talking to an old friend, a gambler from her whoring days, and when she realized the lateness of the hour she had to rush back to start the pot roast for supper. Mrs. Ridenour had decreed: no more stew for at least a week. Pot roast and stew were the only things Sadie knew how to cook.

Her mistress would be furious when she found out that Sadie had failed to purchase the lace trim she needed. Sadie decided to tell her that Keating's Notions was out of the type of lace she wanted, knowing Lucinda was too lazy to check the store herself.

Ten minutes after arriving home Sadie Branch ran back out of the big, gaudy, black-trimmed house and into the street, screaming: *"Murder, murder, bloody murder!"*

Five

Brad Randall spent three hours scouring every saloon, bawdy house, and gambling hall looking for his nephew Kit. Since Leadville was a prosperous mining town where the men outnumbered the women ten to one, there were plenty of such establishments to search.

Finally, he arrived at a small, odd-looking house at the far end of Chestnut Street. This was the easternmost edge of town leading up to the mining district. He did not know at first if it was a brothel, since the sign above the door read BOARDING HOUSE FOR LADIES, but a quick glance at the "ladies" lounging on the front porch hinted that the term meant only that they were not gentlemen. Two women wearing wrappers sat in wicker chairs smoking cigarettes. One had her feet propped up on the porch railing, heedless of the fact that her bare legs, from the knees downward, were on display for all to see.

He asked them if a young man named Christopher or "Kit" Randall might be on the premises.

"Don't know," said the lounging woman.

"He's young," Brad said. "Not very tall, has black, curly hair, brown eyes."

She shrugged.

"Dimples," Brad added. "Deep dimples."

"Oh . . . I bet I know who you mean. That sounds like Bella's sweetie, don't it, Etta?"

"A chatty sort?" said Etta. "A charmer?"

"Definitely," said Brad.

The lounging woman with her feet up instructed him to go to the second floor and knock on the third door to the right.

He went as directed but hesitated at the door for an instant. He heard a young woman's voice inside shout, "For the love of Jesus, get out of bed! You're a mess."

Brad heard a groggy male groan. The voice might belong to Kit. He could not tell for sure.

Brad pressed his ear to the door for more careful listening.

"What's wrong with you?" the girl said. "I don't understand why you've changed so much."

"Don't throw me out, Bella. I need you."

"You *need* to sober up. I hate it when you're like this!"

Brad rapped on the door. He was now certain the male voice belonged to his nephew.

The voices in the room hushed to terse whispers. Brad heard scuffling noises.

"Who is it?" called the young woman in a false-sounding voice.

"Bradley Randall."

More mumbling whispers, more scuffling sounds, then a tall girl opened the door. She wore her blond hair in a half-coiled psyche knot directly on top of her head, making her look taller still.

"Randall? Are you related to him?" She tilted her loose topknot over her shoulder.

"I'm his uncle." Brad looked in and beheld his disheveled

nephew, clad in his underwear, climbing out from under the young woman's bed. Had he been attempting to hide there?

"Maybe *you* can talk some sense into him," she said. "Lord knows I've tried."

Brad entered the small, cluttered room hesitantly. His nostrils were assaulted with the unexpected scent of burning incense. He had not smelled such a thing since he had attended a funeral once in a Catholic church.

This incense was a great deal more pungent and secular than what he had encountered at Christ the King Cathedral. He saw the little cone burning on a small dresser which looked to be an altar of some sort. All manner of objects sat there—a carving of an obese naked woman, little stones of varying colors, candles in red, black, and green, a stone bowl that held the incense, and underneath it all, a pentagram painted directly on the dresser top.

Kit looked only vaguely alert. "Uncle Brad, what are you doing here?"

"You knew we were coming today. You promised to meet us at the stage stop. I've spent half the day looking for you."

The young man yawned and slid back down into the bedclothes as though getting dressed would prove more effort than he was willing to invest.

"Oh, no, you don't," shouted the girl, her topknot bobbing with her words. She rushed to the bed and yanked at his shoulder.

Both she and Brad set to work locating Kit's clothes and shoving him into them.

Though the young girl had seemed perfectly furious with Kit, when he was ready to leave she planted a heartfelt kiss on his mouth and whispered something in his ear. His reply was an uncomfortable smile and a shrug. Brad thought them an odd couple given the fact that the slender girl was a good half foot taller than his nephew. Then again, Kit had never been much ruled by convention.

Once the two men were back out on the street, Brad, whose anger was barely in check, said, "Where are you living?"

"Well, currently I guess it would have to be with . . . uh, Bella. That girl in there. I forgot to make introductions, didn't I?"

"Where are your belongings?"

Kit groaned. "I was staying at a boardinghouse on Oak Street when the landlady caught me with liquor and threw me out. She's keeping all my stuff until I can pay her for the days I owe."

"Well, where can you get cleaned up? You're not seeing my wife and daughter in this condition. Christ, you smell like a distillery."

"There's a barbershop just down the way on State, near the corner."

Brad steered his slightly staggering nephew toward the barbershop in question while wishing he had brought a warmer coat. The fading sun had dropped the temperature. He had not realized the sun set so early in the mountains. He quickly glanced at his watch: only four, so the barbershop would surely still be open.

"Your wife?" Kit said. "When did you two get married? Why didn't you invite me?"

Brad lowered his voice. "We're not married yet. My divorce was granted just before Christmas, but it isn't final until June twenty-first."

"Living 'in sin' are we? I'm shocked at you, Uncle."

"I'm in no mood to be mocked after the day I've had, thank you!"

"Calm down. I was just kidding. Obviously I have no grounds to feel superior."

"Since we're talking about my wedding, that happens to be one of the reasons for coming here. I was counting on you standing up with me."

Kit stopped walking. A flattered smile spread across his handsome, though scruffy, young face. Even the Randall dimples managed to show through the dark stubble.

"Your best man? I'd be honored, Uncle."

"I can't think of a single man on earth I feel closer to than you. In fact, I don't believe she nor I would be alive today to be *getting* married were it not for you."

The boy blushed with modesty. "That was nothing."

"A year ago you saved my life *and* hers. I wouldn't call that 'nothing.' He threw his arm over his nephew's shoulders and gave him an affectionate hug. "We're of course traveling as man and wife, so please don't let on."

"Where are you staying?" said Kit, both men suddenly feeling awkward with all this sloppy emotion.

"The Clarendon House."

"My, my, the toniest place in town. I'm impressed."

Brad sighed. "That was hardly our first choice. All the less expensive places were filled to overflowing. I've never seen a place quite this busy. Even Washington City during the war years wasn't this crowded."

Prospectors, entrepreneurs, and all manner of speculators poured into Leadville from every direction at the rate of two hundred a day. Cheap lodgings were nearly impossible to come by. Saloons and gambling halls, even stables rented out their floor space. Men could pay as much as two dollars for the right to spread their coats on the floor to catch a night's sleep.

"Everybody's getting pretty excited about the railroad coming," Kit said. "That trip over Fremont Pass in the coach is quite a ride."

"I've never experienced anything like it. Good God."

Kit chuckled. "I made the mistake of eating a large lunch and drinking a couple of beers before I made that trip. Spent at least two hours with my head hanging out of the window of the coach, revisiting every morsel—when I wasn't holding on for dear life."

They stopped their conversation as a noisy brass band marched past them. Two young boys in the group carried large signs announcing the opening of a new music hall. When the band retreated far enough for them to talk again, Kit's upbeat mood had evaporated.

"You know, Uncle, you didn't have to come rushing out here. I could have come to visit *you* for the wedding."

"Frankly, I'm concerned about you, Kit. When the bank manager contacted me and told me you'd withdrawn all the money from the your trust account, I had to worry." Brad was no longer Kit's trustee since he had turned twenty-one, but the accountants sent him a quarterly evaluation of the trust. That the young man had tried to borrow against the monthly rentals he received, along with his uncle and aunt, on the Randall Dairy, had prompted Brad's trip.

"Hasn't it occurred to you that my finances are none of your business?"

"Don't take that defensive tone with me. I just care about you, that's all."

They reached the barbershop, where Brad paid for a bath and a shave for his nephew.

"If I go 'round to this boarding house and pay the woman, will she give me some clean clothes for you to put on?" Brad asked.

"Yeah, I've got several nice suits," Kit said as he shucked off his clothes. He slowly eased himself down into the steaming tub. "God, this water is boiling me alive."

Brad handed him a bar of soap. "Wash your hair, too."

"Yes, Mother."

Brad Randall chuckled. Some shadow of the old Kit still remained, though he looked and acted so changed—older, sadder, too world-weary for his twenty-one years.

"Uncle Brad, I need to talk to you."

He wants to borrow money, thought Brad. "We'll talk when I get back."

———

After stopping at Kit's former boardinghouse, Randall did not head straight back to the barbershop, but rather rushed to his hotel.

His soon-to-be wife, Eden Murdoch, rose from her seat near the enormous marble fireplace in the hotel's lobby with a concerned smile.

"Did you find him?" she asked.

"Something's happened." He sat her back down on the small velvet sofa and glanced about to see if anyone was within eavesdropping distance.

"What is it? What's wrong?"

"Where's Hadley?" he asked, wondering about their precocious ten-year-old daughter.

"I let her go exploring. She promised not to cross the street."

"I don't want her out alone. Besides, it's nearly dark."

"Heavens, Brad, what's wrong?"

He set Kit's valise down and paused to catch his breath. "Kit's in trouble. I had quite a chat with his former landlady. The police want to talk to him. Remember that woman he wrote to us about? The wealthy, older woman whom we assumed was essentially 'keeping' him?"

"The one with the son Kit's age?"

"Yes. She's been murdered."

"Oh, dear God!"

At that moment, Kit Randall strode through the ornate double doors of the Clarendon House with his little cousin Hadley riding on his shoulders.

"Look at this street urchin I picked up," he called out with a grin. His still-damp hair hung in black ringlets around his face and down his collar.

"I found him, Papa, I found him!" Hadley said. She was wearing Kit's derby hat, which was so big for her it nearly obscured her eyes. She leaned over and kissed the top of her beloved cousin's head. Her long blond braids dangled on either side of his clean-shaven face.

Eden rose and forced a smile. Kit guided Hadley back to the floor carefully so that he could kiss his future aunt.

"You're looking beautiful as ever," he whispered as he wrapped his arm around her slender waist. "I thought you were bringing me some clean clothes, Uncle. I got tired of waiting and the barber wanted to close up shop."

Though his clothing was stained and rumpled, the bath and shave had improved his appearance immensely.

Brad ushered the entire group back over near the fireplace. Its broad expanse of logs and dancing flames provided a genial warmth against the growing chill of the early mountain evening.

"The police are looking for you," Brad said in low tones to his nephew.

"I know," Kit mumbled.

"Hadley, darling," said Eden to her daughter, "here's some money. Go over there and buy one copy of each of the newspapers from that stand by the front desk, will you?" The city boasted five newspapers of its own. As soon as the girl was out of earshot, she asked tersely, "What's going on? What's all this about, Kit?"

Kit shrugged with a slightly defensive air. "A woman named Lucinda Ridenour was murdered. Somebody stabbed her."

"But this was the woman you lived with, right?" said Brad.

"I was staying with her and her son. I moved out before all that happened."

"Your former landlady told me that she had read in the papers that the police believe *you* might have done it," said Brad. "The woman filed theft charges against you the day before she was killed."

"That's a damned lie!" Kit stood up in outrage. "God damn that whole lying family to hell!"

The manager of the hotel rushed over from the front desk at the sound of this outburst.

"Sir, we at the Clarendon do not tolerate such language. I'm afraid I am going to have to ask you to leave the premises."

"He's a guest here," said Brad. "I would like to take a room for him. We will all retire to our rooms directly and not trouble you further, sir."

The manager was only partially mollified, but led Brad back over to the front desk to complete the registration process for Kit's room.

"Kit, tell me what has happened. You know how much we all love you." Eden placed a comforting arm around his shoulders. He was only a few inches taller than she was.

"Yeah, sure. He loves me plenty. That's why he treats me like I'm nine years old."

"He's just vexed. It's been a—"

"—a long day. Yeah, yeah, I heard all about it." He ran a distracted hand through his curly hair and changed tone. "Look, I'm really sorry I forgot you were coming."

"That's all right. I know that you must be very distracted by what's happened. Let's order some supper brought up to our room. We all need to rest and talk."

Brad returned with an extra set of keys. "I was able to get adjoining rooms. I guess it will be gentlemen in one room, ladies in the other."

"I want to sleep alone," said Kit. He refused to look at anyone.

Brad frowned at his nephew. "All right, if that's what—"

"No, Kit," said Eden. "I'd rather you and Brad share a room."

Kit responded with a disappointed frown, but mounted the stairs without further comment.

Brad gave Eden a questioning look.

She explained. "You need to keep a close watch on him. Didn't you notice his eyes? They're on fire. He's taken some kind of drug. We need to stay with him every moment."

———

Supper was a nearly silent affair with only awkward and meaningless small talk. Kit seemed to direct all his conversation to Hadley, what little there was of it. The girl basked in the attention from her grown-up cousin.

As they finished, Eden tactfully announced that she and her daughter were going to visit the restaurant downstairs in search of ice cream. Brad looked grateful, knowing Eden was trying to give him some needed private time to talk with Kit, who seemed dismal at the prospect.

When the women returned upstairs half an hour later, angry voices could be heard through Brad and Kit's hotel room door.

"Don't be mad at me, Uncle Brad. You don't understand."

"Then *make* me understand," came Randall's exasperated voice. "For God's sake, just tell me what happened."

"I can't. I can't . . ." Kit sobbed.

Eden saw her daughter look confused and upset by this exchange. She hurried the girl into their room and asked her to get ready for bed.

She then rapped on the door between the two rooms.

Brad opened it. "Oh, you're back."

"We could hear you in the hallway," she whispered.

He mock-winced. "Sorry."

He closed the door and only low murmurs filtered through from then on.

Hadley fell asleep almost the moment her head touched her pillow, but Eden sat up fully dressed, hoping to catch a word with Brad. Just before ten, a light knock came on her hallway door.

"Eden?" Brad said softly through the door. "Are you still awake?"

She joined him in the hall. "I'm exhausted, but sleep seems impossible right now."

"I'm the same. Kit's turned in for the night. I thought we might go downstairs and share a cup of coffee."

While Eden waited for Brad to locate a waiter in the hotel's dining room, she took the time to study the grand lobby with its enormous carved pillars holding up the ornately detailed twelve-foot ceiling. Rich blue carpet covered the floor and large gas chandeliers illuminated the huge expanse. The elegant hotel had opened its doors only a few months earlier. She wished she could have enjoyed all this beauty and luxury. How romantic to have spent her wedding night with Brad here. Now Kit's troubles made that impossible.

She had taken a seat on the sofa facing the fire when Brad arrived with their coffee service on a tray.

"You're playing waiter tonight?" she asked with a grin.

"The kitchen closes at ten, but the cook said I was welcome to the coffee if I was willing to serve myself."

They relaxed into the comfortable recesses of the sofa and sipped from their steaming mugs.

"I've at least convinced him to go the police tomorrow

and talk to them, answer their questions. I promised to go with him, of course. He's scared to death."

"Wouldn't you be?"

"Not if I were innocent." Brad shook his head with a disgusted sigh. "There's a part of me that says, 'Let's just leave him here.' He's a grown man. He's gotten himself into this trouble and he can damn well see himself clear of it."

"But you won't."

"I suppose I won't."

"He didn't abandon us in our trouble last year."

"So true. I try to remind myself of that every time he tries my patience."

"He's really still so young, for all his manly posturing. He needs us now more than ever. Besides, it's not like we had anything else to do with our time."

Brad tensed. "What are you implying? You know I'll find a position as soon as we decide where to settle. I'm working on ideas and sending out letters every day."

Eden regretted her careless remark. The subject of Brad's unemployment was a sore one. He had not worked since leaving his post as the Commissioner of Indian Affairs the year before. She knew he deeply wanted to find a new vocation, but after such an exalted position, all normal jobs seemed pale. His only superiors had been the Secretary of the Interior and the President of the United States himself.

How was he now to satisfy the requirements of his pride as a mere bank officer or insurance broker? She ached to help him, but she did not know how.

She tried quickly to steer the conversation back to the

problem at hand—Brad's headstrong nephew. "Should Kit have a lawyer?"

"If they charge him with anything, definitely. I told him not to worry on that score."

"I hate to ask this, but where would we get the money?"

"I know. I've thought about that. If we need money for an attorney, I could contact my sister and the three of us could sell the Randall Dairy."

"That would be a shame."

"I'd be sorry to ask that of Jennetta, but she would do anything for Kit. I'm certain of that much." He shook his head slowly. "That boy is so hopelessly spoiled. And my own mother was in no small way responsible for it. He grew up in a household where his own mother and mine waged a constant tug-of-war for his affections. After my brother was killed in the war, my mother doted on Kit. And Jennetta, she played her role too. She was more sister than aunt to him. He moved in with her after his first semester of college because he thought he was too good to live in a dormitory with the other boys."

"It's awful to say this, but he acts brattiest when he's around you. The pair of you seem to bring out the worst in each other." Eden gave her soon-to-be-husband a sidelong glance. "If I didn't know better, I'd say you were jealous of him."

This elicited only an angry grumble.

"Well, I adore the boy," she said. "I want to help him through this."

"*All* women adore him. That's another one of his problems, if you ask me."

Eden laughed. "You *are* jealous. Kit can't help the fact

that he's cute and smart and has such high spirits. Few women can resist that combination."

"I hope *you* resist it," Brad said to tease her, then he sobered. Mirth soured in the face of such a dire turn of events.

"What did you learn during your talk with him?" she said.

"Not as much as I'd hoped for. He's very reluctant to discuss it, which worries me all the more. He admitted that he and this Mrs. Ridenour were lovers, just as we suspected they were. Odd that her son didn't take issue with that. I can't imagine too many young men who would tolerate one of their own friends bedding their mother—and in their own house. Anyway, Kit and the woman quarreled a couple of mornings ago and he moved out in a huff."

"Why did they quarrel?"

"He refused to tell me. When asked, he just says, 'It's not important' or 'It's private.' "

"The police will certainly want to know."

"I think that's why he's trying to avoid talking to them. At least he's not the only suspect. There's another man the police have questioned."

"Yes, I read about it in those newspapers I bought. I studied them while Hadley ate her ice cream. It seems the Ridenours, the mother and son, that is, had learned that this Jacob Landry had been involved in some sort of plot involving a labor union. Mrs. Ridenour—who apparently had quite a temper, the paper implied—had fired Landry in front of a large group of employees."

Randall did not share her enthusiasm for this theory. He looked so miserable and preoccupied, she could tell he was not paying attention.

"Do you think it's possible that Kit could have done it?" he blurted out suddenly. "He was certainly involved with the woman and, for whatever reason, they parted company on bad terms. I don't know . . . a crime of passion?"

"Oh, Brad, Kit could never kill a woman. To stab a woman in the throat and let her bleed to death—who could do such a terrible thing?"

The gory details from the newspaper stories had sickened her. The sensational crime had knocked the impending visit of former President Ulysses S. Grant off the front page. Grant was on a world tour and was scheduled to be the first passenger on the Denver and Rio Grande train, soon to arrive in Leadville.

She idly wished they could have postponed their own visit to Leadville until the rail service was available. The harrowing stage trip over two mountain passes between here and Denver was a journey she would not willingly repeat soon, if given an option. The bone-jarring ride over Fremont Pass alone was the single most uncomfortable ordeal she had ever experienced in a public conveyance.

"He killed a man with his bare hands a year ago in Kansas," said Randall.

"That was completely different," she said, but the words came out hollow and they both looked at each other in painful silence.

"I know. His goal was as pure as the driven snow, but still we know that, when properly motivated, he is capable of—"

She placed her fingertips to his lips and sleepily shook her head. "I don't know, but I'm too tired to think any more tonight. Let's go upstairs, shall we?"

He took her coffee cup from her and set it on the tray. "I just wish we were retiring to the same bed."

"Me, too, darling, but I think it's important you keep an eye on him."

After Brad returned their coffee service to the kitchen, they climbed the wide oak stairs and each unlocked the doors to their rooms.

She had not yet even hung up her shawl when she heard Brad call her name. She dashed back out into the hallway.

"Brad, what is it?"

"Kit's gone! And so is my new hunting rifle."

Six

Kit waited in the shadows near the boardinghouse of Bella Valentine—the young girl with the bobbing yellow top-knot. Her evening of fortune-telling at the saloons on State Street could last late if she was having a successful night. She had a regular clientele, with appearances at designated taverns on specific nights.

When she finally trudged home, she was delighted to find him waiting for her. When they climbed under the covers, she began to smother his face with kisses, but he did not have romance on his mind.

"Come on, Bella, it's nearly two. Let's get some sleep, all right?"

"What's the matter? In mourning for your lady love?"

"I don't want to talk about that."

"You should never have gotten involved with the sorry likes of her. No good could happen in the Black Lace House. There's a curse on it. You and I had so much fun together before you met Mrs. Fancy-Pants-Eye-Dazzler-Money and that odd-duck son of hers. I could have told you a story or two about her."

"Let's talk in the morning."

She pushed her full lower lip out to make a pouty face. "All right."

They exchanged a brief kiss, then rolled over in opposite directions like a long-married couple.

Bella whispered in the darkness, "I knew you'd come back after Beltane."

Kit's head popped up. "After what?"

"Beltane—the first of May. One of the sabbats."

"You know how I feel about that blather."

"It's not blather. I don't spit on your religion."

"That would be hard to do since I don't seem to have one at the moment," he said.

"We celebrate Beltane with bonfires. Dancing naked under the full moon. It's a wonderful celebration."

"At this altitude? It gets below freezing here at night. I think I'll pass on the opportunity, if it's all the same to you, Pagan Priestess."

" 'Pagan Priestess'—I like that. Now you're sounding like my old Kit." She wrapped her arms around him and kissed the back of his neck, but he refused to turn over to face her. She whispered in a dusky voice, "It's been ever so long since you sent me a love letter."

He had to smile. "Love letter" had been part of their own secret lovers' code for sex. In the first fire of their brief affair, he had said something like, "I've got a love letter I want to give you. Know where I could post it?"

"I've got a letter slot right here . . . as long as you think your letter will fit. It's not too big to slide in?"

"Getting bigger by the minute. We'd better hurry. This news can't wait."

They had delighted in their ribald, nonsensical wordplay and the postal references had grown and embellished themselves to an impossibly silly level. The act of sliding a letter into a real postal drop had lost its innocence for Kit to such a degree he couldn't even watch a stranger mail a letter on the street without wickedly smirking to himself. Sometimes the unwary mailers caught him grinning at them and could only wonder what amused him so.

He pondered whether all lovers said silly things in the secrecy of the bedclothes that they would never dare repeat elsewhere. Then he realized that he and Lucinda had never had a lovers' code. In bed, Lucinda did not like talk; she preferred action.

A part of him wished that he had never left Bella's side in the first place. She would have let him stay indefinitely, but his pride got in the way. When she had rejected his marriage proposal, he felt so hurt and humiliated that he couldn't stand to look at her.

She had pleaded for him to stay, tried to make him understand her radical views on marriage—how it was legalized prostitution, how married women were no better than slaves, how her first husband had spent all her money and left her broke when he died . . . the list of her reasons for her aversion to matrimony went on and on, but he remained unconvinced.

He told her flat-out he could not continue to share a bed with a woman he loved unless they planned to get married. No other course was right, no alternative was honorable, to his way of thinking, even though he had not hesitated a moment the first time she had invited him to return with her to her lodgings. Or the second time, or the third . . . By the end of the first week, she had convinced him to give up his expensive hotel room and move in with her. Pris Hart, the old woman who owned the boardinghouse, raised no objection to her female boarders hosting male visitors, though Bella was the only girl in the house who did not charge for the privilege.

Had he stayed with her he would not be in this nightmarish fix. He would never have met Lucinda, never have moved into the wildly decadent funhouse she called home. He'd had no moral qualms about sharing Lucinda's bed. The word "love" was never spoken between them.

But Bella was a different question entirely. He cared about her too much to treat her with anything less than honor and dignity. When he offered to "make an honest woman of her" and she would not let him, he was confounded, thunderstruck. No matter how long they talked, argued, and debated the issue, she would not bend her principles and neither would he.

So he walked out, silently damning her, damning all women everywhere and thinking love was a pointless waste of time.

Bella's hands wandered over him, still trying to arouse him, but he felt more like sobbing than making love.

"I'm sorry, I'm just tired. Let's go to sleep."

"Beltane is also for the celebration of fertility."

"Neither of us needs to be fertile at the moment. We've had this discussion before."

"Oh! I give up." She turned over and took half the covers with her.

They both tried for sleep, but soon Bella was shaking his shoulder.

"Wake up, blast it. You're making so much noise I can't sleep."

"Huh?" said Kit.

"You were talking in your sleep, making a terrible racket."

"What did I say?"

"I don't know. Mumbling mostly." She thought for a minute. "Cloves."

"What?"

"You said the word 'cloves.' I know I heard that."

The word made Kit squirm.

"Chris Ridenour smells like cloves," she said. "I think he dresses his hair with something made from clove oil."

"How would you know what Chris's hair smells like?"

"He hired me to conduct a séance after his stepfather died. Didn't have much luck, though. I told him we needed to do it in the house of the deceased in order to reach him—it's important to be surrounded by their favorite things—but he wouldn't have it. I think he didn't want his mother knowing. So we had to hold it here."

Kit snorted. "Right here? In your *bedroom*?"

"How dare you suggest—if I didn't love you, I'd smack you one for saying that. This was serious business. And he was a complete gentleman, by the way."

"But you couldn't reach old Ridenour?"

"No, I just faked it like I always do when I can't reach the Other Side. I told him that the old man said, 'Tell Chris I love him and miss him.' That boy burst into tears and cried like a baby. I held him in my arms for nearly half an hour before he dried up. He's a funny one. I like him, though. He paid me double and told me I was gifted."

"Oh, Bella, you're such a shameless fraud."

"I just give people what they want. You should try it sometime."

76

He chuckled and held her tenderly in his arms. He swallowed hard as he tried to work up the nerve to ask her a question that had plagued him constantly over the last couple of days.

"Bella, have you ever . . ."

"Ever what?"

He frowned with the awkwardness of the topic. It was probably a mistake to talk about this to a woman, but she seemed to know the damnedest things. "Have you ever—oh, god, I don't know how to say it."

"Just out with it, for pity's sake."

He took a deep breath and tried again. "Did you ever let your husband—or any other fellow—spend in your mouth?"

"Lord, no. Is *that* what you want?" She sat up and lit the lamp next to the bed. She wrinkled her slender, patrician nose which was her principal claim to beauty. With its finely arched nostrils and chiseled tip, Kit had once told her, her nose had more facets to it than a well-cut diamond. She was fairly sure this was a compliment.

He could tell by her disgusted expression, he shouldn't have asked. "No, no, I was just curious. You've heard of it, though?"

"Gamahuche? Sure. All my girlfriends here are in the lust business. There's not much I haven't heard of."

"There's actually a *word* for it?"

She sighed. "Didn't they teach you anything in that fancy Eastern college?" She narrowed her gray eyes and set her jaw. "I suppose *she* did that for you!"

"Come on, Bella. I don't want to talk about her."

"If that's what you're after, there's a place on State Street that specializes in it."

77

"You're kidding."

"Why would anyone tell lies at this hour? It's upstairs over that saloon next to the Bon Ton. Can't think of the name."

"I never heard about that."

"They don't advertise, dummy. You think they want to get raided by the police?"

Kit hugged her tight and pressed his face into her hair which always smelled like the sandalwood incense she burned. He had once loved that about her. Sometimes he even thought he smelled sandalwood in his dreams. Sandalwood . . . *not cloves*.

"Lots of stuff goes on there that they have to keep secret. Not just from the police, either. That's the least of it."

"Who else do they have to worry about?"

"Blackmailers, of course. They've got boys working there, too."

"Boys?" He sat up, completely shocked. "You mean *boy whores*?"

"Sure, and the girls at the other houses don't like it one bit either. Unfair competition, ya know?"

"Unfair competition? You've lost me there."

"It's not fair at all. Boys don't have to worry about getting knocked up. And they don't have to quit working one week a month when aunty comes to call. 'Course the number of customers who'd rather have a boy is still a whole lot smaller than those who want girls, but if it's a gamahuche they're after, I suppose it doesn't make much difference who—"

"That's all right," Kit interrupted, now wishing he had not brought up this subject.

Seven

Christopher Ridenour sat stoically through the questioning by the police detective, Captain Brace, the third such interview he had been forced to give in two days. He carefully reviewed again the day of his mother's murder and the day preceding.

The two men sat in Lucinda Ridenour's first parlor on the small needlepoint-decorated chairs before the fireplace. Her body had been removed for examination by a doctor, but her dried blood remained about the room in several locations, a mute reminder to the terrible afternoon of two days before.

Christopher could barely stand to enter the room and would not have but for the insistence of the police officers. He found it impossible to sleep in the house. All night he walked the halls with shallow breath and an eye for the windows, waiting for shadows to appear at them.

"Tell me more about this Christopher Randall," said the detective.

"He was a houseguest. He and my mother were . . ."

"Lovers?"

Ridenour winced at the word. "Please don't put that in your report."

"Mr. Ridenour, I know all this must be painful to you, but

it was common knowledge that he was . . . on close terms with your mother. She filed charges of theft against him the day he moved out of here. That fact alone makes him a suspect."

"I think she was mistaken about those theft charges."

"We'll come back to the issue of Randall later. Have the whereabouts of the maid been discovered? It's vital that we talk to her."

"Miss Branch seems to have disappeared. I don't know why. She's not been seen or heard from since the other afternoon when she discovered my mother's . . . body." He bit his lip in an effort to keep from breaking down in front of this policeman.

"Let's talk about the situation out at the Eye Dazzler Mine."

Young Ridenour took a deep breath to restore himself and answered strongly, "The miners presented me with a list of demands today. I've been given twenty-four hours to respond. I asked for more time, given my . . . situation. I don't know what their reaction will be to that."

"Did you or your mother receive any personal threats?"

"No. But as I mentioned, someone took a shot at me last night as I walked home from work at the casino."

"If I were you, I would hire some protection."

"I already have. They're going to escort me to work this morning. When will the police be done with my mother's . . . when can she be released to the undertaker?"

"Soon. Probably tomorrow. The doctor was called away all day yesterday on an emergency. You heard about what happened at the Eclipse?"

He nodded. The hoist cable had broken while lowering a new shift into the Eclipse Mine. The men riding the bucket were killed and two others down below in the shaft were severely injured. The accident had further fueled the seething labor unrest.

Before the two men could discuss the situation more fully, their attention was drawn to a commotion in the front hall of the Black Lace House.

"I must talk to him," came a commanding male voice.

Captain Brace rose from his seat to see who had entered the house.

"It sounds like George Hauser," said Ridenour.

"The banker?"

"He's also an investor in the Lady-Be-Good and the Printer Boy. A couple of other mine syndicates down in the Johnson Gulch, too." With a vague sigh, Ridenour added, "I've been expecting him."

George Hauser, a large man in his fifties, burst into the parlor. Two policemen followed him in, apparently unable to impede his entrance.

"We're conducting an investigation here, sir," said the detective.

"This young man needs support and I am here to offer it," Hauser said in a voice more accustomed to giving orders than following them.

Ridenour glanced up but did not smile. He regarded Hauser with noticeable bitterness. His distressed banker had not rushed to his side to console him at the death of his mother, but now that the Eye Dazzler miners were threatening a strike, his concern was overwhelming.

"How are you holding up, my boy?" said Hauser.

Ridenour, the only man now in the room still seated, merely shrugged.

"Someone took a shot at him last night," said Brace.

"Damned unions." George Hauser spat. "They're at the bottom of this. I'd put money on it. You ought to arrest the lot of them, sergeant."

"Captain," the detective said. "Captain William Brace."

Hauser extended his hand and introduced himself. The two men chatted earnestly about the case while Christopher leaned his head upon his hand. He spotted something gleaming in the morning sun on the lowest shelf of the étagère, something that did not belong there. The whatnot, as Sadie Branch used to call it because she hated dusting it, was crammed with myriad objects—glass and porcelain figurines belonging to his mother, small Greek urns and vases collected by Orson Ridenour on his European travels, plus the odd fossilized rock or crystal formation Christopher had garnered from the mine.

Whatever had suddenly caught the light on that lowest shelf was out of place; he sensed it instantly. He wondered what it could be, but did not care to go crawling about the room with these strange men present.

At that moment, Hauser stepped behind him and grasped his shoulders. "You're going to get through this. I'm going to see to it."

"I think I have all I need for the moment, Mr. Ridenour," Captain Brace said. "I'll be in touch as soon as the doctor gives me his report. Do not touch or remove anything from this room, sir. We are not quite done with our search and it is all potentially evidence. Good day, gentlemen."

George Hauser seated himself in the chair vacated by the police captain and turned now to his true mission.

"How do you intend to deal with the miners and their demands, Ridenour? I represent a consortium of mine managers. This matter must be handled—"

"Mr. Hauser, if you please—I do not feel like discussing business—"

"I know this is difficult, son. I know how you feel."

"No, Mr. Hauser, I don't think you do. Unless someone has murdered *your* mother."

Hauser sat up in the little chair, duly chastised. He studied the room for several seconds, his eyes lingering upon the bloodstained carpet before the fireplace where the police supposed the blow to have occurred, then the trail of stains to the large blue velvet sofa, where Lucinda's body was discovered by her maid, Sadie Branch.

In the current theory of the police the assailant stabbed Lucinda, then fled, leaving his victim to bleed to death, alone in the big house.

"Well, perhaps tomorrow then," Hauser said.

"Yes," said Ridenour. "Perhaps then. Would you mind seeing yourself out?"

"Not at all. Take care, my boy."

The moment he heard George Hauser slam the front door, Christopher was down on his hands and knees. He reached into the shelf nearest the floor of the carved walnut étagère. He pushed aside a rotting, half-peeled apple and retrieved Kit Randall's wolf's-head pocketknife. Its short blade was still extended. He caught his breath as his hands trembled to hold it: the murder weapon. Here it lay, out in the open for anyone to see. This confirmed in his mind that the police investigating the case were utterly incompetent. Why had they not found it when they searched the room? Bumbling fools. Nothing about this investigation had proceeded as he thought it ought to. He was fond of reading detective novels, though he never imagined he would see his own life plunged into the heart of one.

He looked at the knife for several seconds, then closed it and placed it in his pocket. He drew his knees up to his chest and wrapped his arms around them. He hid his face and began to sob.

Kit rose early, careful not to wake Bella. She had laid out a spread of tarot cards at the foot of the bed, but had apparently fallen asleep before she finished reading them. She sometimes pondered a spread so long, her fortune-telling customers grew impatient.

Kit looked over the cards, with their weathered medieval pictures and the French captions which he had translated for her on the night they met. He was originally surprised she could not read these titles, given that she made a living "reading" them.

The cards lay in a pattern Bella called a five-card spread. A central card, known as the focus card, was surrounded by four additional cards, which she called the influences. The middle card was one he did not like, *Le Pendu*—the Hanged Man. She always insisted this card did not signify death. Usually it meant waiting. There was a Death card, too, and she claimed it did not mean death, either. Who made up this senseless stuff, anyway?

Bella took it all seriously. She did a quick reading every morning before getting out of bed to tell her what to expect from her day. She would pull one card from the deck, which lay on the floor next to her bed. She then recorded it in a little journal she kept just for the purpose.

One morning when he had been living with her the first time, she had drawn the Empress card and had immediately pounced on him and insisted they make love. Only afterward did she confess that the Empress represented fertility. This admission had infuriated him and caused him to sweat out the next couple of weeks. He was relieved to learn the cards could be wrong and that nothing procreative had gone on that morning.

He dressed and headed straight for the High Life Club. The casino did not open until noon, but he knew that Chris Ridenour usually arrived at his little office no later than ten.

Kit still had a key to the front door, but found it open. He wandered through the empty casino and immediately noticed that the nude portrait of Lucinda Ridenour had been removed. A tasteful note on the part of her son, no doubt. Kit used to wonder how Chris felt about a portrait of his mother in the altogether hanging up there over the bar for all the world to see. Of course, the average patron would not know the languorous maiden, reclining on the large Navajo blanket of the zigzagging Eye Dazzler pattern, was her. Her face was demurely obscured from the viewer by her arm draped across it in an apparent pose of napping, though all of her remaining charms were on complete and detailed display. A careful observer could note a tiny tattoo on her hip.

Kit had not known that Lucinda had been the model for

the painting until after the first time he had slept with her. He had walked into the High Life Club the next morning, casually looked up at the painting, and recognized the tattoo, having seen it on its owner, having *kissed it* on its owner, the night before. His jaw nearly hit the floor. The bartender, apparently wise to the secret, had chuckled at Kit's amazed expression.

To mask his chagrin, Kit had said to the smirking barkeep, "It's to cover a birthmark, you know. She told me so."

The man had shrugged, unimpressed, and resumed his work.

That he had felt the necessity to boast about his conquest immediately made him feel vulgar and immature at the same time. He wished he could take back the words, though in all fairness, Lucinda had not indicated the matter was confidential in any way.

She had told him she was born with a tiny red birthmark on her hip which she thought disfiguring since she had hoped for a career on the stage, which might involve the wearing of short skirts. A man she met—probably a lover, he guessed—suggested she have the mark disguised by an intriguing tattoo. The design she chose was a red-headed wolf howling at the full moon.

Before Kit reached Christopher Ridenour's accounting office, two large men blocked his path. He remembered one of the men, a tall burly New Mexican named Carlos, from the Eye Dazzler Mine. He served as a security guard when they were transporting large shipments of refined ore to the freight depot.

He did not recognize the other man, but both wore sidearms and carried shotguns.

"I'm here to see Chris." Kit tried to sound nonchalant.

"Mr. Ridenour is not seeing anyone today," Carlos said. He smoothed his hair in a vain manner. Though employed essentially as a thug, he took pains to present a refined image to the world.

"Well, he's gonna see me." Kit tried to push his way past the two larger men without success.

The commotion caused Christopher Ridenour to emerge from his office. He wore a black silk cravat and the black armband of formal mourning over his expensive gray frock coat.

"You!" he cried. "How dare you show your face here? Why haven't the police arrested you?"

"They haven't arrested me because I'm not guilty of anything. It's time we had a talk."

"Should we get rid of him, sir?" asked Carlos.

"See if he's armed. If not, I'll speak with him briefly."

With an angry grunt, Kit raised his arms and allowed the Eye Dazzler goons to search him for weapons, then he was allowed to follow Chris into the small accounting office.

"Look," Kit began, "I'm sorry about what happened to your mother. We parted company on real bad terms, but I'm sorry . . ."

"How dare you say you're sorry, you hypocrite! I know you killed her. I know it! And if the law doesn't bring you to justice, I will!"

Kit had never witnessed so much animation coming from the taciturn Chris Ridenour. Grief had turned the lamb into a lion.

"Are you insane? Excuse me, are you even *more* insane than before?"

"What did you come here for?" Ridenour said as he sat down behind his desk. He pretended to glance at his ledgers, though perspiration glistened on his forehead.

"Could we have this conversation without an audience, please?"

"I've hired these men to protect me. Someone took a shot at me as I left my office at midnight. I don't think it's much of a mystery who fired that shot. Oh, yes, Sadie Branch overheard you tell my mother that you planned to kill me."

"We need to talk about certain matters and I don't think you'll want your new friends to hear what I'm going to say to you. Trust me."

Ridenour nodded for the two guards to leave the room, but cautioned, "Stay close by."

Once the door closed, the two young men sat in silence, glaring at each other. Kit had never seen young Ridenour make so much eye contact in all the previous months of their acquaintance.

The young man's freckled face suddenly twisted up as he came near tears.

"How could you do it, Kit? She never hurt you. She never did anything but treat you with kindness and generosity."

"I didn't kill her. You know as well as I do why I moved out that day—"

"I know that you quarreled with her, but why? What made you so angry?"

Kit almost laughed at the ludicrously innocent pose that

his former housemate was now adopting. "I think you know."

Chris sat blank-faced and silent, his limpid, blue-green eyes still swimming.

"Oh, for God's sake, let's get this out in the open. I left because of what happened that night . . . in her bed!"

"What are you talking about?"

Kit thought he would explode. He no longer cared whether the two goons overheard them. "I may have been pretty far gone on the absinthe, but I knew what was going on. And I'm damned angry about it, you degenerate bastard!"

"I have no idea what you're ranting about."

Kit narrowed his eyes. "Are you claiming it never happened? Are you actually denying it?"

Christopher frowned and brushed his long ginger curls back from his face. "I don't know what you're talking about."

"Look, I asked your mother the next morning. She played all coy and smart, but she didn't deny it."

"*What* are you accusing me of?"

Christopher's belligerent innocence caused Kit to grasp the arms of his chair in exasperation. "Don't make me say it."

"My mother led you to believe that certain . . . that something took place . . . between *you and me?* After you'd passed out in the second parlor?" When he nodded, young Ridenour groaned and looked at his carefully arranged desktop. "My mother was not a well woman. Did that fact completely escape your notice?"

Kit had no answer for this.

"She suffered from delusions and depraved fantasies. Perhaps you would have observed this if you had not been so busy *fucking* her."

The cold fury of these words astounded Kit. He had never heard the boy utter such a crude word before. He had always wondered why Chris had been so accommodating about his affair with his mother. The first week, he had taken great pains to keep his visits to her bedroom a secret. On the fourth such occasion, though, he had lingered in her room past dawn and when he ventured out into the hallway he met Chris face-to-face.

The boy had said nothing, merely ducked his head and hurried on down the stairs. Kit had wanted to talk to him somehow about it, or apologize or offer to move out—whatever Chris thought was right—but he never mentioned it. Lucinda's response was simply a shrug and a "Don't worry about it, darling."

"There was nothing wrong with her," Kit managed to say with ebbing confidence.

"Years of drug use take their toll. A lesson you should learn before it's too late, my *former* friend."

You and your pills and powders. Had he simply imagined it? But it was so real. Too real. How could he imagine something he had never done before or even thought of? With renewed vigor, he resolved not to back down yet.

"You lying son of a bitch!" Kit dove across the desk and grabbed Ridenour by his black silk necktie.

"Carlos! Marco!" the young man shouted.

Kit managed to land one good punch before the bodyguards grabbed him, hoisted him into the air, and threw him out into the hallway, where they punched and kicked him until he lost consciousness.

———

"Eden, do you believe in karma?" Kit asked this as he lay in the hotel bed his uncle had retained for him the day before. His future aunt hovered over him, sponging blood from his hair.

"I'm afraid I've never heard the word, Kit. Sorry, I know this must hurt. Keep holding that cloth to your nose. Pinch the nostrils together hard. It's the only way to stop the bleeding. Is karma something you learned in college?"

"No, I learned it from this girl I know who's obsessed with going to India. It's a belief of the Hindus who live there. They think whatever you do will be rewarded or punished. Your good deeds and your bad—they'll all come back to you at some point."

"And was this your punishment?" She smiled as she asked this, but then saw that the young man was gravely serious.

"I don't know. All these bad things must be happening for some reason."

"Let's open up your shirt and view the damage there."

He lay still as a baby and let her unbutton his shirt and pull up his undershirt to expose his battered ribcage. He flinched as she gently poked and prodded the bruised areas caused by the hobnail boots of Christopher Ridenour's henchmen.

"I don't feel any broken ribs at least. I'm worried that we don't know how long you were unconscious. Are you having any trouble with your memory?"

"I *wish* I were."

She decided to test him. "What did you eat for breakfast?"

"I skipped breakfast."

"Where did you spend the night?"

"Are you testing my memory or checking up on me?" he said with a challenging tilt to his chin.

"A little of both. You know me too well."

"With a girl. A friend of mine. The one who wants to go to India. Her name is Bella Valentine. And she's *not* a whore, by the way. I'm sorry, do you mind me using words like that?"

"No, I don't mind. In fact I prefer it to silly roundabouts like 'soiled dove' and '*nymphe du pavé*' and the like. Just don't talk like that around Hadley."

"I wouldn't do that. Anyway, she's not a whore even though most of the women who live in her boardinghouse are. She makes her living telling people's fortunes with tarot cards. That's how I met her. My first night in Leadville, she was telling fortunes in this bar called the Scarlett. She's trying to save money so she can go to India like this famous spiritualist she idolizes, named Madame Blavatsky." He rolled his eyes. "Anyway, they've written to each other. I saw the letters."

He sighed and grew pensive again. "Eden, do you think everybody's a whore at some price?"

"Define 'whore' for me."

"You *know*." He blushed on the unbruised side of his battered face. He obviously wanted to talk about this subject but it was nearly too sensitive for him to tolerate.

She rinsed out the bloody rag in the basin at her side. She and Hadley had found Kit unconscious on State Street near the High Life Club, just before noon. Brad had not been with them—he had looked up an old army acquaintance named Boyd Whitney, in the hope of learning more local information on the Ridenours and the murder—so she was forced to pay two men to carry Kit back to their hotel.

"I wish Hadley would hurry up with that ice. At least at this altitude, you never suffer from a shortage of ice. The cold will help the swelling on your eye."

His left eye was swollen entirely shut at the moment. "You've decided to change the subject, I see."

She chuckled, then regarded him with a cocked eyebrow. "Do you think *you're* a whore?"

"No. Well, I don't know. Bella says even married women are whores, that they just trade bed for board. She says putting a ring on your finger doesn't really change the transaction."

"Do you agree?"

"I think she's crazy. We've had lots of arguments about this. That's the main reason we went quits the first time. Then again, there's those who would say that's what I did with Mrs. Ridenour." What he did not want to mention was that this idea came from Lucinda Ridenour herself.

"Hmmm . . . I suppose I can see the point."

"But if someone forced you to do something against your will, like when you were captured by Indians and they . . . well, you know—"

" 'Rape' is the word you're looking for." Unlike most, she did not bother to delicately sidestep the word and use "outrage" or some other watered-down bypass. The act was ugly and made no less so by a coy rephrasing.

"No one could blame you because you had no choice in the matter, right? And you'd be justified in taking revenge, right?"

"What are you talking about?" she said with a suspicious frown.

"Nothing. I'm just babbling. Forget I said all this."

She tried to sponge more blood out of his hair. "If Mr. Ridenour believes that you killed his mother, why didn't he turn you over to the police today?"

He shrugged. She could almost swear he had an answer, but he did not want to share it.

"Why did you go see him at all? I don't understand."

"I needed to get something straight. I obviously wish now I hadn't." He sighed again, not so much from pain as from a strange and secret despair. He took her hand in his and whispered, "I think . . . I'm losing my mind."

"Why do you say that?"

"I see things that aren't there. I dream strange things and believe they really happened. Or maybe they did happen, but I can't seem to tell the difference anymore."

"I think you need to rest." She wrung out the cloth once more and placed it on his head.

Eight

Brad walked in just after four and, the moment he saw his nephew, exploded.

"Where is my hunting rifle?"

"In a safe place," Kit said. He avoided looking at his furious uncle.

Eden tensed as she watched the two.

"Where have you been? I did not appreciate spending good money on a room for you in the most expensive hotel in town only to have you sneak out and steal my brand-new rifle—a birthday gift, I might add, from my brother-in-law."

Hadley sat on the other side of Kit's bed, trying to mimic her mother's nursing endeavors, and watched the byplay between Kit and her father with curiosity.

Brad sat on the far edge of the bed and asked, "What happened to you?"

"Nothing" was Kit's surly reply.

"Kit went to see the young man whose mother was killed and the man's bodyguards did this to him," Eden said. "We found him in the street, unconscious."

"Well, I've learned some interesting tidbits from my old friend Boyd Whitney, but we'll have to discuss it all at a later time. For now, where's my rifle?"

Kit reluctantly confessed. "You remember that girl—the

one I was with when you found me? Well, it's under her bed. She doesn't know it's there."

"I'm going to get it straight away."

"I'll go with you," Eden said. She rose to wash her hands though the water in the basin was stained red with Kit's blood.

"I don't think so, dear," Brad said. "It's not the sort of 'house' ladies go visit."

"The sun is still up and I don't believe prostitution is contagious. Trust me, I'll survive." She pulled her shawl around her shoulders against the growing chill of the mountain afternoon.

"Her name's Bella Valentine, Uncle Brad. She's a nice girl, not like the other girls there. You'll like her. Don't rile her, though. She practices witchcraft. She might put a spell on you."

This revelation brought a bemused smile to the faces of Eden and Brad.

"I'm serious," Kit said. "She's a corker. She casts spells and curses and says she can talk to the dead. She'll tell your fortune if you pay her. Don't tell her what happened to me or she'll want to come here and nurse me."

"Don't you want to see her?" Eden said.

Kit looked uncomfortable. "If she comes to a fancy place like this they'll give her trouble. I don't want her to be embarrassed on my account. It's just that they might mistake her for a—" He glanced at Hadley and stopped his sentence.

"Sounds like meeting Miss Valentine is going to be interesting," said Eden.

"Just don't rile her," Kit called after them.

"Duly warned," said Brad, whose anger at his nephew was starting to subside. "You *will* be here when we return, won't you?"

"I'm keeping my eye on him, Papa," said Hadley. "You don't have to worry."

"Actually, I need to go down the hall," said Kit. He referred to the water closet. The Clarendon offered fancy, flushing privies on every floor of the hotel. "Don't worry, I'll come back."

He sat up holding his side, and swung his legs over the edge of the bed, but the minute he tried to rise, he promptly fell flat on the floor. Eden and Brad rushed to his side and Hadley hung over the bed to see what had happened.

"My knee gave way," Kit said in surprise.

"Look at that swelling." Eden saw that Kit's left knee had swollen such that his trouser leg strained at the seams.

"Why didn't you tell me that your knee was hurt?" She looked in her valise for scissors.

"Couldn't feel it. Totally numb."

Brad helped him back into bed. Eden and Hadley left the room so that Kit could make use of the chamber pot. Any future trips to the flushing privy would require help. She wondered where they might be able to locate a set of crutches for him or perhaps a cane.

Eden heard the two men speaking in low voices, then laughing together over some shared joke. She had to note that for all her future husband's harsh opinions on his nephew, he loved him like a son, though only fourteen years separated them in age.

That their laughter died suddenly and was replaced again by serious tones caused her to wonder, though when she was called back into the room the two men did not seem angry.

She went to work with her sewing scissors, opening the seam of his trouser leg so that it might be mended at a later date. She cut off the entire lower portion of his cotton drawers, deciding not to bother saving it. She then swaddled the grotesquely swollen knee with a towel and packed it in ice.

"I don't think anything is broken," she said. "Maybe a torn or sprained ligament. We'll know more when the swelling goes down."

As she and Brad prepared to leave again, Kit called to his uncle, "You'll ask her?"

Brad nodded and steered Eden out the door.

———

"You'll ask me what?" she said as they started their journey through the noisy streets of Leadville.

"He has another symptom. One he was too embarrassed to ask you about himself. When he made water just now there was some blood in it."

"Blood in his urine? Very much?"

"No, I don't think so, but I'm no judge. It appeared to be just a trace, but enough that it scared him into making me have a look." Brad wrinkled his nose with distaste and mumbled, "Just how I wanted to end my day, looking at somebody else's water."

"He's harmed a kidney, no doubt. Those men must have kicked him in the back."

"That sounds serious."

"Kidneys are good at healing themselves. He should be

all right in a week or two, but he'll need complete bed rest. No jostling, no travel on a horse until he is free of symptoms. Even that miserable coach we rode in on would be too bumpy."

"Damn," he uttered under his breath as they waited for the traffic to clear enough that they could cross Harrison Street. "I guess we won't be leaving here anytime soon, regardless of how Kit comes out with the police."

"Not without risking his health, maybe even his life." She linked her arm in his and said, "I won't go to that house if you don't want me to. I just wanted us to have some time alone together to talk. Tell me what you found out."

"Quite a lot and none of it very good. It seems Kit managed to become the paramour of the most notorious woman in all of Leadville."

"Given the wildness of this place, there must have been many contenders for that throne."

"How could the Randall family—Puritan Vermont Yankees to the bone—have produced such an amoral rascal as Kit? Stop laughing—it's not really funny."

"I'm sorry, you're right. The woman is dead and I suppose she should rest in peace, though I'd like to know what in God's name went on in that house—"

"The Black Lace House—that's what the people here call it. I'll show it to you. It's not far from here. Boyd Whitney took me by it. It's a monstrosity. Looks more like a bawdy house than the one we are actually headed to."

"Did Mr. Whitney know the Ridenours?"

"He knew *of* them, but they didn't run in the same social circle. Boyd is a respectable family man with a wife and four children. He owns a hardware store and seems quite prosperous from the look of both the store and the house."

They turned the corner of Third Street and there, standing tall in all its questionable glory, sat the Ridenour mansion. The house was painted a dark shade of red and the elaborate trim was entirely black.

"I've seen red barns and red school houses before, but never a private residence painted that color."

"Boyd told an amusing story to explain that," said Brad. "Rumor had it that the original color was a respectable green, with darker green trim. Mrs. Ridenour accused her husband of being color blind, a charge he vehemently denied. To prove her contention, the wife had the house painted red and black while her husband was in the east on a business trip. Supposedly, he came home and never noticed the change until someone remarked on it."

"It looks like the house itself is in mourning," said Eden as she studied the unusual architecture of the house, which included two large wings joined on a diagonal by a round porch on the ground floor—a look which was repeated on the second floor with a balcony. Every possible angle and edge dripped with depressing black fretwork.

"Boyd knew the late Orson Ridenour. He was a lawyer by profession. He drew up the town charter a few years ago. When his mine struck it so rich, he abandoned his law practice and pursued his investments full time. He was prominent in local government and well thought of about town. Until his scandalous marriage, that is."

"What made his marriage so scandalous? Was there a divorce involved?"

Brad chuckled. "Better than a divorce—a nude painting."

Eden's eyes widened.

"According to Boyd, this Lucinda Ridenour was quite a beauty and a large painting of her—*au naturel*—hung in her husband's casino on State Street for all to see."

She smothered a scandalized giggle behind her gloved hand. "A *married* woman allowed a painting of her displayed to the public?"

"I can't imagine such a husband," said Brad.

"Nor such a wife—"

Their conversation was interrupted by a brass marching band trumpeting down the street with a boastful clashing of cymbals. It seemed the excuse was someone's birthday, judging from the colorful signs carried by some of the celebrants. The musicians appeared to be escorting the birthday guests to the site of the party.

"That's the third brass band I've seen since arriving here," Eden said.

"Leadville loves them, I guess. Kit told me you can't blow your nose in this town without a brass band accompaniment." He was discreetly editing Kit's much more scatological remark on the subject.

They linked arms once again and shifted their direction toward the boardinghouse where Bella Valentine resided.

"Boyd also told me that the late Orson Ridenour took his own life," Brad said. "He was found shot in the head at his office at the mine a year ago last Christmas."

"The family seems plagued by violence and death."

"Yes. The talk among the business community has been whether young Ridenour is really up to the task of running the various family businesses. He's apparently a pious and sober young man, quite industrious and clever with figures, but not a leader. Very shy and reclusive."

" 'Shy and reclusive' does not seem to fit the tenor of this town."

"Hardly," Brad said. "He's barely twenty years old. And there are rumors of labor unrest. A strike has been threatened. They think this will be the young man's true test."

"Oh, dear." Eden tightened her hold on Brad's arm as they turned the corner up onto the busy main commercial thoroughfare of Chestnut Street. "I'd feel sorry for him to have to deal with so much at once—had he not seen fit to have our Kit so brutally attacked."

"This girl, Bella, her house is just down the end of this lane. Not too much farther."

Their attention was once again snagged by the retreating brass band. The group quit playing mid-song and suddenly dispersed in wild disarray.

Eden clutched Brad's sleeve and both strained to see what was happening in the next block. A group of men had ridden up on horseback. There was considerable shouting going on, but they could not make out the words.

"You wait here," Brad said. He pushed her into a nearby confectionery, though most of its occupants now spilled out onto the sidewalk to view the commotion.

She pressed her face against the glass of the store's bay window and watched in horror as a man on horseback with his hands bound behind him was positioned beneath one of the large telegraph poles. A rope was tossed over the lowest crossbar and secured. A noose was placed around the man's neck and his horse was given a kick. The man jerked and swung in the air beneath the pole as the crowd roared its approval.

Eden turned away, sickened by the sight. She seated herself at one of the filigreed, white wrought-iron tables.

Eventually the store's owner and patrons returned, along with her breathless fiancé. He sat down opposite her at the little table.

"I suppose you saw what happened," Brad said.

She nodded.

"The man was accused of killing someone in a town called Dickey. A uniformed policeman stood right next to me and did nothing. When I asked him about it, he just snickered and said, 'Why would I stop it? They're just doing my job for me.' "

Eden shook her head in dismay.

"Shall we continue to our original destination? I don't care to keep you out here past dark."

They left the shop and hurried toward the lodgings of Miss Valentine.

"Eden, I've just come to a decision that I hope you won't find shocking."

She knew exactly what he was thinking. She thought the same.

"I believe in the law," he said. "You know I do."

"But after the rough justice we just saw dispensed, you no longer wish to trust Kit's fate to the local legal system."

"Exactly," he said, relieved that she had put it into words. "I spent an hour last night lecturing him on how important it was for him to go in and talk to the police. Now, all I want to do is get him out of here."

"I couldn't agree more."

He paused and looked down, peering deeply into her eyes. "If he's guilty, that will make us both criminals, too, you know."

"I know."

"Are you sure about this? He's my nephew and I'm going to see this through the best I know how, but I hate making a criminal of you as well. That's more than a husband can ask."

"I couldn't love Kit more if he were my own blood relation. He once risked his own life to save mine. How could I do less for him? The problem is, he honestly should not be moved."

"I have an idea," Brad said as they resumed walking once again. "Boyd's store sold all manner of gear to set up a camp. In fact they even offered whole sets of outfitting supplies for prospectors who want to go up into the mountains and pan for gold on remote claims. They have everything you need—tents, cots, lanterns, cooking pots. When I jokingly complained to Boyd about the shocking cost of the Clarendon, he pointed out the supplies and said, 'Is the family game for a little camping in the wild?' I thought he was joking but he was entirely serious. He says there is a lovely lake near town with incredible views and great fishing."

"It's not as though I've never lived out of doors," she said, with reference to the fourteen years she had spent as the wife of a Cheyenne medicine man.

"Surely we can manage long enough to get Kit into traveling condition. We'll need to hire a rig, but that cost is nothing compared to what we have been paying to stay in town."

"Let's start making arrangements tonight."

He hugged her tight. "I love you so much. Thank you for being so understanding."

When they at last reached the boardinghouse of Bella Valentine, all seemed quiet on the wide porch. Eden waited there while Brad went in.

She watched through the uncurtained front parlor window to see a tall young woman, about Kit's age, descend the stairs and greet Brad. She was not a great beauty, but Eden found a simple, quirky charm in Miss Valentine's wide gray eyes and her wider smile. Eden could not quite picture her and Kit together. Bella's height and her odd manner of dress—the wild topknot of golden hair coupled with her flowing, East India–inspired robes—made her seem far too eccentric for Kit's sophisticated tastes.

Bella and Brad disappeared up the stairs and soon returned with Brad now carrying his hunting rifle. Miss Valentine followed him down the stairs at a strong clip and looked as though she were angry about something. At the bottom of the steps she defiantly placed her hands on her hips. Brad's reply was to shrug his shoulders, then abruptly make for the door.

He retrieved Eden from her post on the front porch and they hurried into the gathering twilight. Eden glanced back just once and realized that young Miss Valentine had followed them out onto the porch and now stood observing their departure.

"She had heard all about Kit being attacked by young

Ridenour's bodyguards. She demanded to know where he was, but I declined to tell her. She got a bit belligerent about it, as though she had the right to know. I finally lied and said that he had disappeared again after telling me where he had stowed my rifle." Brad frowned to himself as they walked along the crowded sidewalk. "Soon Kit will have us lying to everyone in town."

Nine

Brad and Eden purchased all manner of camping gear from an outfitter competing with Randall's friend so as not to let anyone know their plans. They hired a wagon to stow all the goods and smuggled Kit out of the Clarendon before dawn.

They waited at the edge of the forest north of town for enough light to negotiate the slim path that led to the alpine lake. They located a suitable campsite with surprising ease, a flat clearing far enough from the wagon road to allow privacy, yet near enough to the water so that it needn't be carried long distances.

Kit had suffered through a bad night before they left in the hired rig. Eden and Brad took turns sitting up with him. He had finally fallen asleep on the rough journey into the forest, having giving in and taken the pain-killing drugs he had first rejected.

Eden noted that he seemed to be making a show of this drug refusal. She assumed he was trying to make a point to his uncle that he sincerely intended to reform his dissolute habits.

Eden and Randall pitched the large canvas tent while Hadley gathered firewood from dried slash upon the ground. Eden made mental note of provisions they would need to see them all through the next week or two.

Once Kit was put to bed on his cot, they returned to town to check out of their lodgings at the Clarendon.

As they rode into Leadville with Hadley wedged between them in the wagon's driver's seat, the little girl said, "Kit will be a lot happier staying in that tent than in our hotel."

"Why's that, honey?" Brad asked.

"No mirrors."

Eden grinned, thinking this was the lead-up to some sort of joke. "And why would our handsome Kit not like mirrors?"

"He's afraid of mirrors."

"What do you mean?"

"The other day when you and Daddy went to get his rifle back, Kit looked in the mirror over the chest of drawers and got all scared and thought someone else was in the room with us. He said, 'Do you see him? Do you see him?' and I said, 'See who? There's just us here.' Then he made me stare straight in the mirror and said, 'You don't see a boy with blond hair?' I looked and looked, but I didn't. Then he pulled the bedcovers over his face and I think he started crying."

Eden held her daughter close and patted her shoulder. "I think he was just in a lot of pain, darling." She looked over Hadley's head to Brad and mouthed the word, "Drugs?"

He nodded sadly, then sighed.

When they entered the Clarendon to settle their account, the desk clerk announced that Brad had a telegram waiting for him. A worried look crossed both their faces.

Eden unconsciously held her breath as she watched Brad read the message. Telegrams only brought bad news, it seemed to her, and his expression did nothing to alleviate this fear.

"It's from Amanda," he said. "B.J. is gravely ill. She asks me to come at once."

"Oh, darling, I'm so sorry. That's terrible. You must go."

"What a time for this to happen. I don't know what to do. Are you certain Kit can't travel?"

His distraught face told so much of his history. The long illness and agonizing death of his little daughter, Sarah, had done much to destroy his marriage to Amanda. The couple never recovered from the tragedy.

"It might kill him to move. There's no doubt in my mind. I just hope the trip into the woods didn't hurt him too much." With a sad sigh, she knew what must happen. "You have to go back there and be with your son. I'll stay here and look after Kit."

"Certainly not. I could never leave you to fend for yourself in this hell hole. No man in his right mind would leave the woman he loves in such straits."

"Don't be ridiculous. I have 'fended for myself' all my life. You know that better than anyone."

"But—but—"

"I'll be fine and so will Kit. Now stop worrying."

"The Western Union office is just around the corner. I'll need to wire my sister and tell her she's about to have an unplanned houseguest."

"Two houseguests," Eden said.

"What?"

She pulled him into a corner of the lobby away from the

milling guests. "I think I'd feel better if you took Hadley with you."

"I'd love to take her east with me, but—"

"Please, Brad. It would make my job of looking after Kit a lot easier."

"Jennetta has been asking when she would get to meet you and Hadley."

"I've been longing for Hadley to meet her brother, though it's unfortunate the circumstance. Still, she's a good little nurse. Will Amanda . . . will she be kind to her?"

"I honestly have no idea. She never brought up the subject of Hadley in the divorce proceedings, not that she was in a position to make a fuss on the score. I'll see to it that it's not a problem, but still, leaving you here to fend for yourself . . . I just can't see my way clear—"

"What's the matter? Afraid to leave me alone with your wayward nephew?" She smiled teasingly. "Worried he'll seduce me as he seems to do every other woman he meets?"

"I don't think he poses much of a threat in his present condition." He pondered the situation. "Still I think we had better keep one of our rooms here at the hotel, don't you? I mean, it's not that I don't trust you—"

"Yes, all joking aside, I believe everyone would feel more comfortable if I slept in town. Kit can get up if he needs to with the help of that cane we bought. I'll go out and check on him every day and bring him food and such."

Despite all their comments on mutual trust, she had mentally breathed a sigh of relief when Brad had mentioned staying at his sister Jennetta's house. She trusted him, but his formidable first wife was another matter entirely.

"Promise you will get yourselves to Denver the moment he can travel?"

"Of course. The matter is settled. Go east and nurse your son back to health. When he's better, we'll all be reunited . . . *and* have a wedding to celebrate."

When she had kissed them both good-bye, the two people she loved most in the world, and struggled against the tears filling her eyes, she stood alone at the stage stop and felt the oddest sense of . . . relief. She was free. At least for the next several weeks, she was free to do as she pleased, free to untangle this terrible puzzle enmeshing Kit.

As she walked from the stagecoach station to the livery to retrieve her hired rig, she heard the newsboys on the streets shouting the latest local developments.

"Dazzler miners go on strike! Read all about it."

She bought a paper and scanned the Eye Dazzler story. The night shift had voted to strike, then met the day shift at seven the previous morning and convinced them to join in. No work was done at the Dazzler and the miners, some three hundred in number, had marched up and down Harrison Street to trumpet their solidarity, then headed straight for Christopher Ridenour's office in the back of the High Life Club on State Street.

Ridenour met them, flanked by his armed guards, and refused their demands: a wage of four dollars a day, an eight-hour work day, and the right to choose their own shift bosses.

Ridenour declined to be interviewed. The paper expressed sympathy for the recent loss of his mother and criticized the union for taking advantage of the situation and exploiting the tragedy for their own ends. They trod close to the libel laws, in Eden's estimation, by hinting, almost suggesting, that the unions may have been responsible for Lucinda Ridenour's murder.

She read an interesting history of the current labor situation on an inside page. One George Hauser presumed to speak on behalf of the grieving young man now at the helm of the current crisis, though his connection as banker to the Ridenour interests did not appear to give him authority to claim this honor.

Hauser stated that the collapse of the Little Pittsburgh Mine earlier that spring precipitated much of the unrest in the Leadville mining district. The Little Pittsburgh's stock had traded in New York for more than thirty-five dollars a share the year before, when Horace Tabor sold his interest for one million dollars and the mine was syndicated.

Then the Little Pittsburgh, which in its heyday produced as much as two thousand ounces of silver for every ton of carbonate lead dug out of the ground, took a downward turn.

The fatal words "played out" were soon heard on Carbonate Hill and the stock dropped to less than two dollars a share. New investors would be impossible to find in the current climate of doubt and fear. All the mine owners and investors were anxious. If the Little Pittsburgh could fail, would the Eye Dazzler or the Chrysolite or the Robert E. Lee be next? The mine owners were in no mood to be generous in dealing with their employees.

Hauser opined that the arrival of the railroad would bring in still more cheap labor and vanquish the unions, a worry voiced by a striking miner who refused to be identified in the article.

Eden wondered if the newspaper was right to suspect the union might have been involved in Lucinda Ridenour's murder. Would these men—could these men—many of whom seemed more refined than she would have guessed prior to seeing them firsthand, really stoop to murdering a woman, however much they disliked or disapproved of her?

She hurried to her tasks, buying a few items at a mercantile, then picking up some foodstuffs at the grocery.

A perplexing question arose when she noticed Miss Bella Valentine on the sidewalk outside both stores while she shopped. Was it a coincidence or was the girl following her? Did she remember her from the other day when Brad came to claim his rifle?

Eden hurried on her way, set her purchases in her wagon, and waited until she saw absolutely no sign of Miss Valentine before returning to Kit at the tent in the woods.

———

"Do you know Jacob Landry?" she asked Kit as they ate bread and cheese in his humble temporary home—quite a comedown from the grand and glorious Clarendon, not to mention the Black Lace House. The newspaper article on the strike had mentioned Landry several times, but she could not figure out on which side of the labor divide to place him.

"Not really. He was the superintendent of the Eye Dazzler Mine until Lucy and Chris fired him a few days ago."

"Why was he let go?"

"I'm not sure. She told me they had caught him in some

kind of wrongdoing but she didn't say what and I didn't bother to ask. I think maybe he stole the Ridenours' personal account book. The union got a hold of it from somewhere. He's a real turncoat, if that's true. He should have been loyal to the Ridenours, but that's another story."

"One you'd better tell, I think." She watched him grimace at the prospect of talking about his former hosts.

"All this is servants' gossip, you understand," he said. "Lucinda's maid, Sadie Branch, told me a long and crazy story one day about Lucinda and Jake. They carried on quite a love affair even though both were married to others at the time. Why old Ridenour put up with it, I have no idea. Apparently it was the talk of the town so there's no way he could have been in the dark."

She hesitated to ask the next question, but had to know the answer. "Why did they part? Uhm . . . because of you?"

"No, no, I came later, though . . ." Kit pushed aside the remainder of his supper and lay down again on the cot.

She could tell he felt miserable and opened her bag to locate some laudanum. She handed him the bottle. He seemed to have less hesitation about drug-taking now that his uncle was no longer present.

"Sadie used to tease me and say Lucinda took up with me just to spite Jake. I guess Lucinda thought once her husband was dead and she inherited all that Eye Dazzler money, she and Jake would just run off together or something, but that didn't happen. I don't know why. It wasn't something she or her son ever talked about."

"How did Orson Ridenour die?"

"Shot himself. Christmas Day, a year and a half ago. A suicide. At least they *assumed* it was a suicide. He was found dead in his own office out at the Eye Dazzler workings on Carbonate Hill. There were no witnesses. Christmas Day was the only day of the entire year the mine was closed. There was no evidence of foul play. No sign of a struggle. No theft. His petty cash box sat open in the room with every dollar accounted for, seven hundred and eighty-four dollars, in fact."

"No suicide note?"

"Nope, but lots in town speculate. Christopher thought it was an accident. I think the police officially listed it that way, too." Kit made a face to indicate he thought this an unlikely circumstance. "How do you *accidentally* shoot yourself in the temple?"

"Murder was never discussed?"

"Nobody could come up with a motive. He had plenty of money right there in his office, so there was no theft. I guess his wife had the most to gain, but she had an alibi. She and Chris were both seen in church that morning." Kit chuckled mirthlessly. "I never saw Lucinda set foot in church all the while I knew her. Now Chris is a Sunday morning regular at the local Presbyterian church, but not her. I never saw her leave her bed before noon on a Sunday. Saturday nights in the Black Lace House tended to stretch into dawn."

"How did you learn all this about Mr. Ridenour's death?"

"Sadie Branch told me some. Enough to make me curious. It started to give me a chill, so I went down to the newspaper office and went into their archives to read about it."

"How did the young man—Christopher—get along with his stepfather?"

"Obviously better than I get on with mine." Kit tried to smile. "Of course, that wouldn't be hard, would it?"

"What *is* the problem between you and your stepfather? May I ask it? I've always wondered."

He shrugged. "He's a son of a bitch."

"Was he cruel to you?"

"You could say that."

She did not know how to penetrate the evasive wall he always threw up when asked about the difficulties between him and his mother's new husband. "Did he . . . beat you?"

"Yeah, a couple of times, but that's not it."

"I don't understand."

With a disgusted sigh, he finally said, "He essentially made my mother choose between him and me. I guess it's obvious who she chose."

"I'm sorry. I had no right to ask. We were talking about Christopher and Mr. Ridenour."

"They got on fine, I think. The old man adopted Chris. He never had a father he could call his own before that." He suddenly stopped to laugh. "Would you believe he got taken on their honeymoon?"

Eden raised her eyebrows at this. "You're kidding."

"It's true. Swear to God. And Chris was *fourteen* at the time. Ridenour took them on a three-month tour of Europe. They talked about it constantly. You would have thought it was six months ago, not six years ago, they went on about it so much. It must have been the biggest thing that ever happened to them."

Eden shook her head in added disbelief.

"I sure wasn't invited on *my* mother and stepfather's

honeymoon trip. Of course, it would make some kind of sense if you were to believe what Lucinda said about—"

"Yes?" she said.

"Nothing. Never mind. She said lots of preposterous things. Her own son said she was a loony, that she suffered from 'depraved fantasies.' "

"What do *you* think?"

He sighed. "I think I'm even crazier than she was."

———

Eden spent the morning looking for another hotel room. She did not like the fact that she was still registered under the name "Mrs. Bradley Randall." She decided she must register at another hotel as "Mrs. Eden Murdoch" in order to avoid anyone making the connection between her and Kit and possibly following her into the woods.

She spent a fruitless three hours walking up and down the streets of Leadville and being told by every hotel and boardinghouse that accepted women guests that they were full to bursting.

She bought a newspaper to see if any private homeowners were advertising for boarders. She decided to walk past the Black Lace House out of curiosity and suddenly found a novel solution to her housing problem.

A sign posted in the front window of the grand home announced:

HOUSEKEEPER WANTED

She smiled at this stroke of luck. If she could land the job she would have virtually unlimited access to the house and its secrets. What might she find? Gossiping servants? Letters and diaries? Her pulse raced with the possibilities that might present themselves to discover what had really gone on there. Maybe she could clear Kit's name, remove him as a suspect in Lucinda Ridenour's murder. Brad would be so relieved, not to mention Kit, of course.

Before she could enter the front yard, two men stepped out of the house and paused upon the large covered porch. One was a very tall, slender young man with wildly curly ginger-colored hair plastered back from his forehead with some sort of hair oil. Because he wore a black armband of mourning, Eden assumed he must be Christopher Ridenour.

The smaller, middle-aged man with whom he spoke looked to be a tradesman of some sort, too well dressed to be a miner, but too solicitous of the younger gentleman to be a social acquaintance.

A large, rough-looking man sat lounging in a porch chair. He had a rifle braced across his lap. She assumed this must be a bodyguard, perhaps one of the men who had beaten up Kit.

The visitor replaced his black top hat and said in a European accent Eden could not place, "Worry not, dear sir. I shall see to every detail. You must soon provide me with an appropriate frock for your mother's final rest."

Young Ridenour wrung his hands.

"The less bustle the better, and no train, if you please," continued the little man, who Eden now realized was the undertaker. "High-necked, of course, for—uhm—obvious reasons." He thoughtlessly touched his own throat at the site of Lucinda Ridenour's fatal neck wound to illustrate his point. He instantly regretted this blunder, withdrawing his hand and plunging it into his pocket as though to punish it for its misbehavior. But he was too late.

Christopher Ridenour winced visibly. The bodyguard had the tactless impudence to smirk at this, which annoyed his young employer.

"Carlos, you're dismissed for the remainder of the day. I will see you this evening at the High Life prior to closing."

The hired guard frowned and nodded, then left the darkened porch of the Black Lace House. He squinted into the fierce mountain sunlight as he seemed to re-enter the outside world. He glanced down at Eden as he strode past her on the sidewalk. She pretended to study the newspaper she had been carrying.

The undertaker delivered his practiced refrain of condolences, then departed as well, leaving the young Eye Dazzler heir alone on his front porch looking like as forlorn a boy as Eden had ever seen.

He sat down in the chair the bodyguard had just vacated and covered his face with his hands in a despairing gesture.

Eden boldly approached.

"Excuse me, sir. Perhaps I can help."

Ridenour looked up, startled and wary. Grief aged his young face.

"Forgive me, but I overheard your conversation with that gentleman and perhaps I can help you with this . . . difficult task. In matters of dress, a woman might see things a man does not."

"A high-necked gown—where am I to locate that?" he

asked in a pleading, exasperated tone as though he expected her to understand this.

"An appropriate frock shouldn't be hard to find."

"You don't know my mother." He shook his head in such a defeated way, it seemed almost a caricature, but he was obviously not the type to joke about such a thing.

"Let me help."

"Excuse me, but—who are you?"

She pointed to the sign in the window. "I've come about the position."

"Oh." Ridenour relaxed and tried to create a smile, for the sake of civility.

"If you take me to your mother's room, I promise you I'll find an appropriate gown."

———

After being led to Lucinda Ridenour's spacious closet and darting through several dozen dresses, Eden quickly realized why the son felt such hopelessness at locating a high-necked gown to clothe his mother for her last repose.

Who was this woman who dressed like a music hall entertainer even in her own home? Did she bare her bosom at the breakfast table, for heaven's sake?

Eden glanced out to find her future employer. The young man sat in the bedroom on a chair before a cold fireplace. He stared at the floor, lost in his thoughts.

Above his head loomed a large oil painting of a woman with dark reddish hair holding a parrot. Was this the notorious Lucinda Ridenour herself? Eden wondered. The woman was beautiful in a lush and sensuous way. Her immodest dress in the painting, while not so shocking as the nude portrait on the Eye Dazzler rug that Brad had described, was still highly provocative. No decent matron would pose for a likeness with her blouse hanging open exposing nearly all of her bosom.

What became of the parrot? she wondered. A brass parrot stand stood silently in the corner of the room. The tray beneath it lay covered with seed husks and droppings, but no bird was in sight.

"I think the best choice might be this soft blue silk, Mr. Ridenour. Here is a white lace shawl. I can cut and style it into a jabot at the throat."

He looked up with a flicker of hope in his pale, blue-green eyes. She saw them for only an instant before he dropped his gaze down again. "You're certain this will work?"

"Yes. Uhm . . . does this mean you wish to employ me, sir?"

He turned a sweet smile on her and stood up. "It seems you are already indispensable to me, Miss—?"

"Mrs. Murdoch." She extended her hand and he shook it.

"Are you sure you don't mind working here? All the other servants have left, you see. Because of what happened. I assume you know all about that?"

"I read about it in the papers, yes. I'm deeply sorry for your loss. I'm afraid we have one dreadful thing in common, sir. My own husband, the late Mr. Murdoch, was also a victim of murder, so I believe I have some understanding of your situation."

"Oh, my. I'm sorry to hear that, ma'am. I'm grateful for your offer of work. I need someone to see to the house and cook my dinner for me. I don't require breakfast and usually dine out at midday. Hopefully, the work will not be too trying until additional staff can be hired."

"I'm nothing if not resourceful. I'll do my best."

He then took her on a tour of the house, mentioning various items like hours and wages, the list of stores with which he held trade accounts, but Eden barely heard him, so intent was she on studying the house and trying to find a way to unlock its disturbing secrets.

Though not large by eastern standards, the house was grand in ornament. The large double doors bore the interlocking triangles of the Eye Dazzler company insignia in their etched glass inserts, as did a set of china in the long dining room with its table seating twelve in comfort.

A beautiful library and well-furnished kitchen occupied the back of the house, together with a bathing room whose tub was supplied with hot water heated by the gas-fired kitchen stove on the other side of the wall. Ridenour graciously offered Eden the use of the bathtub, whenever he was not home. He also mentioned she would have the Ridenour family carriage at her disposal for any shopping trips, should she desire it, though most local stores offered delivery. His generosity impressed her.

A splendidly carved staircase in the front hall led to the upper floors, with Lucinda's grand boudoir and two smaller, more masculine-looking bedrooms on the second floor, and some austere servants' quarters on the third. She was told her room would be here. She peeked in and found a large dormitory-style room capable of accommodating at least six women. A similar room on the other side of the dark hallway presumably housed the male members of the staff. She had to smile to think she would occupy this entire floor by herself.

Before leaving the third floor, she noted a small, back staircase that must lead to an attic and wondered if it might hold any items of interest.

They returned to the main floor and her new employer briefly pointed out the back parlor, which held a beautiful grand piano as well as the famous rug, which hung upon the wall.

"This is what the Eye Dazzler Mine is named after," he said. "It's a Navajo rug. The pattern is called an 'eye dazzler' because it makes one dizzy to look at it."

"It's interesting," she said to be courteous. The brightly colored pattern indeed seemed to vibrate. "Have I seen the entire house now?"

"No, there's one more room." He looked troubled and led her to the closed doors of the front parlor. "This room still needs to be cleaned."

She parted the gorgeously carved pocket doors and peeked in. She saw immediately why the young man was loathe to look inside. Dark bloodstains covered the Turkish carpet and the sofa.

"If you do not feel you can do it—"

"Mr. Ridenour, by tomorrow night when you return home from your office, you will find no trace of what happened in there. Rest assured."

"You are so kind, Mrs. Mur—"

Their discussion was interrupted by an insistent knock at the front door. Eden saw the apprehension in young Ridenour's face. He seemed in constant fear for his safety, but the tightness in his jaw relaxed when the caller made his identity known.

"Ridenour? George Hauser here. Are you in there, son?"

"Yes, Mr. Hauser. One moment." He turned to Eden apologetically. "My banker. I must meet with him."

"I'll busy myself getting acquainted with the kitchen," she said.

Ridenour hurried to the front door, admitted his guest and ushered him into the dining room. Eden lingered just out of sight, but within hearing distance of the two men.

"I came as soon as I heard that the Dazzler shut down," said Hauser.

"We tried opening with a skeleton crew this morning, but they were waylaid before they could arrive. So much for nonviolence, I guess."

"Tabor's volunteering the use of his private militia."

Eden had read about H.A.W. Tabor, the current Colorado lieutenant governor. Perhaps the most famous of the Leadville silver kings, the shopkeeper-turned-millionaire had raised his own private military force, with uniforms and light artillery. She could not tell from the newspaper article the exact reason a private citizen would feel compelled to do this, but his action had inspired other wealthy men to emulate the activity. She had trouble understanding how such extralegal forces were allowed to openly exist.

"I don't think that will be necessary. I ordered the main shaft of the Dazzler barricaded. The strikers were threatening to storm the mine and shut off the pumps."

"Good Lord, have they lost their minds?"

"The shutting of the pumps was Jacob Landry's idea," said Christopher. "I can't believe it. He, of all people, would know the damage that would do. If the pumps were shut off for even an hour the lower shafts would flood. Think of the costly damage. The cleaning and the refitting necessary. It would be ruinous. Why do they think they would benefit from such havoc?"

"They're mad. All of them. And stupid. You are going to stand with us, Ridenour, aren't you? You know they have closed every mine on Carbonate Hill, Fryer Hill, California Gulch—their numbers are now rumored to be three thousand."

"Yes, yes, of course. I'll hold out for as long as I can, but you know my financial situation. The debt service on those new hydraulic pumps is killing me, Mr. Hauser. If the bank could see clear perhaps to a renegotiation of the loans . . . ?"

"What about a syndication of your interest in the Dazzler?"

Eden thought Hauser's tone unforgivably brutal, as though he was exploiting the dire situation. She pitied the poor young Mr. Ridenour, dealing simultaneously with the death of his mother and with what was undoubtedly the biggest business crisis he had ever faced in his brief tenure as a mining mogul.

"I've thought about it, sir, but after the collapse of the Little Pittsburgh, the New York investment community has little interest in Leadville at the moment. Besides . . . my stepfather never had to syndicate. I would feel like I had let him down. His memory, that is."

Ten

Bella Valentine wondered why Kit Randall's aunt seemed to be living at the Black Lace House. What was she up to? A light, chilly rain commenced just as the funeral cortège turned onto Third Street. She saw Christopher Ridenour watching for it from his bay window in the parlor.

Few mourners were expected for Lucinda Ridenour, given the strike and now the inclement weather. Ribbons of clouds, as thin as smoke, clung to the sides of the nearby hills, ghostly sentinels to the somber day. Steam rose off the horses' backs and spouted from their nostrils as they pulled the funeral coach down the muddy street.

Bella tied her colorful shawl more tightly about her shoulders, then struggled to open her umbrella. At least her umbrella was black. It represented the only item she owned that carried the requisite color of mourning. That would have to suffice as she planned to attend this funeral on the off chance Kit Randall might show up. She could only wonder what shape he was in. People she had spoken with in the various saloons where she read tarot cards said Chris Ridenour's bodyguards had done fair work on him and that he was unconscious when they left him.

She knew he was alive and that he was still in town. The

cards had told her that much. If only they could give her his location.

She recoiled at the memory of the sorry way they had parted last winter. She had been flattered nearly to tears when he had asked her to marry him the week after he had moved in with her, though she had feared his motives sprung more from his notion of propriety than a well thought-out desire to make her his wife.

She had put off answering for as long as she could, always teasing out a reply or deftly changing the subject. After three weeks, he had finally delivered an ultimatum. He wanted an answer or he was moving out.

She had labored to make him understand her admittedly exotic philosophy of life, but had not succeeded. He was, in the end, too conventional in his thinking. She could tell his pride was bitterly wounded, but she could not make him believe she was serious in her opposition to marriage. He was convinced she simply did not want to marry *him*. The following morning, he announced without passion that he was leaving.

He had sullenly wished her good luck on getting to India and she had watched him walk down the porch steps and out into the street without a single back-thrown glance.

She refused to give up so easily and had set to work, casting a love glamour on him so that he would not forget her, only to have it somehow backfire. He was snatched up by the predatory Eye Dazzler heiress the very next week. She had labored to undo the miscast spell ever since, consulting her grimoire over and over.

At least he had found his way back into her arms on the

terrible day the newsboys were shouting out the murder of Lucinda Ridenour. The Leadville populace, already in a fever over the impending strike and now confronted with a sensational murder, was in a state of near frenzy. Kit was a suspect. The papers all said the police wanted him for questioning.

He had stumbled, literally, to her door on an absinthe bender like she had never seen before. She took him in without question.

Once he sobered up enough to carry on a conversation, he seemed genuinely shocked when told of the murder. He asked if he could stay for a day or two. She realized at that point that he was evading the police. She also knew if she helped him this would make her an accomplice of some sort, but she didn't care. The cards had told her on the night she met him that he would be the one to change her life. Even though everything had gone spectacularly wrong for them, she could not forget those cards.

He was so troubled, yet if not by the murder of his mistress, then what? He was an absolute wreck. He couldn't make love to her, he tried to stay drunk around the clock, he refused to bathe or change clothes. And why had he acted so strangely about mirrors? Insisting she drape a sheet over the looking glass above her washstand? It seemed an odd superstition, completely out of character for him.

What had that Lucinda Ridenour done to him, anyway? That hag, that shrew, that man-wrecker, she deserved to die.

Bella quickly crossed herself. Such negative thoughts were beneath her, she lectured herself. The woman was dead. The story was over. Ill feelings were a waste of her time.

The funeral procession stopped in front of the Black Lace House and Christopher Ridenour, clad in formal attire including a tall top hat draped with a black mourning sash, emerged from the house followed by that woman, Kit's aunt. Both she and young Ridenour opened their umbrellas.

Two large, unfriendly-looking men flanked Ridenour as he stepped into the street to join the Presbyterian minister behind his mother's casket. Bodyguards, Bella guessed. She joined the small procession as it headed up Third to Harrison Street, a convoluted route, to her way of thinking. The cemetery was located in the northwest corner of town, at Tenth and James.

A few more mourners gathered behind the funeral coach as it wound its way through Leadville. A dozen or so. Bella recognized most to be employees of the High Life Club. Only a couple of foremen from the Eye Dazzler made an appearance, plus one of the mining engineers who had probably never met Lucinda Ridenour, but thought himself obligated to show his respects to the new, young owner who was now his boss.

The drizzle faded into light, wet May snow chilling the entourage as they continued their solemn journey. The noisy bustle of Harrison Street slowed to a quiet rumble in deference to the somber procession. George Hauser, the banker, joined the cortège at Sixth. He brought with him his stolid-looking wife and three pale daughters.

Bella had met the oldest girl, Georgina. She had come to her room one day in March seeking advice from the cards on a matter of the heart. She was in love with a young miner who was active in the secret local union. He would certainly not be George Hauser's first choice for a son-in-law, so the complication was obvious. The girl wanted to know if she eloped with her sweetheart, would they have a happy life together?

Bella had told her frankly that the future did not look bright. The girl had left in an indignant huff, as unaccustomed to bad news as her blustering, blowhard father. And Bella hadn't even told her the worst of it. She had sugarcoated the reading to spare the girl grief. The Queen of Pentacles had dominated the spread. That could only mean "heiress," "marriage of convenience," and above all, "greed."

The procession had nearly reached the cemetery before Bella got the nerve to maneuver herself to Kit's aunt's side and whisper, "What are you up to?"

Eden blanched at the frankness of this question and glared at her.

Bella sighed. She realized she had shot the question too boldly. She ducked down a bit to place her face nearer her much shorter walking companion and said more softly, "We're on the same side."

A puzzled look was the only answer she got. The woman quickened her pace to place her directly behind Ridenour and his bodyguards.

Bella would not be so easily put off and marched directly up to the woman once again. Before she could speak further, a loud commotion spilled from a small house at the end of Sixth.

"No! No, you won't go!" shouted a woman's voice.

Bella gazed over the heads of the other mourners to see what was going on. Everyone began to mumble.

Jacob Landry stood in the small front yard of what must be his own house, Bella assumed. He did not wear a coat, nor hat, nor tie. With his collar open, his face unshaven, and his hair wildly uncombed, he stood in sharp contrast to the dapper superintendent of the Eye Dazzler Mine that he had been until a scant few days ago.

What a difference a week makes, Bella thought cynically. She had never had any personal dealings with Landry, but she had seen him many times in the High Life Club. She often went there to tell fortunes. The weeknight floor boss let her in on evenings he did not expect Mrs. Ridenour to drop by. He demanded in return ten percent of her take, which she agreed was fair. The weekend boss was not so easy to deal with. He wanted more than money and that she refused to give, on principle. She would not submit to sexual extortion; it did not reconcile with her complicated system of morality.

She thought Jake Landry a handsome individual for a man of his age. He was thirty, at least, which she considered old. She also found him proud and vain, two traits she had little use for in a man.

She had even less use for his pious wife, that noble do-gooder who ran the orphan asylum and thought herself too righteous to speak to ordinary mortals who did not share her rigorous views on morality and religion. That Bella had something rather crucial in common with Ellen Landry—they had both lost their men to Lucinda Ridenour—made her curl her lip in disgust.

Mrs. Landry clung to her errant husband's arm, trying to yank him back into the house.

"Please, Jacob, for the love of all that's decent, stop this!" the poor woman cried, but her husband ignored her.

The unseemly little commotion made the funeral party

uncomfortable, especially as virtually all of them knew about the past connection between Landry and the woman they were about to bury.

Two policemen rode up on horseback and entered the Landrys' yard without bothering to dismount. Bella had not previously noticed that they had been silently escorting the funeral group down the street at a discreet distance. They no doubt expected union violence or at least a demonstration, not a domestic dispute.

Bella observed the reactions of the rest of the group. Christopher Ridenour grimaced painfully at the sight of Landry and his wife. She could not tell if he was embarrassed or affronted by the display.

Kit Randall's aunt watched with sharp eyes, taking in all that was happening. Bella had to find a way to meet with her, talk with her. She must know Kit's whereabouts.

Ellen Landry gave up trying to persuade her husband to re-enter their house and hurried back inside, away from the staring eyes. Her husband spoke calmly to the police officers and they departed, resuming their vigil at the back of the group.

The funeral procession continued on its determined journey to the cemetery, but Eden and Bella both looked back as they walked along. They watched the curious sight of Jacob Landry standing in his front yard, heedless of the wet snow pelting his distraught face.

———

Eden wondered who the man and woman were who had stood in their little yard making a spectacle of themselves. She overheard other mourners mention the name "Landry" and had to think this was the fired superintendent of the Eye Dazzler, of whom Kit had spoken.

She also worried that Kit's girlfriend knew her. This was potentially disastrous to her current plans. If her connection to Kit was known by anyone she could never learn the secrets she needed to prove his innocence.

At the Evergreen Cemetery at last, Eden looked about the small crowd. Some seemed merely to be spectators. Others appeared to be attending for polite, business-related purposes only.

Fancy wrought-iron fencing marked out the Ridenour family plot. A small gate permitted entrance to the eight-by-twelve-foot burial ground where Lucinda would be laid to rest under the imposing marble headstone so recently carved for her late husband.

The pillarlike stone was emblazoned across its base with the family name. Up its midsection it carried the inscription: "Orson Walter Ridenour, born September 2, 1828—departed this life December 25, 1878." Another name, one Zachary Ridenour, was carved beneath it. That man's life had spanned the years 1832 to 1873.

Lucinda's name would be added at a later date, no doubt. There was room for many Ridenours on the tall sculpture.

A carving of a Grecian vase decorated the top of the pillar, but instead of the key design such vases usually carried, this carving was embellished with the interlocking triangles of the Eye Dazzler pattern. Eden questioned the taste of adorning one's gravestone with a company insignia rather than the more expected religious or pastoral motif, but as everything else in the Ridenour house bore this symbol of the origin of its wealth, perhaps this prideful designation pleased the man who now rested beneath it.

Christopher Ridenour held his emotions in check as befitted a man of his station. Eden noticed him look very directly at Bella Valentine.

The girl smiled at him in a respectful way to acknowledge his gaze. He did not smile back, but nodded slightly, polite, but formal, as seemed to be his habit.

Eden wondered how they could possibly know each other, then remembered Kit saying that Bella told fortunes in the various saloons around town. Maybe the High Life Club, owned by the Ridenours, also hosted her services.

After the short ceremony was concluded at the graveside, Eden watched the hovering presence of George Hauser descend upon the Eye Dazzler heir. She was surprised to note how deftly Ridenour disentangled himself and sought instead the company of Bella Valentine. Eden followed the pair at a careful distance while the rest of the gathering dispersed in various directions.

Ridenour glanced back and saw Eden. He motioned for her to come closer.

"A carriage will be here in a moment, Mrs. Murdoch. Allow me to transport you home again."

"Thank you, sir."

He turned to Bella. "May we drop you somewhere, Miss Valentine?"

"Thanks. I need to go back up to Harrison, is all."

The carriage pulled up and the three climbed in.

"I suppose you ladies have not met. Excuse me for failing to make introductions."

"Mr. Ridenour," said Eden. "We can hardly expect you to

attend to social minutiae on such a day as this." She secretly wished he would not introduce her and mentally squirmed at the possibility of compromising her anonymity.

"Miss Valentine, this is my new housekeeper, Mrs. Murdoch."

"Pleased to meet you, ma'am." Bella extended her hand and Eden shook it. The two women eyed each other suspiciously.

Bella's destination arrived before any further conversation could take place. As the carriage jostled on toward Third Street, Eden asked as tactfully as possible how Christopher knew Miss Valentine.

"A business acquaintance" was all he would say.

Eden spent every minute her young employer was away from his home examining it for information. She found distressingly little. The grand house, so richly decorated and detailed, looked like a museum, untouched by human beings.

The only unusual item she turned up initially was a photograph of Kit under Chris Ridenour's bed. Why did he keep a picture of a housemate in such a secret location?

The photograph did not do its subject justice. He looked so serious and sober as many such portraits seemed to look and nothing could capture the spirit of its sitter less. Kit without his classic smile and constant dimples was simply not Kit Randall.

The next day of digging led to the attic. There she found what she assumed to be the famous Eye Dazzler portrait of Lucinda Ridenour. The son must have removed it after his mother's demise.

It was a classic nude, she supposed. She had not visited many saloons or gambling emporiums, but she assumed this lascivious painting must be typical. The artist made pretensions toward fine art, perhaps to disguise the main purpose of the painting—pure titillation.

She did not exactly know what thoughts of lust wandered through men's minds when they viewed such paintings, but she imagined this work of "art" filled them with the expected stimulation. Mrs. Ridenour's form possessed a lush and generous sensuality she presumed men liked. The one odd chord struck was the noticeable tattoo on the woman's hip. It seemed to be a howling wolf in the image of the full moon. She had never heard of a woman decorated with a tattoo before.

The more Eden learned about Lucinda Ridenour, the less she felt she understood her.

Her next discovery was a trunk filled with Orson Ridenour's personal correspondence. Most of it was pretty boring, letters from businessmen and tradesmen, advertisements for the latest in mining equipment, surveyors' and geologists' reports, political material from many local and national campaigns.

Then a letter. It proved to be a small gem, making her long day of dusty searching well rewarded. The letter was from a Mr. Nathaniel Burke, Esquire, of a law firm in Denver. Ridenour had apparently sought legal advice on a highly personal matter that he did not wish to share with a local attorney.

> *. . . after much research, I fear I must agree with your original assessment. I cannot ascertain any*

manner by which you could make your adopted son your sole heir. As you know, your wife acquired what is know as "dower rights" upon your marriage. She cannot be disinherited without her knowledge and consent. She retains these rights and may exercise them to elect against the terms of your will, should you choose to exclude her so long as your marriage remains intact at the time of your demise.

Your only route to achieve this goal would be to take legal steps to end the marriage. As we discussed on the day of your visit, a divorce proceeding often disintegrates into a most unpleasant and unseemly event, unfortunately very public in nature, particularly so for a man in so prominent a position as yourself. . . .

Eleven

Kit was napping when sounds in the surrounding woods awakened him with a jolt. It was not the police that he feared. They might come to arrest him, but that was not what plagued him the most. He worried that the ghost of Ian Greene had come to steal him once and for all. But Greene's ghost had not yet ventured out into the woods. It only appeared to him in mirrors. First that night at the saloon, then Bella's room, then Eden and Brad's hotel room.

He grabbed his uncle's rifle from under the cot and removed the safety. He aimed it straight for the opening flap of the tent and waited, afraid to breathe. Nothing. Perhaps it was an animal in the pine and aspen forest surrounding him.

He was groggy and not thinking clearly. He had taken more morphine than he should have, but he had only himself to blame for the pain he was in. All morning, memories of that last night in Lucinda's bed had tormented him.

He wanted to believe Christopher's denials. He longed to think he had just imagined it, the wicked absinthe at work. Yet the memories were so vivid, and what was worse—they never failed to arouse him. The guilty thoughts came on him when he least expected it, just popped into his mind. No matter how hard he tried, he could not halt images of

Christopher with his mouth upon him. The visions both revolted and excited him. He could not understand this paradox.

Are you upset about what happened last night ... or that you enjoyed it?

Sometimes the shameful arousal was so powerful and profound it forced him to seek relief by his own hand, thereby compounding the sin. Yet he had to do something to abate his vicious torment, even as he despised himself every moment of the ignoble act.

Such vice was supposed to be the province of misbehaving schoolboys. How his dormitory bunkmate, Ian Greene, had lectured him on this very topic. They had become friends on the first day of school. Both were sixteen, younger than all the other boys in the dormitory and both away from home for the first time in their lives.

Good old Greene, who let him win at chess. How angry and humiliated Kit had been when he learned the truth of this. Greene had actually allowed Kit to think he had taught him to play the game, until he had happened onto Greene outside the library competing in a chess tournament one day. The competition was in the final round with Greene effortlessly triumphing over the upperclassman who challenged him.

"I thought it would make you like me," Greene had tried to explain away the little deception when Kit confronted him.

"That's just stupid. And I would have liked you if I had won or not."

Greene looked so relieved by this he had nearly wept and they never mentioned the incident again. But they never played chess again either.

Kit found a poem under his pillow the next day. And the next. The gushy praise Greene heaped on him in these poems embarrassed him a little, though he liked being the center of attention.

Had they been love poems? This thought had never occurred to him at the time. Yet it was Greene's secret good-night kisses under the covers that usually inspired the prohibited activity of self-abuse.

Such chaste kisses, Kit recalled. They never once parted their lips. He wouldn't learn of that pleasure until years later when he started making love to girls.

"You know what Father Logan says about it," Greene had scolded one night as Kit indulged. "He calls it *self-pollution.*"

"But I *want* to," Kit panted, already having found the perfect rhythm.

"It's dangerous. You'll harm yourself. And we're only born with a finite number of spendings. If you waste them all now, how will you ever father children when the time comes?"

"I'll jump off that bridge when I come to it. And I don't think old Logan is an expert on procreation. He took a life-long vow of chastity, now didn't he?"

Greene grabbed Kit's wrist. "I won't let you do this."

"Let go."

"I care about you. I'll protect you from yourself, if I have to. We promised to keep our friendship pure. Remember? No vice of any sort."

Even as he spoke these words, Kit had disengaged Greene's hand from his wrist and held it tight while he resumed his illicit stroking with his other hand.

In the darkness, Greene's face was so close to his that his hair hung down and grazed Kit's forehead. He wondered what expression his straitlaced friend's thin face carried as he squeezed his hand tighter and tighter.

The wooden bunk bed creaked with the increasing commotion. He tensed, then shuddered, then spent—gloriously, and relaxed, still holding Greene's hand.

The room was filled with a brittle silence as though not a single boy were breathing.

Then came Macmillian's voice from the bunk on top of them. "Now that Randall's successfully shucked his corn, maybe we can all get some sleep!"

The room erupted in laughter and Kit pulled the quilt over his face, a mortified blush burning his cheeks. He realized in an instant he would have to join the joke or remain the butt of it. He chose the former.

"Pleased to provide you with this evening's entertainment, gentlemen. I live to amuse."

More laughter. Lots of mumbling. Kit could not resist laughing along. The absurdity of the situation was apparent even to him, but his bunkmate did not think it was funny. The frost had begun to clot the air already. Greene would not speak to him for days to punish him for this dangerous folly.

After Greene died, Kit came to adopt his dim view of self-abuse. He was seldom successful at talking himself out of it, but at least he now tried. Lately he had come up with a new method of avoiding the vice. He would force himself to stand up and put weight on his injured knee. He punished his swollen kneecap until tears stung his eyelids and extinguished his troublesome bout of deviant lust.

He drifted to sleep again and when he awoke, he found that Eden had left a basket of food for him along with a jar of lemonade. He looked to the food eagerly as he had not eaten since the day before, but stopped and listened when he thought he heard the sound of an approaching horse.

He grabbed the rifle once again, and waited.

"Kit?" came a familiar voice. "You in there?"

"Bella! How did you find me?" Relief washed over him like a sweet, refreshing waterfall. Bella, his angel, his only confidante in this whole terrible nightmare world.

"I followed your aunt out here. Don't worry, she didn't see me. I played quiet as an Indian." She entered the tent opening lugging a large wicker basket. She held it with two hands and pushed it forward with her knee as she walked. He wondered how any picnic on earth could be so heavy.

"I'd get up but I'm supposed to stay in bed all the time. I have bruised kidneys."

Bella twisted her lips. "That doesn't sound good. What made you want to hide out here in the first place?"

"You know why. They say the police are looking for me."

He peeked under the large linen napkin which covered the basket. He found cold fried chicken, a half dozen biscuits and a small bottle of whiskey.

"This is wonderful! Hey, what do you think of my beard?" He had not shaved since the day his uncle had summarily sent him to the barber. He now had a fresh growth of scruffy, itchy stubble to show for it.

She frowned at him, wrinkling her elegant nose. "Looks like your face is dirty."

"I thought it would make me look older."

"Not really."

"Distinguished?"

"Nope."

He rubbed his prickly chin for the millionth time.

"How can you tell if you've got bruised kidneys?" she asked as she buttered him a biscuit.

"Trust me, you don't want to know."

She reached down into the bottom of the basket and produced what had caused her to strain to carry his dinner in.

"Watermelon!" he said. "I haven't had one since I was a kid. Where did you get it?"

"The greengrocer on Harrison got in a whole wagonload. I stood in line for an hour to buy this. You know they say that once the rail line comes, we'll get all manner of fresh produce. Won't that be lovely?"

"How did you know my aunt?"

"I know everything."

He theatrically slapped his forehead to gently mock her. "I keep forgetting."

Usually this made her mad, but today, she was determined to keep her temper. "Why does she call herself 'Mrs. Murdoch' if she's married to your uncle?"

Kit raised his eyebrows suggestively. "They're not married yet. My uncle's not quite unhitched from his first wife. The divorce has been granted but there's some kind of waiting period. Don't repeat that. They don't want people knowing, of course."

"How interesting," said Bella with a challenge in her voice. "So this uncle you idolize thinks it's all right for a man

143

and a woman to live together without tying the knot—legally, so to speak."

"That's not what's going on. They *plan* to get married."

"But they managed to have a ten-year-old daughter somehow. This *perfect* uncle who never does anything wrong."

"Bella, I don't want to dredge up these old arguments again. I'm in no mood." They sat in silence, continuing their meal until Kit thought of something less personal to talk about.

"When you said, 'quiet as an Indian,' just now, I bet you didn't know that Mrs. Murdoch used to live with the Indians."

"Really?" said Bella.

He launched into an entertaining tale of Mrs. Murdoch's unorthodox history, how she had been kidnapped by warring Indians as a young bride, but then came to live amongst them willingly, even marrying into the tribe. Kit devoted a long portion of the narrative to his uncle's role in her recapture on the banks of the Washita in '68 when Brad Randall served as aide-de-camp to the famous boy general, George Armstrong Custer. Brad was assigned to return her to civilization, a task that proved more challenging than anyone would have imagined.

The willful Eden had dared to contradict Custer and the entire U.S. Army over their version of the events at the Washita. The case had made national headlines and was the subject of a congressional inquiry. Brad Randall grew to love his headstrong charge and the pair enjoyed a bittersweet romance before she learned her Cheyenne husband was not dead.

She helped him escape army custody and disappeared with him into the wilderness. Brad would not learn for another decade that their brief affair had given them their daughter Hadley.

"How come Mrs. Murdoch is living at the Black Lace House?" Bella said.

"What?"

"You didn't know that?"

"She's supposed to be staying at the Clarendon."

"She's Christopher Ridenour's new housekeeper."

"The hell you say. Why on earth?"

"Maybe she's trying to find out who really killed you-know-who."

"She shouldn't be—"

"Hold still." Bella reached over and cleaned a crumb of fried chicken crust from his cheek.

"How come you're so good to me?" he said, grinning.

"I care about you, remember? I wish you'd asked me before you got tangled up with *her.*" She did not deign to speak Lucinda Ridenour's name. "If you had, you wouldn't be in this fix. The things I could have told you."

"How would you have call to know Mrs. Ridenour?" He tore into a chicken leg, happily ripping the flesh from the bone. "She doesn't exactly seem like somebody you'd be friends with."

"She was a friend of Miss Hart's, not mine."

Kit frowned in confusion. Priscilla Hart was the aging bawd who owned the "boardinghouse" where Bella roomed, but why she would have a reason to know Lucinda perplexed him just as completely as Bella's claim.

Bella could tell by his confounded expression that he had not read her meaning. "You know how Miss Hart makes a living, don't you?"

"Renting rooms?"

Bella hooted at his innocence. "Old Pris has a sideline. A room in the back that brings her more cash than any real estate she's ever let." Bella's tone turned coy. "She provides a service that nobody talks about but every town needs."

Kit waited, still in the dark.

Bella could not believe how dense he was. "Girls come to her in a fix and she gets 'em out of it. I'm talking about inconvenient babies, blockhead."

Kit's dark eyes widened. "Pris Hart's an abortionist?"

"A pretty good one, too. Not many are. That's why she makes so much money. Women travel in from all over to visit her. They go home a little bit lighter."

"And Lucy Ridenour got an abortion?"

"More than one. Back when she and Jake Landry were the talk of the town, she was coming in once or twice a year. They say that old Ridenour knew all about her running around, but didn't care a pin so long as she didn't disgrace him with any bastards. Who can imagine such a marriage as that one?"

"I can," Kit said. He stared at the quilt at his feet, not happy at further confirmation of his suspicions about Lucinda's marriage and every other unnatural thing about her.

Bella folded her hands in her lap and weighed whether to deliver her last shocking bit of news about her darling boy's former sweetheart. A sudden pinch of jealousy, even of a woman who was now dead, forced her to say, "The last time Mrs. Ridenour paid a visit to Pris was hardly more than a month ago."

She studied his reaction. The implication of these words did not sink into his brain for several seconds, but when it did, he could not disguise his utter shock. "You mean . . . ?"

"I guess she never told you," Bella said.

He shook his head slowly, stunned. He had gotten Lucinda pregnant? She had discreetly secured an abortion and never even mentioned it? He searched his memory and recalled an incident of a month ago when she had taken to her bed for a week with a mysterious illness that she would not discuss with her son or her lover.

Christopher had grown worried and he and Kit had marched into her bedroom one morning and demanded the right to summon a doctor.

She had dismissed them with an annoyed pout, confessing the malady was merely a "female indisposition" and did they really want the details?

Both young men had been too embarrassed to inquire further and the matter was dropped.

"Why are you so surprised?" Bella said, unable to resist the temptation to stab a little deeper. "Did you think she was so old it couldn't happen?"

"No. I didn't think that. I just . . . didn't think at all, I guess."

"I suppose you would have insisted on marriage, knowing you."

"Of course I would have. That would have been the only honorable thing to do." He let out a long, painful sigh. "I guess she had no interest in that."

She realized she had pushed it all too far and now knew what needed to be done. She cleared away the picnic food, gathering up the chicken bones in her napkin for possible later use in an enchantment. She collected all manner of artifacts for magical uses. "What's wrong with your leg?"

"Chris's goons managed to smash me pretty good." He pulled the quilt away to display the swollen, discolored kneecap peeking out of his opened trouser leg.

Bella pretended attention to the nasty-looking injury, but found better sport sliding her hand up the leg of his cotton underwear where it had been cut away just above the damaged knee. She massaged his thigh. "This feel good?"

"What are you up to?"

"Oh, nothing." She unbuttoned his fly with the deft efficiency of a nurse, then untied the drawstring at the waist of his drawers. She smiled.

"There's my good soldier, standing at attention just like he should." She drew up her skirts and climbed onto the cot to straddle him.

"Excuse me, miss, are you trying to force your attentions on me?"

"I'm actually trying to force *your* attentions *into* me at the moment."

He laughed with delight even though laughing hurt his bruised rib cage.

"You complaining?" she said.

"No, ma'am."

He smiled up at her as she gently rocked up and down. Her tousled blond topknot swayed with her as she made little sighing murmurs like the lapping of water at the edge of a lake. She was wearing a lavender taffeta dress he knew was her favorite. That she would risk her best frock on a trip into the woods on horseback was a stronger testament to her feelings for him than the sexual treat she was currently bestowing.

Deep in her sweet warmth, he longed to enjoy himself, but he could not. His inability to surrender to the moment had nothing to do with the pain in his ribs or his knee, but rather a festering sore deep in his soul.

He grabbed her waist to slow her down. "Bella, I didn't kill her. You believe me, don't you?"

"Of course, I do, honey." She leaned down and kissed his cheek.

"I'm certain I didn't."

Bella stared at him in horror. "What do you mean by that?"

"Nothing, I mean . . ."

Bella gracefully dismounted and snuggled in next to him on the small cot. Her seventeen yards of lavender taffeta took up more than half the space.

He held his side and edged himself into a sitting position. "Truth is, I can't remember a single thing about that day. That's why I don't want to talk to the police. I don't have an alibi."

This was not the first time he had lost his memory. Years ago, when told of Ian Greene's death, he had fainted in the chancellor's office. He hit his head on his way to the floor and woke up three hours later in the school infirmary. All his memories of Ian's last week on earth had vanished. He could not retrieve them, no matter how hard he tried.

"Why can't you remember it? Were you drunk?"

"Maybe. I guess so. Sometimes when I've been into the

absinthe, I lose track of time. I lose whole nights. I wake up places and don't have a devil of a clue how I got there. Once I lost two days."

"Oh, Lord," she murmured.

"But I know I could never have killed her. I said a lot of bad things right after I left her, but I was just mad at her and Chris. Now I realize that the things I accused them of— maybe they were all in my mind. The truth is, I think I'm sick in the head. I imagine things that aren't real and I think I know why."

"I don't understand."

"If I tried to explain it, you'd *know* I was crazy."

"Try me," she said.

Kit knew by her tone that she just might be the one person in the whole world who could understand. "There's this ghost—at least I think I see a ghost."

"The one you said you saw in my mirror?"

"Yeah, and he's determined to punish me for . . . I don't know, things that happened a long time ago. My mind has come right off its hinges and I think it's him that's causing it. I swear it."

"Oh, come on now. I won't let any ghosts hurt you." She put her arms around him for a long good-bye kiss.

Twelve

"What the devil are you doing at the Ridenour house?" Kit said the moment Eden stepped into the tent the next day.

"How did you know that?" she said.

"Bella told me."

"When did you see her?"

"She followed you out here."

"Oh, no! Soon everyone will know I'm connected to you."

"Don't worry about Bella. She won't tell."

"We can't have anyone knowing. That will ruin everything."

"Ruin what? What's going on?"

Eden heaved a guilty sigh. "I know your uncle won't approve, but I am determined to learn more about Mrs. Ridenour's death so I took a job as the housekeeper at the Ridenour mansion."

"You can't do that. It's not safe, for God's sake."

"It's the safest place in town. Christopher has guards posted at his front and back doors all night. And who else is there to unsort this, Kit? Someone has to. And no one, except your friend, Miss Valentine, knows about this."

"It's too dangerous. Not only is there a strike on, there's a murderer on the loose."

They debated the issue several minutes more, then finally reached a stalemate. Kit knew he was in no position to stop her and she was not a woman to be bullied. She made him lie down while she set out a supper for him of chicken soup and vegetables.

"So what's it like to be a servant at the Black Lace House?" Kit asked.

"Pretty easy, really. Christopher is seldom home and he makes little work when he is there." She found her young employer to be unfailingly polite and self-effacing. He carried an air of not always having had servants. Whenever he asked for work he did so in a hesitant, apologetic way.

His only annoying habit was his piano practice. He would start a piece over from scratch every time he made the slightest error. Late into the night, she could hear the endless refrains repeated incessantly until she was forced to bury her head beneath her pillows. She mentioned this and Kit laughed out loud.

"Chris and that damned piano!" he said. "Even his own mother was driven nearly to distraction. But he wouldn't stop. Old Ridenour gave him that piano as a gift. Imported it all the way from Europe."

The piano in question was a thing of beauty in its own right, a work of art, in fact. The carvings on the front legs of the large square grand piano were so intricate, it took her nearly an hour to dust them properly. The fine rosewood of the soundbox gleamed with a rich finish and the nameplate indicated the instrument had been built in Vienna.

"Did you know that Orson Ridenour had consulted an attorney in Denver on how best to disinherit his wife in order to make Christopher his sole heir?" she said.

"Hmmm. That's interesting. No, I never heard a bit of it. Chris sure never said anything. Of course, he was so broken up by Orson's death, he couldn't even mention it without getting all teary. He was such a girl about it."

This reference caused Eden pause, but she did not pursue it. "He's holding up pretty well, given the stress of the labor situation."

"You know this whole strike might have been prevented if not for Chris wanting to start a health insurance plan. They were all griping about that."

"Health insurance? What's that?" She had never heard of being able to guarantee one's continuing health.

"If a miner gets hurt on the job—which happens about every day—the Ridenour Company would pay his doctor bills for him."

"That seems awfully generous."

"Oh, they all had to donate some money from their pay, got it held back, each week."

"Everyone? Healthy or hurt?"

"Yep. Then if one gets hurt, the fund pays for his care, regardless of how much it is. Oh, and the injured miner also agrees not to take the company to court over the accident."

"That sounds very complicated," said Eden.

"Chris is a real progressive thinker, but those miners were too stupid to understand the advantage of it; that it was for *their* benefit. He was always two or three steps ahead of the herd at figuring things out, always coming up with wild, new ideas that would never occur to anybody else. He's so quiet, though, most people never get to know him well enough to figure out how smart he is. But old Ridenour did, I bet."

She nodded, deep in thought on this point. They spoke for some time on various minutiae involving the Ridenour family and she tried to pretend nothing was amiss, but she proved a poor actress.

"What's wrong, Eden? You're not yourself."

She tried to smile to dismiss his concern, but he knew her well enough. "I'm fretful about him."

"Uncle Brad?"

She nodded. "I know I should be concentrating on your troubles, not mine—"

"Nonsense. I'm sick of my troubles. Tell me yours to distract me."

"I fear for the little boy, of course. If he loses him—"

"It may not be as serious as she makes out, Eden. Aunt Amanda dotes on that boy and ever since their little girl died, she's overprotected the kid. She thinks every little chest cold is pneumonia."

"I hope that's true, Kit." She hesitated to state her more selfish concern. "This is terrible to admit, but I can't help thinking, what if she wants him back?"

"Come sit with me." He patted the corner of the bed and she approached. He knew she had once met his uncle's stunning, if faithless, wife. "You know it's you he loves. You don't have to worry."

"I tell myself I'm being silly. But still, she's a very beautiful and strong-willed woman. I imagine if she wanted something she could find a way to get it. My worry is, she wants him back."

"I know my aunt Amanda better than you, and you're right, she's plenty strong-willed. But don't forget, it was she who broke the marriage. She's the one who committed adultery. What man would want a woman back after she'd disgraced him like that? And with a young fellow who worked for him?"

"But their son is ill. A crisis like that could draw them back together."

"That's just not going to happen," Kit said.

"It's impossible to know what might pass between them." Another couple's marriage was a foreign country. No outsiders were ever admitted.

"Stop worrying. It's you he loves."

"I just get afraid. If I lost him again . . . I don't know what I'd do."

"Hey, you'll always have me." He grinned at her and playfully pinched her elbow. "I may not be much, but I have to be better than nothing."

"It's good to see those Randall family dimples again. I've missed them."

This innocent comment produced an effect she never would have guessed. Kit suddenly twisted up his face and looked near tears.

"Kit, what's wrong? I didn't mean to upset you."

He held his breath in a effort to keep from sobbing out loud, but his dark brown eyes glistened with tears.

"It's nothing. It's just that *she* said something like that to me the last day. . . ."

"Mrs. Ridenour?"

He nodded, unable to speak.

"I'm sorry, Kit. But I don't understand. Just a week ago, you said you hated her."

"I did. I mean, I do. I mean . . . oh, I'm a damned fool. I don't know what I feel."

"Why did you quarrel with her? Can't you tell me?"

He glanced up from under his thick dark brows. "No."

"But I've shared with you my darkest fears today. Can't you do the same?"

He just shook his head.

She noticed a book at the foot of the cot. "*Isis Unveiled*. What's this?"

"A book Bella gave me. She thought it would help me convalesce."

Eden thought the book might be a saucy tale to entertain a young bachelor, given the title, but when she read the subtitle, she realized she could not have been more wrong. *Isis Unveiled* announced itself to be: *A Master-Key to the Mysteries of Ancient and Modern Science and Theology*, by someone named H. P. Blavatsky.

"Not exactly light reading," she murmured as she thumbed the chapters and noted they dealt with such matters as the kabala, the Vedas, Buddhism, psychical phenomena, French savants, and mesmerism.

Kit grinned. "You're telling me!"

She noted that the last third of the tome was devoted to India, calling it "the cradle of the race," and recalled Kit telling her how Bella wanted to visit the exotic east.

"Your Miss Valentine sounds . . . most interesting."

"She's interesting, all right. Most people just say 'odd.' "

Christopher Ridenour stood waiting in his entryway for his housekeeper to return home.

"Mrs. Murdoch, where have you been? I need you this minute."

"I'm sorry, I—"

He grabbed her by the elbow and guided her into the house, taking her hat and shawl from her as they headed for the kitchen.

"They'll be here any minute and I need refreshments for them."

"Who, sir?"

"The Committee for Public Safety. George Hauser volunteered *my* house for the meeting." He did not look pleased by this development.

"How many are expected?"

"I've no idea. Ten? Twenty? All of Leadville's most powerful men."

"I'll brew some tea and . . . and prepare some cold meats and cheeses?" she said.

"Do we have any pastries? Pastries and coffee, I think."

"I'll dash off to the bakery on Harrison—"

"There's no time. Just do something. Anything."

"There's some brandy in the parlor," said Eden.

"Brandy's an after-dinner drink. Oh, this is awful. Don't they realize I'm in mourning and unable to accommodate guests?"

"Of course, they'll understand, Mr. Ridenour. These are extraordinary times, what with the strike and all."

"Yes, you're right. They will simply have to understand."

"They'll be grateful to you for putting the welfare of the community ahead of your own personal sorrow."

By the time they reached the kitchen the front door bell was ringing with the first arrivals. Christopher bid her stay busy in the kitchen while he answered his own door.

She quickly assembled a tray of small sandwiches that

would not require silverware and carried it into the dining room where the gentlemen now congregated.

The number shocked her. More than a dozen were already present with a steady stream heading in through the front door, some gathering in the parlor as the dining room filled to its capacity.

She smiled like a modest domestic as she walked among the finely outfitted men, the powerful and influential of Leadville. Her young employer stood hovering behind George Hauser, content to remain in the older man's shadow, figuratively, if not literally.

She picked up pieces of the men's conversation as she passed among them handing out her refreshments.

"Why can't they arrest Landry?" said a portly gentleman. "Isn't he a suspect in that tart's murder? Getting him behind bars would be the first step toward securing the peace."

"Don't call her a tart, Kent," said the man at his elbow. "We're standing in her son's dining room, for heaven's sake."

"But Lord, she was an eyeful, wasn't she? Ever see that painting of her in the High Life Club?"

"The High Life isn't my sort of venue."

"Never thought Ridenour was the type to have his head turned by a pretty face, though."

"Hard to say, but I admit I was surprised by the marriage myself."

Eden moved on, amazed that her lowly status as a domestic made these eminent guests ignore her existence to the point of gossiping liberally in her presence.

"Grant will arrive in just a few weeks' time," said the next gentleman she served. "How will it look for Leadville to be in the grips of martial law?"

"Dreadful, simply dreadful," said the man next to him. "It will undoubtedly make the national press. As if we needed this on the heels of the failure of the Little Pittsburgh. Eastern investors will never regain their confidence in us at this rate."

"And I am the head of the Union Veterans Association. I am in charge of all the decorations, as well as coordinating the bands, and the speakers for the welcoming committee. Mayor Humphreys—"

The men's conversation was diverted when the meeting was called to order by George Hauser. Everyone seemed to speak at once. She could not hear what he was saying over the general din so she moved in closer.

"Look, Ridenour," said a gentleman Eden did not recognize but who conducted himself with an air of disdainful authority, "if you stand up to these hooligans, I have the personal assurance from Tabor that his own military company will keep the peace."

"If I should hire strike breakers, you mean?" Ridenour said.

Eden knew that every day the Eye Dazzler sat idle, its owner moved one step closer to bankruptcy. Did Jacob Landry know this and long to see the Ridenour fortune in ruins? Would he garner some sort of indecent pleasure from this collapse? Was he working in collusion with George Hauser? The banker was the only one who would profit from such a failure.

"I'd be grateful for the help of Mr. Tabor's private army,"

said young Ridenour. "I don't have the funds to finance security for the mine at present."

"We'll see heads bloodied over this before we're through," shouted a man in the dining room with altogether too much glee. The others heartily concurred.

The sight of these comfortable men conspiring like schoolboys disgusted Eden. It was just a game to them, a momentary diversion from the monotony of their counting-houses. They enjoyed the luxury of *watching* the mischief they plotted. *Their* heads were not the ones that might be bloodied.

She noted with approval that her young employer did not join in their merriment and enthusiasm, though he stood to benefit from their plotting.

"Gentlemen," he said. "I'm not eager to incite violence. My family has already been its victim."

This remark made his audience uncomfortable, but not repentant.

"You surely don't expect to reason with these strikers, do you, Ridenour?" said a tall gentleman in a police uniform.

"That would be disastrous for us all," said another man, obviously another mine owner.

"Governor Pitkin has promised to send in the state militia," a man in the crowd announced. "Should it come to that."

"He won't back down," said Hauser, placing his arm around the much taller Christopher. "He'll stand as firm as anyone, won't you, my boy?"

Ridenour said nothing and seemed to shrink back into the wallpaper as the meeting swirled on without him. The Committee for Public Safety was duly organized and a pledge was drafted to be signed by all those present. As the meeting filled the house and spilled out onto the front porch, they decided to adjourn to Tabor's Opera House.

The men quickly filed out and Eden was left alone with Christopher Ridenour. He slumped down onto a sofa as she fussed about cleaning up the refuse of the meeting. She noted with disapproval that many of the men had seen fit to knock their cigar ashes on the expensive imported carpet.

"They're having a lot of fun," he remarked.

She smiled sympathetically. "At least someone is enjoying this."

They both chuckled at their own cynicism, then Christopher turned dark once again.

"I have nothing but contempt for them all," he said. "Orson Ridenour had more intelligence and education and refinement than all the men who filled this room put together. Yet they chose to exclude *him*."

"How so?" she said.

"Denied him membership in the Argot Club, for one thing. That's why he opened the High Life. To spite them. They never understood or appreciated him. They weren't capable of it." He shook his head bitterly. "Have you ever met Tabor? He wasn't here tonight."

"No, I haven't." She had read about him in the newspaper often enough, but he remained only a name on a grand opera house that stood next door to the Clarendon Hotel.

"Don't worry, you haven't missed much. Our *esteemed* lieutenant governor has the manners of a mule skinner. How Orson used to laugh at him behind his back. He used to say Horace Tabor was living proof it was better to be lucky than smart."

Though she typically did not approve of strong drink, she poured the young man a brandy.

"Thank you," he said as he took the glass. The weak smile he gave her sagged under the weight of his returning bitterness. He frowned into his glass before finishing it. "Argot Club."

Eden continued to explore the Ridenour mansion one room at a time. She left the library for last. The impressive space, situated at the rear of the home where it occupied two stories, was lined floor to ceiling with carved mahogany bookshelves. She decided it must hold some clue to this confounding family. The rest of the house had yielded so little.

She addressed the library systematically, resolving to open every single book, knowing that people often placed stray items between the leaves. Four hours later, she was still only a third of the way through the volumes.

Most of the books were on legal topics, no doubt a remnant of Orson Ridenour's days as a practicing attorney, but a surprising number focused on the classics. The world of the ancient Greeks must have fascinated him. Countless tomes by and about Plato, Socrates, Pythagoras, Parmenides, Thales, Empedocles, and Heraclitus lined the shelves behind the massive desk. The Greek poets like Anacreon, Alcaeus, Strato, and Ibycus were also well represented. She seated herself in the comfortably upholstered chair there and began to note that many volumes carried bookmarks and folded-down pages.

Stories from Greek myth featuring elaborate descriptions

of the love affair of Zeus and Ganymede and the passion of Apollo for Hyacinthus had been marked out for particular interest.

At some point, she began to shift uncomfortably in her seat. A passage attributed to someone named Achilles Tatius was double-underlined: "Boys' sweat has a finer smell than anything in a woman's makeup box."

Her interest was kindled still more when she came across a passage by Solon, the Lawgiver of Athens: "You shall love young boys, with all your body and mind, until the hair grows on their faces."

A Greek poet named Pindar was singled out in a heavily underlined passage: "I, like wax of the sacred bees when smitten by the sun, am melted when I look upon the fresh-limbed youth of boys." A lengthy description of a beautiful youth named Theoxenus was included and by the look of the wear upon the pages, had been read many times.

"Mrs. Murdoch?" called Christopher Ridenour, who now stood in the open double doorway of the library.

Eden was so startled she dropped the book she was perusing with a guilty vengeance.

"Please forgive me, Mr. Ridenour. I . . . I came in here to dust the books and am afraid I became caught up in them and forgot the hour. Please feel free to dock my wages for such shameless time-wasting."

To her surprise, the young man smiled warmly. "I don't blame you a moment. This is an extraordinary library, is it not?"

"The finest in Colorado, I'm certain."

He strode into the room and glanced about the shelves

with a wistful look on his face. "This was my stepfather's favorite room."

He traced his fingertips lovingly along the leather-bound spines on the shelf nearest him.

"I imagine you are something of a scholar yourself, sir."

He smiled bashfully. "Not really. I try to read widely. When I was fourteen and my mother married Mr. Ridenour, I could barely read or write."

"Really?"

"We traveled around so much, you see, my mother and me, I'd never had the chance to attend school very regularly. Orson was shocked at my ignorance and immediately began to remedy the situation. He hired tutors of every discipline to instruct me in math, history, literature, music."

"How fortunate for you."

He nodded and looked impossibly melancholy.

Eden could not mistake the obvious love for his stepfather in the young man's voice. This made her squirm all the more to have read the countless references in Orson Ridenour's library to love between grown men and young boys.

———

Christopher Ridenour was the last person Ellen Landry expected to knock upon her door on the bright, sunny last day of May. He had never done so in all the years her husband had worked for his family.

"Yes?" she said as she opened her door a crack. He looked younger than she remembered him. She had not caught a real glance at him during that embarrassing interlude at his mother's funeral procession.

"Mrs. Landry, I am Christopher Rid—"

"Yes, sir, I know who you are."

"Is your husband at home, madam?"

"No."

The young man seemed to debate what to do next. "Might I have a word with you?"

"I don't think it appropriate for me to allow a gentleman into my house when my husband is not present."

"I understand, but if you could just speak to me for a moment. Here on the porch if need be. I need to know . . ." He drew a long breath to build his courage. "Mrs. Landry, has your husband had any dealings with Mr. George Hauser? You know . . . the banker, the mine owner?"

Ellen Landry stiffened. "I don't think so. Why do you ask?"

Christopher swallowed and looked supremely uncomfortable. "There are rumors circulating that perhaps the strike was instigated by certain mine owners who feared their holdings were losing value. That a diversion was needed so that they might dump their shares quietly before the values dropped. A strike would provide a convenient diversion."

"I have no idea what you are talking about, sir. You unjustly terminated my husband's employment. That is the only thing I know for certain." She tried to shut the door, but Ridenour held it open a few inches.

"I had ample reason to discharge your husband, madam. If he told you the truth of it, you would not say this."

"We both know the real reason he was dismissed," she said. "That harlot you called a mother—"

"Mrs. Landry," he interrupted, his jaw clenched, "might I suggest that you were not the only victim of their unfortunate liaison."

"Good day, sir!" She slammed the door.

"I need to see Mr. Ridenour," said Sergeant Sorel Weston as he stood on the shadowy porch of the Black Lace House.

"I'm expecting him momentarily," said Eden in her best housekeeper voice.

Weston looked annoyed. "Look, I don't have all day here. I got my supper to go home to and a wife who don't like to be kept waiting. If I gave you something, could you make sure Mr. Ridenour gets it?"

Eden bristled at the man's rude tone. "Of course, sir."

"We made a raid on the union headquarters this afternoon and found this." He handed her a large brown ledger book.

Eden was surprised to learn the unionists even had a headquarters. The rumors about town hinted that the strikers met at various secret locations, never the same place twice, to avoid detection and the disruption they had obviously faced today. The city government was firmly in the grasp and sympathies of the mine owners. Ridenour and the others enjoyed the full cooperation of the local police force, though it was now well outnumbered by the strikers.

Before Weston could leave the porch, Eden called out, "Is it true that the governor is going to declare martial law in Leadville?"

The policeman shrugged. "You know as much as I do, lady."

Eden's hands nearly trembled with excitement at the thought that she could gain a peek into the Ridenour family finances. She hurried to her room on the third floor and sat on a wooden stool near the window for good light.

The entries in the ledger dated back three years and two hands were distinctly noticeable in the writing. Prior to December 25, 1878, the records were kept in a careful, masculine script that must have belonged to Orson Ridenour. After that date, after Ridenour's death, the writing style was more artistic, distinctly feminine in quality, the spelling erratic and haphazard.

Eden guessed that Lucinda took over the check-writing duties after her husband's passing. From the entries—bank notes to greengrocers, dressmakers, farriers, drapers, haberdashers, and pharmacies—she deduced this ledger represented only the Ridenour family's personal accounts. The books of the Eye Dazzler and the High Life Club must have separate records.

The balance in the account varied widely from week to week, ranging from a high of forty-eight thousand dollars to a low of two hundred.

The weekly salaries of the Ridenour household staff were listed. Eden recognized several names she had learned from quizzing tradesmen on the former employees of the Black Lace House. None of the entries excited interest, save one: Sadie Branch. Beginning on January 1, 1879, Mrs. Branch began to receive a salary of one hundred dollars per week!

Quite a raise from the ten dollars she had previously earned in Lucinda Ridenour's service. Eden had been stunned when Christopher offered her twelve dollars a week with every other Sunday off. She knew that Leadville wages—like everything else in the rollicking town—were higher than to be expected. Female domestic servants in large cities would be happy to make even *five* dollars a week.

But one hundred dollars? There was more going on here than domestic service. Blackmail? Illicit doings? Something justified the extraordinary wage.

And where was this Mrs. Branch now? Eden hated to speculate. The possibilities worried her too much. What had been the consequence of Orson Ridenour consulting an attorney on how to disinherit his wife?

Was he planning to kill himself and seeking to leave his wealth to his adopted son?

Or did Lucinda Ridenour anticipate her husband's plan to divorce her and take her own action before he could?

Thirteen

"Do you believe in the occult, Mrs. Murdoch?" Christopher Ridenour unexpectedly asked as she cleared his dinner dishes from his place at the table.

"I don't really have a developed opinion, Mr. Ridenour."

"I didn't want to shock you, but I've invited someone to come to the house tonight. She's a medium. A young woman in touch with the spirit world. I know that some would dismiss this as a humbug, but I believe she really can contact the other side—the world of the departed."

"Do you have some proof of this, sir?"

"Indeed, I do. I asked her to reach my late stepfather after he . . . crossed over. There are those who would say it's all folly, that the spirit world doesn't exist and that mediums and spiritualists are all charlatans, but what I learned that night helped me to cope with the loss. It gave me the solace I needed. Now I want to contact my mother. To learn the identity of her murderer, of course. I have to know if what I believe is . . . the truth."

"You have a notion of who killed your mother?"

"Yes."

"But who is it? Have you shared this with the police?"

He shook his head. "Not yet. I'm hoping I'm wrong."

Eden tried not to appear too interested, but ventured

cautiously, "Do you think it's that young man who lived with you? Kit Randall?"

Ridenour's tousled ginger head jerked up. "Why would you say that?"

"The newspapers. They mentioned him."

"Let's see what my guest has to say. Would you like to participate? She says the more people we have at the table, the stronger the . . . spiritual essence, or something."

"I would love to join you."

"You're not afraid?"

"No, indeed. Who is your guest, by the way?"

"Her name is Miss Bella Valentine. The girl we met in the coach after the funeral."

———

Ridenour moved a small table in his mother's bedroom to its center and set three chairs around it to accommodate the séance group. Eden placed a white tablecloth over the finely polished wood of the table in accordance with the directions her employer had received.

Lucinda must have used this little table for her tea. Eden glanced up at the portrait of the woman. This beautiful room, her room. Had she been happy here? She sensed that the spirit of Lucinda Ridenour was restless, even though she had never met her in life.

Ridenour nervously bustled around, showing more animation than Eden had seen him exhibit in the preceding week. Just after dark, the heavy door knocker clanked briskly.

Eden and her young employer both dashed downstairs and arrived at the door simultaneously. He smiled self-consciously as though reminding himself that the master of the house did not answer his own door, but rather allowed his servant to do it.

Bella smiled with narrowed eyes to see Eden at the door, but said nothing. The two women scrutinized each other in a different light now that both had talked to Kit. Eden played the dutiful housekeeper and took Bella's brightly colored shawl.

The girl carried a large leather pouch over her shoulder and was dressed in a clinging, elaborately draped costume, somewhere between classical Greek and East Indian in fashion, which ended at her lower calf. Beneath the gown she wore close-fitting silk trousers. Her bare feet were clad in woven straw sandals.

Eden thought this exotic garb helped her carry out the pretense of being someone in touch with otherworldly forces. Eden, on the other hand, was of a stubbornly realistic frame of mind. This resistance to the supernatural had often caused friction in her marriage to a Cheyenne medicine man who drew few distinctions between the spiritual and temporal in life. Still, she would play along and pretend to believe whatever transpired tonight.

"Miss Valentine," said her host. "I have everything you requested all ready and set up. Mrs. Murdoch has agreed to join us. Do you wish some refreshment first or shall we—"

"I'd prefer to start immediately, if you don't mind," Bella said.

They all adjourned to Lucinda Ridenour's bedchamber. The drapes were drawn, though the window was left open at Bella's request. This made Eden suspicious.

"The moon is full tonight," the girl explained. "I prefer a

171

new moon, but we will have to make do. Sometimes a full moon has its own power, though I don't want it to shine in on us."

The only light in the room was a lamp in the middle of the little table which sat beneath the portrait of the late mistress of the house.

Bella gazed up at the painting for a moment to study it.

"Where's the parrot?" she asked.

"I don't know, actually," Ridenour said. "He disappeared from the house the day after she—the day after the . . . murder."

Eden saw the young man almost flinch to say the word "murder." The thought of it still troubled him so profoundly, he could not speak about it without emotion. That was surely to be expected from one as sensitive as Christopher Ridenour, she supposed.

"What was his name?" said Bella.

"Mr. Sparks." He gazed up at the portrait for a moment and added with distaste, "Old Sparky. A nuisance. I can't say I miss him. Except that . . . well, *she* loved him."

Bella walked over to the brass parrot stand. She knelt and picked up a red feather from the tray beneath it.

Eden and Ridenour seated themselves at the table. He tapped his foot incessantly as Bella made her slow tour of the room, pausing to touch things, sometimes hold them in her hand, even occasionally sniff them. She carried with her a lit stick of incense in a little porcelain bowl. The scent of sandalwood soon filled the chamber.

The young spiritualist approached the table and turned the lamp to its lowest flame, plunging the large room into near darkness. She then drew a small candle from her pouch. She lit it and placed it at the center of the table, then extinguished the lamp. The tiny flickering light made their forms cast enormous, swaying shadows on three separate walls.

Bella told them all to join hands.

The girl's slender hand felt cool and delicate to Eden, but Ridenour's grasp was clammy. She could feel the agitation in his muscles as he held her hand more tightly than she would have wished.

Bella closed her eyes and began to sway back and forth slightly with each deep breath she drew. Eden glanced at Christopher, whose anxious eyes were fixed on his guest.

Bella began to speak in a low, unnatural voice. "Oh, spirits, admit this unworthy one back into your domain. We seek to commune with the spirit of our departed sister Lucinda."

She then made a moaning cry that sounded as though she were in pain, but Ridenour turned and gave Eden a look to indicate this was part of the ritual.

Part of the show, Eden secretly smirked.

"Dear Lucinda, if you walk among us, give us poor mortals a sign."

A knock was heard in the room. Both Ridenour and Eden jumped at the sound.

"Is she here?" he asked. "Mother, can you hear me?"

Another knock.

He glanced about the room, waiting.

No more knocking. Eden wondered how the girl managed it. She must have a confederate lurking outside the house.

"This room is filled with longing," said Bella. "And lust."

Ridenour gave Eden an uncertain look at the mention of this last.

"The air is thick with craving and inconsolable loss."

"Miss Valentine, is she here or not?" he asked.

Bella did not answer, in fact she now looked somewhat different, bizarre in fact. Her eyes were still closed, but her mouth sagged open. Her breath came in a short, swift meter.

A sudden gust of wind blew the curtains wide and extinguished the flame of the little candle. The frosty breeze continued, filling the room with a terrible chill. The pale sliver of moonlight caught the features of Miss Valentine, who looked strangely tormented.

She's really good at this, marveled Eden. How does she manage these superb effects?

When she noticed that Christopher looked concerned, she whispered to him, "Is this to be expected?"

"I don't know. She didn't act this way last time."

Bella panted like a hungry animal, faster and faster. Eden feared the girl would black out with too much oxygen in her brain.

"I see . . ." Bella's voice no longer carried the altered, theatrical quality she had first adopted. It was now her own voice, but weak and strained. Her breathing became labored. "I see a bed. A bed with shiny, black carvings of the ocean."

Christopher and Eden simultaneously glanced over to Lucinda's bed, since it mirrored the girl's description.

"A satin sheet . . . delicate and shimmering. See how the lamplight glows upon it?"

"What is she talking about?" Eden whispered.

"Hush, please," he said.

"A young man lies in the bed. The silky sheets caress him. His eyes are closed but he is not sleeping."

The girl became more agitated, rocking back and forth again in her seat. The legs of her chair knocked against the floor with a clatter. Her head tossed from side to side, in counterpoint to her body. Beads of perspiration glistened on her smooth forehead in the moonlight, though the room was far from warm.

Eden wondered what to make of this. She had seen people in trances before when she lived among the Indians, but usually their altered state of consciousness was induced by drugs or fasting.

"My darling boys." The sound of her voice had subtly changed. It now carried the hint of a Southern accent.

"What are you talking about?" Ridenour said.

Bella's own voice returned. "The other young man leans over the bed and kisses him."

"What the devil?" He released both women's hands.

"Kiss him again. You know you want to," said the simpering Southern belle voice.

"Miss Valentine! Stop this nonsense immediately!" He stood up.

The increasing panic in her young employer's voice frightened Eden. She pushed back from the table. Bella continued, oblivious to the agitation she was causing.

"He does kiss him again, more passionately and is surprised by the ardent response."

"Miss Valentine? Miss Valentine, do you hear me?"

The Southern inflection returned. *"See how he wants this? Just look at him."*

175

"Shut up! Get out of here!"

"My darling boys," she drawled, in a singsong that was both sad and sweet. *"My two darling Christophers."*

He grabbed the edge of the little table and overturned it. The loud crash as it hit the floor woke Bella from her trance.

She blinked and looked about her as though she was not sure where she was.

"Get out!" Ridenour shouted. "Get out of my house."

Bella realized she might be in danger and leaped to her feet. She ran from the room and Eden followed her, both racing down the stairs.

Bella stopped at the door and turned. "My bag. I left it in the bedroom."

Eden blocked her from trying to fetch it. She feared for the girl's safety. She had not previously thought Christopher Ridenour capable of such violent emotions. Now she had to wonder if he might be a suspect, too.

"You need to leave now. I'll get your bag and bring it to you at your lodgings tomorrow."

Bella frowned, but nodded and left the house.

Eden debated whether she should stay or go. She heard the sound of Christopher descending the staircase. She kept her back to the door with her hand on the knob to aid in a hasty exit, if need be.

He carried Bella's bag and now looked entirely composed. Almost. His curly ginger hair was in wild disarray.

"She . . . she forgot this." He handed the bag to Eden. "I apologize for my behavior. It's not like me to lose my temper. I'm quite embarrassed."

"We needn't speak of it, Mr. Ridenour."

"She upset me. Those silly things she said. It was absurd."
He ran his hands through his long curls, attempting to control them.

"Perhaps you should turn in early tonight, sir."

He nodded and mounted the stairs once again, heading
for his room, which lay just below Eden's. She was not sure
she wanted him in between her and the door tonight. That
and she had no appetite for sleep after such a tumultuous
evening, so she wandered into the kitchen. She sat down at
the table with a fresh orange. Sniffing the pungent citrus
scent as she slowly tore away the skin, she tried to sort out
Bella's "trance."

She had never believed in mediums and frankly thought
the young girl to be a charlatan. Still, once Bella began
breathing strangely and talking in such an eerie voice, Eden
had to conclude she was either an extremely talented
actress or something strange had indeed happened.

The voice had a strong southern accent—was it Lucinda
Ridenour's voice? Kit had told her that Lucinda was born in
Tennessee. Her son's voice still held traces of his Southern
childhood, though the influence just crept in around the
edges of his speech. A certain softness around the r's and
a's.

Bella had probably met Lucinda at the High Life Club and
had learned to mimic her accent. But what about the scene
she described? One young man kissing another? Kit and
Christopher?

My darling boys. My two darling Christophers.

She did not see this development coming. The thought
of this scene gave her a shiver. Yet something had to explain
Kit's terrible despondency and his refusal to talk about it.

And what about those odd remarks he had made about rape? Had he been forced to do something against his will? Or had he engaged in some activity that he now regretted?

A knock at the kitchen door caused her to jump. She held her breath, yet did not even know what she was afraid of. Where were Christopher's bodyguards tonight? Had he dismissed them to keep this evening's occult interlude private?

The light of her lamp cast ominous shadows on the walls of the large kitchen. The knock came again, this time more insistent. She grabbed a large carving knife along with her lamp.

The glass panes of the door cast enough light onto the back porch for her to see Bella's tall, thin form. She relaxed and opened the door.

"I saw the light," Bella said. "I really need my bag. I left my key and all my money in it."

"Yes, I'll get it," Eden whispered with a smile of relief. "Please come in, but . . . shhhh." She placed her finger to her lips.

Bella nodded, understanding Eden's desire for secrecy.

Eden returned to the kitchen with the bag and the two women sat at the table. She offered Bella an orange from the large bowl and the girl eagerly took two, placing one in her bag, then starting to peel the second.

"What did I say that riled him so much?" said Bella.

"You don't know?"

"I just asked, didn't I?"

"Excuse me. I'm not used to dealing with clairvoyants. I was surprised you didn't know what happened." Eden was not at all sure she wanted to repeat it. She did not wish to belabor such a startling accusation against Kit. No use publicizing something that was probably not true anyway.

Yet Eden knew Kit trusted Bella completely. Perhaps the girl could be a useful ally. Eden needed one. She felt severely handicapped so far by her lack of knowledge of Leadville and its inhabitants.

"Well, you said some fairly shocking things. At least the implications were shocking."

Bella leaned forward with interest as she tossed a large piece of orange rind on the floor. "Do tell."

"You described two young men kissing."

Bella grimaced. "On the mouth?"

"I guess so. You used the word 'passionate.' "

Bella made a low whistle. "I assumed Kit would eventually get tired of her, but I never guessed *that's* who he'd leave her for."

The girl's blithe acceptance of the scandalous scenario stunned Eden even more than the possibility it could be true.

"You mean you think that Kit and Christopher—?"

Bella shrugged. "What do *you* think?"

Eden did not know. Kit had been sexually adventurous from a tender age, according to Brad. He had always so guilelessly reveled in his own animal spirits, he had seemed more wayward than he really was. She had assumed his interests did not stray beyond the typical misbehavior of a virile, young bachelor. His family had never doubted for a moment that he would sow a few wild oats, then settle down and marry like all good young men of his background were expected to do.

"Did you ever know Kit to . . . engage in such behavior before?" Eden said cautiously.

"No, but just recently he asked me about that sort of thing." Bella stopped separating her orange sections long enough to puzzle over her recollections. "He didn't act like he knew much about it. Then again, in my book, he was living with the Queen of Decadence, so who knows? Anything's possible in this house."

Eden wanted to say, *not my Kit*, but could she? Did she really know him anymore? She quietly chewed the pulpy flesh of her orange section.

"I know you've seen Kit," Eden said. "He told me you visited him the other day."

"Don't worry." She winked. "I won't let anyone know."

"I think it's better if we don't mention to him what you said at the séance tonight. I'm afraid it will just upset him like it upset Mr. Ridenour."

"Kit's not like Chris. He's not so . . . fragile. He'd probably laugh."

"You might be surprised. Please swear to me you won't tell him what we learned tonight. We both want what's best for him, don't we?"

Bella impulsively grabbed Eden's hand. "We're going to be great friends. The cards told me so."

"I hope so," Eden said. She tried to make some neutral conversation. "What brought you to Leadville, Bella?"

"A man. What else? My husband. He was bound and determined to get rich quick. All he was good at was spending my money. His name was Ben Valentine."

She suddenly chuckled. "Kit doesn't believe that's my real name, but it is. My married name, at least. Anyway, I grew up in Denver and I'd still be there if I hadn't met Ben. I owned my own house there. It was a really nice house, too, but Ben mortgaged it to buy a lumber business, which failed, then the bank foreclosed and we were out on the street . . . so we moved to Leadville. It was a lot smaller then, three, four years ago. Just starting to boom. Everybody said, here's where all the opportunity is, so off we went."

Bella shook her head sadly. "Ben never got rich. Never even got the chance to file a claim of his own. Just went to work in the mines like all the rest of the get-rich-quick blockheads. The dampness didn't agree with him. Filled up his lungs. In six months, he was dead."

"I'm sorry."

The girl's story took a bitter turn. "Not half so sorry as me. I was dead broke. Had to earn a living any way I could so I decided to become a spiritualist for money."

"Kit says you're a witch. He's just kidding, isn't he? I can never tell with Kit."

"I'm *not* a witch." The girl seemed offended, but not necessarily at Eden. "I practice an ancient religion. After my folks died, I was taken in by a neighbor. Her name was Mamie, at least that's what I always called her. She grew up on a little island off the coast of Ireland, a place so isolated they called Christianity the 'new religion.' I suppose you're going to tell me I'll go straight to hell for all of this."

"Quite the opposite, Bella. I lived among the Cheyennes for fourteen years, married to a medicine man who was certainly not a Christian. I'd be the last to judge you."

Bella relaxed and a broad smile spilled across her thin face. "Then I'll speak frankly."

Eden hid her amusement at this remark. The young woman had not so far spoken with anything but frankness.

"Tell me about Mamie."

Before Bella could reply, a loud thud, like a piece of furniture hitting the floor above their heads, caused them to jump up from their seats.

They both headed for the central staircase, where Eden motioned for Bella to wait. She did not want Christopher to know she was in the house.

She tried Ridenour's bedroom door and found it unlocked. She threw it open and saw Christopher Ridenour hanging by the neck from a ceiling beam.

Fourteen

He was alive. Jerking, kicking, and flailing as the noose slowly but efficiently choked him, but still alive. His face glowed a grotesque shade of dark red, his tongue protruded, and his eyes bulged from their sockets.

Eden plunged into action. She glanced about the room and spied a pocketknife on the bureau. She grabbed it, then righted the chair the young man had just kicked over beneath him and jumped up on it. He tried to shove her away, but was losing consciousness. She managed to sever the silk drapery tie he had fashioned into a rope and he crashed to the floor, shaking the entire room as he hit.

"Is he dead?" Bella whispered from the doorway.

"No. Please leave. I'll handle this and talk to you tomorrow."

"There's a restaurant just across Chestnut from my boardinghouse. It's called Mrs. Julia's. Noon?"

Eden nodded as she pulled Christopher's head into her lap and loosened the cord from his throat. Apparently he did not know how to tie a proper slip knot. He might have strangled to death eventually from his own weight upon the knot, but it would have been a terrible, slow process, had she not interrupted it.

"Mr. Ridenour? Can you hear me?"

He managed to groan between deep gasps for breath. The violent dark red faded from his face and his breathing soon slowed to a near-normal level.

When he recovered himself enough to recognize his surroundings, he tried to sit up. His ginger curls hung in his face as he massaged his bruised and swollen throat and coughed spasmodically.

"Why did you do that?" he said, though his voice was so hoarse she could barely make out the words.

"You were making a mistake."

"You don't know anything about me."

She rose to her feet. "That's true. I have a purely personal motive for seeing that you stay alive."

He looked up at her and waited.

"I came to work here under false pretenses."

"A spy for the union. I knew it! I knew you didn't have the manner of a housekeeper."

She shook her head with a weary smile. "I have no connection to your labor problems, Mr. Ridenour. I want to find out who murdered your mother."

"Did you even know my mother?"

"I know Kit Randall. I'm engaged to marry his uncle and we want to see him clear of this trouble."

"Where is he? Is he still in Leadville? I don't think those lazy misfits on the police force are even looking for him."

She remained silent.

"I'm sorry to tell you this, Mrs. Murdoch, but I have evidence Kit killed my mother."

"What sort of evidence?"

"I found the murder weapon. His own knife. That one

there." He pointed to the pocketknife on the floor, which Eden had just used to cut him down.

"The newspapers didn't mention the murder weapon being found." She bent down and picked it up to examine it. The knife blade was small and wide. It tucked neatly into a silver handle with the carving of a wolf's head on it.

"I haven't told the police about it."

This was a surprising admission, she thought. Why on earth would he not turn over the supposed murder weapon to the police? It made no sense at all. Didn't he want his mother's killer to be punished? She resolved not to end this night until she had some basic answers.

"If you come down to the kitchen, I'll fix you some mint tea. That might soothe your throat."

He glanced up at her with a wary expression, then slowly nodded. She could tell he wanted to talk, needed to talk. She knew now just how terribly alone he was.

———

He sat slumped at the kitchen table as she poured him his tea.

"It smells like sandalwood in here," he said.

She did not wish him to know Bella had returned to the house.

"You're probably smelling Miss Valentine's valise. She left it, remember?"

He nodded as she sat down across from him.

"Why would a handsome, wealthy young man of twenty want to kill himself?"

He chuckled sadly. "I'm not handsome. You needn't try to flatter me. And soon I won't be wealthy, either."

"You have financial problems in addition to everything else?" She pretended ignorance of the topic.

"Yes, if you're actually interested. I went into a staggering amount of debt last year to buy new hydraulic pumps for the Eye Dazzler. All the upper shafts are played out, you see. We've been forced to go deeper and deeper and with every foot down, the water problems have increased. The pumps have to run continuously or the lower shafts would flood in an hour." He sighed. "I'm sure this is all quite boring to—"

"You can't meet your debt payments unless the mine is producing."

He looked up. "You do know a thing or two about business."

"I'm sorry. I've been eavesdropping on you and your banker, Mr. Hauser."

"You wouldn't be the first servant in this house to eavesdrop."

Eden thought instantly of Sadie Branch, Lucinda Ridenour's personal maid. The one who began to make one hundred dollars a week after the mysterious death of Orson Ridenour.

"Does Mr. Landry know the financial situation you are in?"

"As a matter of fact, he knows everything about our—I mean, *my* finances. He stole my personal accounting ledger and shared the information with the workers, no doubt to convince them I was hoarding vast sums of money while denying them a fair wage. But I'm sure he didn't tell them the whole story. Then they would know that I put up everything I owned as collateral to buy those pumps. If I can't pay the interest on the loans, the bank will soon foreclose on the Dazzler."

"I can understand his vengefulness *after* he was fired, but why *before*?"

"I believe he was trying to ruin me . . . and my mother. I think he wanted to show her he was—I don't know—powerful or something. They were constantly fighting. An endless game of tug-of-war, but I don't, for the life of me, know what the prize was. Sometimes they acted like they hated each other and then they would behave like they couldn't live without each other. Ever since my stepfather died, the contest had taken on insane proportions. And her . . . friendship . . . with Kit just rubbed salt in the wound—"He broke off suddenly.

"I know all about Kit's relationship with your mother. We can discuss such things openly. I'm not a delicate lady, sheltered from the world, and this isn't a tea party. I also know a little bit about your mother's 'friendship' with Mr. Landry."

"I'll speak plainly, then. No need now to pretend it didn't happen. My mother carried on an adulterous liaison with Mr. Landry throughout her entire marriage to my stepfather."

"Did *he* know? Your stepfather, I mean."

"He must have. We didn't talk about it. Some things just aren't talked about. But *everyone* knew. Landry and my mother . . . they weren't particularly discreet."

Eden shifted the discussion back to Kit. "I don't understand why you haven't told the police about finding the knife."

Ridenour propped his elbows upon the heavy oak table and rested his chin in his hands. He gazed down at nothing and refused to answer.

"Why are you certain that was the murder weapon?" she continued.

"I found it in the room where she died. It had been thrown onto the bottom shelf of the étagère."

"Was there blood on it?"

He raised his eyes at this. "No, there wasn't."

"But the room was . . . uhm . . . quite bloody—?"

He jerked back in his seat and looked distraught.

"I'm sorry. I didn't mean to upset you. I know that talking about this must be very hard. Still—"

"Kit Randall murdered my mother! I just have to make myself accept that. And I suppose that you will, too."

"You liked Kit, didn't you?"

He ducked his tousled head, but nodded. "He was the first true friend I ever had. When I was growing up, my mother and I had to travel from place to place. I never got a chance to meet any children my own age. Then we settled here, but I still never . . . oh, it doesn't matter now."

He sipped his tea, grimacing as he swallowed. The flesh of his throat was so bruised and swollen, he couldn't have buttoned his collar if he had wanted to.

"Life in this house was so gloomy after my stepfather passed on. Then we met Kit and everything changed. He was so sunny and full of life. In the evenings, I would play the piano and my mother would sing for us. She was once a professional singer. Quite gifted. Not that anyone ever appreciated her for that. Sometimes Kit would sing, too. He has a lovely baritone voice. My mother taught him how to perfect it." He sighed. "How I miss those evenings."

He turned his cup round and round in his hand and faintly smiled at the memory. "Kit was very kind to me. I'll never forget the night he made me get my tooth pulled."

"Tell me about it," Eden said, sensing the boy was at last relaxing enough to speak candidly.

"A couple of months ago, I had a terrible toothache, and I'm an awful coward when it comes to dentists. Mother and Kit pleaded with me for three days to go get the tooth pulled, but I was too stubborn. Content to live in unspeakable agony rather than face the inevitable.

"On the third night, when I was nearly ready to climb the walls, I was suffering so, Kit marched into my room and told me to get dressed, that I was going to get that tooth pulled or else. I said, 'Where do you plan to find a dentist at this hour?' It was nearly two in the morning. He said, 'I have a plan.'

"He led me to the High Life Club, of all places, because he had met a professional gambler there who claimed to also practice dentistry. Holliday was his name, I think. Everyone called him 'Doc,' so maybe he really was a dentist. The only thing I knew for certain was that he was profoundly intoxicated. Kit said, 'Doc, are you too drunk to pull a tooth?'

"The man took offense at the very notion of it. 'Sir, I'm never too drunk to pull a tooth and damn any man who suggests it.' Kit shoved me and my aching jaw toward him and asked what he charged.

"This Holliday fellow was not interested in pulling teeth at the moment and said, 'Maybe tomorrow.' He had a poker hand demanding his attention, so Kit said—and this is the brilliant part—'I've got twenty dollars says you can't pull a tooth out in less than two minutes.' The dentist-gambler put down his cards and said, 'Let me see the tooth.'

"I opened my mouth and he wiggled the molar that was tormenting me, then said, 'Make it fifty and I'll have it out in *one* minute.'

"Soon all the men were placing bets on whether Holliday could make good his boast. He returned from his hotel room carrying his bag of dentistry tools. They made me drink all the whiskey I could hold. I normally hate the taste of hard liquor, but I was so desperate to end my torment, I was willing to do anything. They sat me down in a straight chair with my head laid back against the edge of the bar. The bartender got out his watch and yelled, 'Go!' and fifty-six seconds later I was minus the offending molar!"

Eden laughed with him at this. His affection for Kit was plaintively obvious. Soon she sobered, though, and said directly, "Why haven't you gone to the police with the knife?"

The downcast red-gold lashes again—he refused her question and she feared for the answer. Did he worry more about Kit saying something about him, about them? About all three of them? What?

"I'll tell you flatly, Mr. Ridenour, I don't believe Kit Randall is capable of murdering your mother or any other person in cold blood."

"I don't think it was cold blood, exactly. I think she tormented him into it somehow. Just like she used to torment every man who loved her. She drove that witless Jake Landry to distraction. She must have done the same to Kit."

"*How* did she 'drive him to distraction?' I think Kit was infatuated with your mother, but not necessarily in *love* her. At least not the violent, all-consuming love that would drive a man to murder."

"I think she told him lies. Told him things happened that didn't happen. And he believed her."

"What sort of things?"

He refused to answer.

"Things about you and him?" she asked. "Things he might not remember clearly because he'd been drinking?"

He looked up with a painfully twisted expression on his freckled face.

"Mr. Ridenour, was Miss Valentine's vision about you and Kit?"

"Don't be absurd."

"Did you kiss him in your mother's bed?"

"How dare you ask me that!"

"Did *he* kiss *you*?"

"Stop it!" He stood up. "Leave my house!"

"I won't leave your house. I won't leave you to finish what you started tonight."

"Why do you care if I live or die?"

"Because I need you alive. I want to find out the truth."

"I want you to leave here immediately!"

"No," she said in a quiet but firm voice.

"What makes you think I won't *force* you to leave?"

"Because I'm the last friend you've got."

Fifteen

The following morning at ten sharp, Eden and Christopher Ridenour were ushered into the office of a Dr. Chandler, the surgeon who had examined Lucinda's body.

"How do you do, Mr. Ridenour," said the surgeon, a young man of perhaps thirty, with a full blond beard and an already receding hairline. "What can I do for you?"

"I've come seeking the details of the wound that . . . that . . ."

Eden was glad that Christopher had allowed her to accompany him. He was clearly not yet up to handling this on his own. She could tell that he was somehow as anxious as she was to rule out Kit as a suspect, though she did not fully understand why.

"Mr. Ridenour would like to know exactly how his mother died," she said.

The young doctor frowned at her and obviously wondered who she was.

Ridenour noticed this and said, "This is Mrs. Murdoch. She is . . . a family friend."

Eden was impressed with his quick thinking in introducing her so. Suggesting that she was there merely to lend moral support to the grief-stricken young man made a great deal more sense than any truthful explanation could have.

The doctor shuffled through some papers on his desk and located his notes.

Ridenour cleared his throat and stared at the floor as he asked a delicate question which was apparently important to him. "I hope I don't offend you, Dr. Chandler, but are you fully versed in pathology?"

The older man smiled slightly with a hint of condescension. "I would guess that not one man out of fifty in this town would even have known the word 'pathology,' sir. You must have an extensive education."

"No, doctor, I just read a lot."

"Rest assured that I am well trained in the art and science of morbid anatomy. I am a graduate of Johns Hopkins and did a great deal of study in the scientific investigation of wounds while serving on the staff of a hospital in Chicago prior to opening a private practice here."

Ridenour nodded, satisfied with the doctor's credentials.

Dr. Chandler consulted his notes, then looked up. "Do you mind my being forthright? Some do not have the stomach for it." He looked pointedly at Eden when he said this.

"Sir, don't abridge your remarks out of deference to the delicacy of my sex," she said. "I served as a nurse during the War of the Rebellion. I will neither flinch nor faint."

"Fine, then," said Chandler. "I performed the autopsy approximately forty-eight hours after death occurred. Not optimal, but the delay was unavoidable due to an accident at one of the mines. I'm sure you will agree I must focus my efforts on those who can still benefit from my services. That said, the late Mrs. Ridenour died of massive blood loss due to a single knife wound to the throat which—by chance or design—severed the carotid artery."

That would account for the amount of blood in Lucinda Ridenour's parlor. Eden knew that the opening of the carotid artery in a living person would literally spout blood like a fountain. The assailant could not have escaped some of that crimson spray after making the wound.

"Death was not instantaneous," Chandler continued, "as there was blood over several areas of the room. The blow was probably struck near the hearth. The victim then managed to approach the sofa on the far wall, where she collapsed and ultimately died."

"Did she suffer long?" Ridenour asked, still directing his questions at the floor.

The young doctor's face softened for a moment. He added, probably more out of kindness than truth, "Very little, I'm sure."

"Was there any sign of a struggle?" Eden said. She had read in the newspaper accounts that a fight between Lucinda and her attacker was not thought to have occurred, but she wanted the doctor's verification in that she did not trust journalists. She had too often been the subject of their fanciful fact embroidery and felt they placed a greater value on entertaining the sensation-hunting masses than serving the cause of truth.

"None whatsoever. The body carried no defensive wounds at all. That is, no cuts and the like on the hands or arms, either in fighting the attacker or simply warding off further blows. I even examined under the fingernails for signs of having scratched the assailant. It is my opinion that the murderer delivered the single, fatal stab wound and then fled the scene immediately."

"What was the size and angle of the wound?" she asked.

A groan escaped Ridenour at this question. She looked over to see him, head down, covering his eyes with his hand, then his mouth. She worried he might get violently ill and decided they must quickly end the interview.

"Unusual," said Chandler in a tone that seemed to indicate he was warming to his topic. Was he an amateur detective? Eden wished he would remember that he was talking in the presence of a bereaved family member instead of giving an interview to the press.

"The weapon was at least seven inches in length and pierced the entire breadth of the neck. The blade was not particularly sharp, but was long and very thin, with a sharp point on the end. The angle was a downward trajectory, implying that the attacker was taller than his victim. Not unlikely given that Mrs. Ridenour was only five feet—" He paused to glanced once more at his notes. "—two inches in height."

"What was the exact width of the blade?" Eden pressed on though she saw in the corner of her eye that Christopher was growing paler by the minute.

"No more than one half inch at its widest point."

With growing confidence, she pulled Kit's pocketknife from her wrist bag. "Could this knife have made the wound?"

The surgeon took the knife and extended its blade. "Absolutely not. This blade is no more than three and a half, four inches long. And broad from tip to base. This could not possibly have made the wound in question."

Christopher looked up, then glanced over to Eden. They

exchanged faintly relieved looks and thanked the doctor for his time.

———

Mrs. Julia's Restaurant, the site Bella had chosen for their meeting, was too crowded and noisy for Eden's taste, but she had not yet found any dining establishment in Leadville that was not crowded and noisy.

Bella rushed in breathless, causing more of a scene than Eden would have liked. She toted her large bag and bumped several diners with it as she passed them. This, plus her exotic manner of dress, caused every patron in the small establishment to glance up at her.

"Did he live?" said Bella as she sat down.

"Yes. A little bruised and shaken, but alive."

"That's good, I guess."

A waiter approached their table and took their luncheon order. They both chose the beans and bacon with dark bread.

"Mr. Ridenour and I had a long talk last night, but I didn't learn as much as I had hoped."

Bella leaned forward and whispered, "What did he say about him and Kit?"

"Not much. He flatly denied anything improper took place."

"Of course, he'd have to say that. If only we could get our hands on Sadie Branch. Bet she could tell a tale or two about the Black Lace House."

"Do you know Mrs. Branch?" Eden had asked all the tradesmen she had encountered since taking over Sadie Branch's duties, but no one seemed to know what became of Lucinda Ridenour's maid since the day after she discovered the body of her mistress.

"I'll ask around," Bella said. "I'll ask every girl on State Street, if I have to. She came from there, you know."

The girl could tell from Eden's unchanged expression that she did not understand the reference to State Street, so she added, "Most of the women on State Street are—" She lowered her voice once again. "—ladies of . . . negotiable virtue."

Eden nodded her understanding. She wondered whether to share her belief that Sadie Branch was a blackmailer. There must be some explanation of why her salary increased by a factor of ten after Orson Ridenour's death. She decided to wait for a more secluded moment to discuss this issue and changed the subject.

"Do you know anything about this Jacob Landry?"

"Not really," said Bella. "What I saw of him, I didn't like. He was proud. Proud and arrogant. He and that Ridenour hag made a perfect pair."

Eden tried not to smile at the young girl's obvious jealousy. "Do you know anything about Landry's wife?"

"I know *of* her. She runs the local orphan asylum. Quite the noble doer of good deeds. No children, so I suppose she has time on her hands. Always getting written about in the paper."

"Do you suppose she would know anything of interest to us?"

Bella propped her pointed chin up with her elbow, ignoring social etiquette with such casual abandon, Eden had to immediately like the girl. She sensed this blithe attitude of hers was part of what attracted Kit.

"I never gave her much thought until the day of the funeral. Has to be embarrassing. Having your husband in love with another man's wife and not even caring who knows it."

Eden shifted in her seat. She was, after all, in love with another woman's husband. But where Jacob Landry heedlessly exposed his wife to public humiliation, Brad Randall took great pains to shield his family from such pain. He was the original injured party in the divorce proceedings. His wife had been unfaithful to him.

Brad could have taken their son from his wife and publicly revealed her sins to feed the hungry gossip-mongers of Washington City. Most in society would have supported him in this. But he would not do it. His love for his child was too great. He decided his son needed a mother more than his own vanity needed vindication.

The couple agreed to part as quietly as possible, with him taking the legal "blame" in the courts so that Amanda could retain at least a portion of her social standing. It would never be the same, of course. A divorced woman would never be received in certain circles, but she would keep her fine house on K Street and raise up their son in it.

"I'm sure the woman's situation is very difficult. One has to feel sorry for her. She must be very devoted to her husband to give him a convenient alibi, if it weren't the truth, that is."

Bella hooted at this suggestion. "That mousy thing? I'm not surprised. I don't think she's got enough gumption to argue with a butcher she caught with his thumb on the scales. She probably would say anything her stupid husband told her to say. She let him run after Lucy Ridenour for *six years*, after all, without complaining. That's about as tame as it gets for a woman who still draws a breath."

Eden decided she would pay a call on the orphan asylum after she finished her meal, nonetheless. Having viewed the scene in the Landrys' front yard gave her to know much trouble still brewed in that little house on Sixth Street, despite its deceptively proper and nondescript appearance.

"I wonder why she did put up with it?"

"Probably had no choice," said Bella. "Most married women don't, you know. No money. Nowhere else to go. That's why you'll never catch me getting married again. Not for anything."

"Not even for love?"

"*Especially* not for love. I'm in love, at this very moment. Don't care who knows it either."

"I wonder if I can guess with whom?"

Bella grinned. "I'm pretty sure you can. But if we got married, it would spoil everything. Trust me."

"We were interrupted the other night when you were about to tell me about the woman who raised you."

"Mamie? She was a funny old thing. She saw the whole world as something magical and I liked that about her. She taught me the power of the seasons and to respect the wisdom of the ancients. Worshiping a goddess makes a lot more sense than worshiping a god, if you ask me. Kit makes fun of what I believe. But if he would sit down and read some of Madame Blavatsky's writings, he would understand."

"That book you gave him, *Isis Unveiled*?"

"Yes, it's so important to know these things."

"Bella, I'm not sure Kit has a very metaphysical slant to him. You're asking a lot."

"He could stand to be more liberal-minded *and* less judgmental. The thought of him acting so morally superior, after all he's gotten up to with Chris Ridenour—"

"You mustn't spread such slander. We don't really know anything. I have reason to believe Kit is very upset about whatever it was that happened. He may not have been a willing participant."

The young woman quieted at this and their conversation dwindled into silence. They finished their meal and agreed to meet again in a few days' time to share any new information.

Sixteen

The Presbyterian Orphan Asylum was located on the second floor of a building on Chestnut Street, just above a laundry. Eden studied the building and who came and went from it for several moments before deciding to approach.

She mounted the stairs on the side of the building as the laundress had instructed her to do, but when she entered she was told that Mrs. Landry had taken some of the children to the local school yard for exercise.

She headed straight for the school and found Ellen Landry supervising some toddlers and young children playing in a sand pile. The woman was much taller than Eden remembered from the brief scene at her house the day of the funeral. She was taller even than Bella Valentine, who towered over both her and Kit.

"Excuse me, Mrs. Landry?" she called out.

Ellen Landry turned with a severe look. "Yes?"

"Good day, ma'am. I am Mrs. Eden Murdoch. Your assistant told me I could find you here."

"What is it?" The woman's watchful gaze turned back to monitoring the children.

"My husband and I are thinking about adopting a child. I was told to speak with you."

"A baby or an older child? We have plenty of both."

Eden thought the woman talked as though she were selling horses. A draft horse or a trotter?

"Well, I'm not really sure. I thought that I might spend some time at the asylum and get to know the children and then choose."

"I'm not sure that's wise. Once the children know you are looking to adopt they all get their hopes up only to have them dashed. I won't have that. Better to take one home on trial."

"Perhaps if you would permit me to come to the asylum to help out occasionally, no one would need know my motives."

Ellen Landry thought about this. "I suppose that would—"

Her sentence was cut off by the booming of a brass band. She and Eden both turned to see a large gathering of men carrying signs behind the band as they made their way up the street. Mrs. Landry's orphans gathered about to watch as well.

The pro-union slogans on the signs quickly identified the marchers as miners on strike from the Eye Dazzler, the Chrysolite, and other mines in the district. The band strutted to military-sounding music and passersby on the street began to shout encouragement and taunts in equal measure.

Soon a uniformed group of men on horseback rode in from the opposite direction. Screams and shouts now ricocheted from every direction. The band music ended on a sour note as the musicians scattered for cover. The striking miners, however, were primed for a fight.

The horsemen charged the crowd, whacking heads with

truncheons. Some of the uniformed men, who Eden noted were not city policemen, but must be from one of the private militias she had read about, were successfully dragged off their horses and attacked by the crowd.

As Ellen Landry tried to gather her panicked charges about her, one curious little boy of five ran from her toward the fracas, excited rather than frightened by the action.

"I'll get him!" Eden said and ran after the boy. She caught up with him before he reached the street and scooped him up in her arms.

He fought and kicked wildly as she made her way back to Mrs. Landry. He shouted amazingly adult oaths at Eden and even managed to bite the side of her hand. She yelped at the unexpected pain and nearly dropped him.

"Broderick!" said Ellen. "Stop that at once. I apologize, Mrs.—"

"—Murdoch. Shall we return to the asylum?"

"Yes, please. Oh, dear, you're bleeding. I will take care of it as soon as we get back there."

The two women huddled together and escorted the group of children down an alleyway to escape the violence on the street. They both jumped at the crackling sound of pistol shots being fired.

When they turned back onto the main road, the riot had already played itself out. Bleeding men streamed in all directions.

"Nell?" a man shouted. "Nell!"

They turned to see Jacob Landry following them at a limping pace. He held a handkerchief to his bloody cheek.

Ellen glanced back at her injured husband, then hurried on down the street pretending she had not seen him. Eden followed, wondering why a woman would turn her back on her own husband as he called for her aid.

They reached the orphanage and mounted the steps with all the children accounted for. When Mrs. Landry's assistant was able to oversee the group, she took Eden into her office to examine the bite on her hand.

"It's nothing, really," said Eden, though the bleeding hand was smarting sharply.

"Let me bandage it for you." She removed a roll of cotton dressing from one of her desk drawers and pulled off a length.

"I want to apologize again for this happening."

"Don't mention it. I'm a—" Eden stopped when she realized she was about to ruin her disguise by saying, I'm a mother. "I was glad I could help at such a dire moment."

"I thank the good Lord you were there. I don't know what I would have done."

"Well, it's over now," Eden said. "I worry that some of those men were seriously injured. Maybe killed."

"This strike is ridiculous. Those men deserve what they got today. If they had any sense they would go back to work like they should."

Eden thought this a very odd statement coming from the wife of one of the most prominent strike leaders. She decided to change the subject. "Might I come back tomorrow and help again for an hour or two?"

"I would be pleased for you to return, Mrs. Murdoch."

As Eden left the orphan asylum and Ellen Landry's chilly smile, she pondered the fact that she had met two women this week who could not be more opposite had they been spawned from different species, yet alike in that both bore a grudge against the late Lucinda Ridenour.

———

Bella rose early to begin her search of the State Street amusements, both low and high, to find Sadie Branch. She had never ventured out much before mid-morning and was surprised to discover the unsavory sight of saloonkeepers sweeping out the dirty sawdust from last night's floors onto the sidewalks and streets.

Young boys gathered like maggots on a festering corpse as they set about their daily chore of sifting the sawdust hoping to find a coin or two among the detritus of a raucous saloon night. Spent tobacco juice, vomit, bits of food, and general litter filled their "mine tailings" of choice.

"A double eagle!" shouted one boy of ten or so.

Bella raised her eyebrows. Combing through filth had its rewards. She had not made that much last night from telling fortunes.

She glanced up at the garish signs of the saloons around her and sighed with frustration. HATTENBACK'S, BORDEN & MCELHENY, CASSADY & O'ROURKE'S, W. H. JONES, J. W. ALEXANDER'S—and that covered only half of one block. Where to begin? She had never met Sadie Branch and so did not know who her friends might have been. All she knew for certain was that several years ago, Sadie had "graduated" from one of the local houses of ill repute into the less well paid, but much higher social milieu of Third Street domestic service. The change had caused a modest level of gossip on the street. Etta, one of Bella's boardinghouse neighbors, remembered the event well and thought Sadie had perhaps been working at one of the music halls, most of which advertised "waiter girls in short skirts."

She first tried Cassady & O'Rourke's saloon, reasoning that Lucinda Ridenour's maiden name was O'Rourke, so maybe she had been related to the owner.

She knocked on the window after finding the door locked. She kept on rapping until a tiny man with long white hair and a cherublike face ringed with white whiskers opened the door.

"What the devil do you—oh, hello, milady, never too early in the morning for a breath of beauty."

Bella chuckled at the old Irishman's flirting. He looked exactly like a leprechaun. Old Mamie, the woman who had raised her after her parents died, had told countless stories about these wee folk and swore they existed, though even nine-year-old Bella had a few doubts.

"Such a tall drink of water, but I do like 'em tall, dearie," he said with a wink.

"Look, old man, I'm not searching for company. I need a favor."

"Anything, anything, my lovely, so long as you promise to marry me straight after."

She groaned, but could not help but smile. "Would you be Cassady or O'Rourke?"

The puckish man finally sobered. "Neither, I'm sorry to say. Both are long gone. Sold the place to me. Sean McGee, at your service."

"Pleased to meet you, Mr. McGee. Would you happen to have known Lucinda O'Rourke? That was her name before she married old Ridenour."

"The lady who was killed? Oh, my, no. Never met her. She was no relation to O'Rourke that I know of."

"What about a woman named Sadie Branch? Ever heard of her?"

"I've seen Sadie now and then. She likes to raise a glass or two when someone else is paying."

"Have you seen her lately?"

"No, not for months. Why?"

"I need to talk to her. Know anyone who might be friends with her?"

McGee twisted his face like a prune to try and pull forth a name. "She had a friend she used to make the rounds with. Can't think of her name, though. A floozie. She might work in one of the music halls."

Bella thanked the man and felt some encouragement that Etta's music hall reference might be correct. Inquiries at the Bon Ton, the Comique, and the Coliseum elicited only the slightest hint. She roamed all the way to Fifth Street to the house of the notorious Mollie May who, with chilly courtesy, directed her down the street to the brothel of her arch rival, Sallie Purple.

A surly and very hung-over woman there told her to seek out a girl named Betty—no last name was remembered—who worked at the Columbia Beer Hall and lived in a room above it.

Bella trudged back to State Street, her sandaled feet getting filthy from so much walking. She knew she should wear more conventional attire, but Leadville's summers were so short, she was determined to enjoy the freedom of wiggling her toes in the open air during the few weeks the weather permitted it.

Besides, wearing sandals made her feel close to her idol, Madame Blavatsky, who frequently adopted East Indian dress and occasionally ancient Egyptian attire. At least, some of her writings suggested this. Plus she had sent Bella a photograph of her, a full-length portrait in which the stately Russian-born matron wore an elaborate gown, trimmed in rich ornament. Over her head, she sported an exquisite hood, heavy with eastern embroidery. A fur neck piece completed the ensemble. Bella tried to copy each element of her fashion, to the extent her limited budget would allow.

Once a month, she received by mail Helena Blavatsky's monthly periodical, *The Theosophist*, published on the other side of the world in Bombay, where she currently resided. The magazine took six months to finally reach Leadville, Colorado.

Mixing with the lowly female denizens of State Street wore on her mood. It was not the toothless mouths or whiskey-soaked stink of them that bothered her so much as the hard-worn, hollow look in their kohl-rimmed eyes, with the paint still smeared from the night before. If only she could enlighten them. But she had not even succeeded in awakening college-educated Kit Randall to his higher potential in life; what hope did she have to reach these sorrowful creatures?

By the time she reached the Columbia, her feet were aching and her sandals nearly ruined. She gritted her teeth and entered the lavishly decorated drinking emporium which was just opening for its business day at the stroke of noon. She strode past the elaborate bar with its many pretenses to elegance, from the carved Corinthian-style columns to its mirrors coated with diamond dust.

A man wiped out whiskey glasses, while another tinkered with the absinthe fountain, reputed to deliver the iciest water in town to pour through a slotted absinthe spoon. The fountain made her think of Kit in the most painful way.

"Hi, there, sweetie," said the man cleaning shot glasses.

"Hi, yourself. Can you tell me where to find Betty?" She prayed there was not more than one Betty, since she did not have a surname for the woman.

"Upstairs." He jerked his head ceilingward.

She glanced around the back recesses of the long, narrow room.

"No," he said. "You gotta go up the stairs off the alleyway."

She thanked him and headed to the alley the local girls called Stillborn Street. She glanced around the foul-smelling lane behind the Columbia, half fearful she might actually see a dead baby among the rubbish heaps piled next to the rear doors of each business. Of course, it was probably just a rumor that the unfortunate women who worked these brothels and cribs disposed of their ill-conceived progeny out here. Yet the rank smell was bad enough to conjure up visions of rotting flesh.

She climbed the wooden stairs to the second floor door and knocked. She heard a commotion inside and possibly voices, though the noise coming from State Street in the form of band music, cries of street peddlers, and the incessant crack of freight drivers' whips over the heads of the weary oxen did much to drown out her eavesdropping.

After a minute, a woman appeared at the door. She seemed to be a typical resident of State Street: tattered finery showing more than ankle, face paint not yet washed off from the night before, plus a distinct odor of cigar smoke, probably from a bed partner rather than a tobacco habit of her own.

"Yeah?" said Betty, who did not invite her visitor in but rather stepped out onto the small landing, preventing Bella from getting a look into her lodgings.

"Hello. I'm looking for someone. An old friend, Sadie. Sadie Branch. You know her?"

"Used to."

"Know where I can find her now?"

The woman shrugged and backed through her door.

"Wait. When did you see her last? It's real important that I find her."

"You and everybody else in town. I ain't seen her in a while, so skedaddle. All right, sugar?"

"Thanks," Bella said and was about to depart when she heard a strange, squawking voice in the room behind the woman.

"Time flies, time flies," a nonhuman voice repeated over and over.

Betty turned her head inside the room and snarled, "Shut up, you damned—"

"You've got a bird? A talking bird?" said Bella with pretended enthusiasm.

"Yeah, so?"

"Could I see him?" She hoped this would encourage an invitation to enter.

Betty glanced back into her house uncertainly. "Maybe another day."

"Please, Betty. I just love those talking birds. I've never seen one up close before. Please."

"Oh, hell, why not?" The woman made an accommodating face, then turned and closed the door with a gesture that she would return.

Bella frowned with disappointment, but then smiled when Betty opened the door again. She held a brightly hued parrot, red-bodied with magnificent wings of blue, green, and yellow. She seemed uneasy with her pet, holding him out from her body as though she feared being pecked.

"Oh, he's a beauty," said Bella. She reached out to touch the bird.

"He bites."

Bella retracted her hand with lightning speed, startling the bird, which began to squawk and flap his wings. Betty grasped the bird's feet, but grimaced in fear.

"I gotta go," she said and rushed back into her room, slamming the door behind her with her foot.

"Time flies, time flies," Bella heard the parrot say through the door.

She stood on the little landing in the broiling noonday sun and wondered why the bird seemed to trigger something in her mind. She made her way back down the stairs, her brain spinning with possibilities. By the time she reached the last step, the memory came alive: The bird resembled the parrot in the painting of Lucinda Ridenour that hung above her bedroom fireplace. Christopher Ridenour had said that the bird had disappeared after his mother's death.

What if Sadie Branch had purloined the bird the day she left? She and the bird might both be staying with Betty.

Bella looked up at the silent door and wondered how to find out if her assumptions were true.

Seventeen

Dearest Brad,

I received your letter this morning and am filled with shock and dismay. Had I predicted your reaction to my suspicions about Kit and his relationship with Christopher Ridenour, I would never have shared them! How can you even consider severing your bond with this boy whom you have known since his birth? Who was raised up in your own mother's house like a younger brother to you? You have told me many times how fond you are of him and how you felt a duty to act in your late brother's stead as a mentor and protector to him.

Are you really willing to destroy this precious attachment based on a mere suspicion I had? An unproven suspicion based on the "vision"—one could as easily say hallucination—of a young woman who was not even present at the scene she described?

All that said—what if my suspicions are true? Is that really so unforgivable? I suppose I forget the rigid dictates of our own society since I have lived so long outside them, but my years among the Cheyennes did teach me many things.

They are more—what word to use?—"accepting"
of human nature in all its rich variety. To begin
with, they are not harshly critical of intimate rela-
tions pursued for their own sake, as opposed to
merely a "necessary evil" required to propagate the
species. They do not label such actions "fornication"
and therefore a crime and a sin.

Such liaisons as Kit and Christopher may have
engaged in were spoken of openly and without
shame among the Cheyennes.

She rested her pen a moment and debated whether to
try to explain the customs of the Cheyennes, given Brad's
horrified reaction to the news that young Ridenour and Kit
may have merely kissed. She had already been careful in her
remarks and choice of words so not to alarm him, but she
had obviously not gone far enough.

She was forced now to remind herself of her own shock
at learning of such matters. She had gradually noticed that
certain men of the tribe seemed to form their closest bonds
with other men, rather than women. They shunned the tra-
ditions of their own sex and at times exhibited the tem-
peraments of both genders. This seemed to upset no one in
the tribe, though she was bewildered and needed the matter explained to her.

Her late husband told her such men were regarded as
spiritually blessed, in that they were thought to embody the
divine ideal of synthesis. The fact that they chose as their
companions, even lovers, other men of the tribe, rather than
women was treated with a mere shrug.

The topic had first been broached because of a person in

a neighboring lodge named Youngwolf. Eden had actually mistaken Youngwolf for a woman. Advancing the confusion was that fact that Cheyenne pronouns have no gender. "He," "she," and "it" are all the same word.

Many young men visited Youngwolf's lodge and she soon realized something intimate was going on in there, judging from the remarks others made about these visits. Though she never fully accepted the free and easy way her Cheyenne friends talked and even joked about sexual matters, she had learned to tolerate it.

That Youngwolf sometimes led sacred dances and even accompanied the men on war parties further confused her. No women were ever allowed such duties. When she asked her husband about this, he was astonished to realize she did not know that Youngwolf was not a woman. Not that he considered him a "man" in the traditional sense, either. The tribe believed there existed more than two genders. Youngwolf fell into a category considered to be a third sex, a hybrid in a sense. This was not looked upon as an anomaly, but rather a special gift, and celebrated as such.

How could she ever get Brad to understand this? Kit was not in any way similar to Youngwolf, but Christopher Ridenour? Hmmm . . . she had to wonder.

He obviously did not adopt feminine dress or habits, yet he exhibited the same delicacy of manner she recalled in Youngwolf. If her suspicions were true, she pitied the young man the accident of fate which saw him born into the white world rather than the red.

With misgivings, she continued her letter:

I believe Kit's natural love of life leads him to express it with everyone he cares about without regard to their gender.

All that said, I am not certain he willingly participated in any such activity. His natural animal spirits could be misinterpreted by those who do not know him well. I fear he may have been taken advantage of while in a state of inebriation, though perhaps sedation might be a better term. Miss Valentine reports that he far too often indulges in a devilish concoction called absinthe. As you know, I never partake of strong drink so I am not in a position to know the particular effects of this libation, but Miss Valentine assured me it was considerably stronger than the typical alcoholic beverage and frequently produces hallucinations.

This drink was apparently such a favorite in the Ridenour house that they had commissioned a set of slotted absinthe spoons designed with the Eye Dazzler insignia on them. (This pattern adorns nearly everything associated with the Ridenours, from their etched glass front doors to the carvings on the family gravestone!)

I have much more to say, but time does not permit me to put it on paper at this moment. The labor unrest in Leadville is taking on increasingly violent proportions. I wish I could leave here, but Kit is still unable to travel. He is restless in his confinement, but he needs constant bedrest for at least another week if his damaged kidneys are to heal.

I am grateful that B.J. is responding to the doctor's treatment. That aspect of your last letter gave me some joy at least. Take care that Amanda does not overfeed him once his appetite has returned. I will write again tomorrow. Give Hadley a kiss for me and tell her I am proud of the way she is helping out your sister in minding her two little boys.

Yours as ever,
Eden

———

"Kit, you're supposed to be in bed." Eden set her basket of foods on the little wooden camp table and marched over to her patient.

"I'm going crazy here! It's been more than a week."

"I said a week or *two* of bedrest. Do you want to die?"

He slumped back down on the cot with a disgruntled moan. He watched as she laid out his supper. "What's the latest news from town?"

"I brought you some newspapers. Christopher is thinking of hiring strike breakers. He's desperate to reopen the Dazzler. Apparently his banker will call in his loans soon because he cannot make his payments."

"Good old George," Kit said.

"You know Mr. Hauser?"

"He was wined and dined a lot by the Ridenours. They were always trying to borrow money. Lucinda's spending habits were even beyond the reach of the Eye Dazzler money at times."

"Good grief, how could anyone spend that much?"

"It's amazing how quick you can learn to," he said. "Old Hauser used to bring his daughter, Georgina, to those dinners because his wife wouldn't set foot in the Black Lace House. That Georgina was a fast piece. She used to flirt with me and it made Lucinda furious."

"Not furious enough to stop courting the banker's money?"

"Nope. The Ridenours didn't really have a choice. They got hit with a bad break last year when the lower shafts started flooding."

"Yes, Christopher told me he had to buy all new hydraulic pumps."

"They cost a fortune. Chris wanted his mother to rein in the spending for a while, but she wouldn't hear of it. They must owe money to everybody in Colorado and half of New York and Chicago."

Eden sat at the table and nibbled on a biscuit while Kit attacked the meal she had brought him. She watched him with a mixture of curiosity and pity. That she may have caused a rift between him and his uncle pained her, a feeling made worse by the thought that it might all be illusory. Perhaps nothing inappropriate had transpired between Kit and his mistress's son.

"Kit, does Christopher Ridenour like young women?"

"Why wouldn't he?"

"Have you ever known him to express an interest in the opposite sex?"

He thought this over, then shrugged. "Not really, but he's shy. He wouldn't talk about things like that."

"I suppose, but—"

"But what?" Kit's tone turned defensive. "It's not a crime to be shy."

"There were rumors that Christopher and his stepfather were . . . a little closer than usual."

"I never heard anything like that." He sat back on the bed and adopted a casual face.

"You were the one I heard it from first."

He debated whether to share what Lucy had told him about why old Ridenour had married her in the first place.

Imagine the irony, she had said with such a bitter smile, it chilled his blood.

He even wished for half a moment he could share with Eden—with anybody—his fears about what had happened that last night in the Black Lace House. Who was lying? Christopher or his mother?

Why did Eden care whether or not Chris Ridenour liked girls?

For some reason, his thoughts wandered back to the night he had talked that gambling dentist, John Holliday, into pulling Christopher's aching tooth.

That was the first and only time Kit had ever seen Chris Ridenour drunk. He sipped a glass of brandy or sherry after dinner occasionally but never took his liquor as seriously as his hard-drinking mother.

They had staggered home together at four in the morning singing snatches of songs from the State Street music halls. At least, Christopher tried to sing along but was still chewing on a handkerchief he had stuffed into his mouth to stem the bleeding from his pulled tooth.

They stumbled noisily up the stairs of the mansion. When they reached the door, Christopher grabbed him by the shoulders and proclaimed, "You're the best friend a man could ever have, Kit Randall."

He then smothered him in a bear hug, crushing Kit's face against his shoulder. They drunkenly rocked back and forth, neither of them too steady on their feet. Christopher planted a friendly kiss on the top of Kit's curly head, then rested his cheek there for a second.

A shapely figure appeared in the etched glass of the double doors and threw them open. The startled boys jerked apart.

"What are you doing out here?" Lucinda hissed. "Have you both lost your minds?"

All the merriment drained from Christopher's swollen face in an instant. He ducked his head and dashed upstairs to his room.

Lucinda grabbed Kit's elbow and jerked him into the house.

"What are you so sore about?" he said.

She did not answer, just stomped off to her bed, leaving him standing in the entry hall wondering what the hell was wrong.

———

He desperately wanted to change the subject and so plucked an apple from Eden's basket. "Do you have a knife? I don't like the skins."

She pulled his wolf's head pocketknife from her bag. "Been missing this?"

"Where did you get it?"

"Christopher found it in his mother's first parlor. He assumed it was the knife you used to kill her."

Kit opened his mouth to make a furious denial, but she silenced him with a wave of her hand. "I know this is not the murder weapon. Christopher knows it, too, now. We spoke with the surgeon who examined Mrs. Ridenour's body. She was stabbed with a much longer blade. Your pocketknife could not possibly have made the wound."

Kit looked strangely relieved and slumped back onto the bed again to peel his apple.

"Christopher wants to talk to you," she said, watching for his reaction carefully. "Now that he agrees with me that you didn't kill his mother. He thinks there's been a terrible mistake or misunderstanding and he wants to clear it up."

"There's been a mistake, all right. Me moving into the Black Lace House to begin with."

She wanted him to calm down. "You were right about Mrs. Ridenour not keeping a journal or diary. I've searched every inch of that house and found nothing."

"I can't recall Lucinda ever writing a letter, the whole three months I lived there. Or *reading* a letter or a book. She could write, though. Checks, that is. And IOUs."

"That's too bad for us. I want to know more about her affair with Jacob Landry."

"Why isn't *he* a suspect? He had a reason to be mad at her."

"He has an alibi. His wife claims he was with her that afternoon."

"That's not very convincing," said Kit.

"I agree. Still it's better than—"

"Better than nothing, which brings it all back to me, doesn't it?"

Eighteen

Eden smiled nervously at Ellen Landry as she helped her collect the orphans' breakfast dishes.

"You are doing a fine job, Mrs. Murdoch. You needn't look to me for approval."

"Dealing with these children must be heartrending, Mrs. Landry."

"Indeed, it is. I confess I have to harden myself to a certain degree in order to handle the sadness of their little lives. It brings me great comfort to watch when one of them gets adopted by a loving family, though. I feel satisfaction in that. And you will provide such a family, I am sure of it. When will I be allowed the honor of meeting Mr. Murdoch?"

"He is very busy right now. The labor troubles and all."

Ellen Landry shook her head. "This strike is a terrible thing. The violence we saw the other day—it is just the beginning, I fear. And I was so looking forward to this summer, with the arrival of the railroad and President Grant and all. Now it's been spoiled by that stupid miners' strike."

She bid one of the small boys come over and sit on a tall chair. She wrapped a towel about his shoulders and began to trim his unruly hair.

"Is your husband involved, too?" Eden asked, playing the

innocent. She watched Ellen wield her shears with practiced grace. The little boy squirmed in his chair and yelped when her comb caught a tangle. She firmly reseated him.

"No, thank heavens. He is free of all that. He was once the superintendent of the Eye Dazzler Mine. I'm sure you've heard of it."

"Yes, I have," said Eden. Her mind raced for a likely introduction to the topic she longed to speak on. "It seems I am the neighbor of the owner of the Eye Dazzler Mine."

Ellen Landry's pale eyes widened at this. "You know the Ridenours?"

Eden thought it curious she would refer to the Ridenour family in the plural, given that only one of them remained alive, but she let that pass. "Not really. We're so new in town. I know almost no one. In fact . . ." She ducked her head in a pretended show of modesty. "I do hope you and I might become friends, Mrs. Landry."

Ellen Landry smiled in a haughty, almost condescending way. "I'm sure we shall."

"Then I must ask you a delicate question. If I may confide?"

"By all means," said Ellen.

"I have read about the shocking murder of my neighbor, Mrs. Ridenour. Should I fear for my own safety? Third Street seemed to my husband and myself to be the model of refinement in neighborhoods."

"Put your mind to rest. You have nothing to fear from Lucinda Ridenour's killer. Whoever he is, he should receive a medal."

This bold assertion shocked Eden. And just when she believed she was becoming shockproof. She was about to respond when the child lost his patience with his haircut and tried to wiggle free.

"Sit still," Ellen Landry snapped. She grabbed the boy's shoulders and jerked him back into the proper position.

He continued to fidget. Her annoyance grew and the color flamed in her pale cheeks. She began to squeeze the boy's shoulders so tightly Eden feared she would harm the child. Instinctively, she stepped nearer.

Ellen turned a furious face on her. "I don't need help, madam!"

"I'm sorry, I just—"

"Sit still this instant, Michael, or I shall whip you again!"

"No, no," cried the little boy. "I'll be good. Don't hit me."

Ellen's composure returned as quickly as her temper had flared. She resumed her trimming.

Eden waited a few moments before recommencing their conversation. The woman was obviously under a lot of personal strain, and who could blame her, given all that had happened?

"I'm sorry, Mrs. Landry, but I find your opinion about the late Mrs. Ridenour very difficult to understand. I didn't know the woman, but surely—"

"No, you did not know the woman," said Ellen. She finished her trim of the child's hair and removed the towel from his shoulders. Once freed, he gratefully dashed off to rejoin his playmates. "Nor would you wish to. She was not the sort of woman who would be received in the homes of decent women like ourselves. Forgive me for the coarseness of my emotions on this subject. I was just trying to be candid for your sake."

"I'm sorry, but I still don't understand."

"Let's just say that if Mrs. Ridenour's murderer goes free, justice will not unduly be wanting."

Eden shook her head, completely confused.

Ellen took her by the arm and led her to the far corner of the orphanage room, far from the ears of the toddlers and the other women tending them.

They stepped out onto a back fire exit of the building. The stairs were rudimentary and a bit precarious. Eden had never suffered from a fear of heights, but the tension of her conversation with Ellen Landry, added to the thinness of the mountain air, made her tingle with unease.

"I fear I have spoken out of turn and upset you, Mrs. Murdoch." Ellen shook out the hair-covered towel in the breeze. "I'm sorry for the indelicate things I said. But you should know the reason I said them."

Eden braced herself, wondering if Ellen Landry were actually about to confess her true grievance against Lucinda Ridenour. This seemed so out of character. She could not imagine a woman admitting to any but a relative or a closest friend that her husband had been unfaithful.

Ellen Landry placed her lips just inches from Eden's ear and whispered, "Lucinda Ridenour murdered her own husband."

Eden gasped. She did not expect this announcement, of all the possible disclosures Mrs. Landry could have made.

"You know this to be a fact?"

Ellen drew back with a superior smile. "Indeed I do. So do not judge me too harshly when I fail to lament the death of such a woman. She got what she deserved, didn't she? It was probably that young man she had living with her. They behaved most scandalously. She thought money could take the place of a reputation, but that's a false notion, isn't it? Decent women like us know better. Consort with the gutter and you will end up there."

"But how do you know that she killed her husband? Why didn't the police bring charges?"

Ellen Landry sighed and looked off into the distance. The cold high mountain range to the west of town spread itself out in majestic opulence. Travelers might journey days to behold such a sight, but the inhabitants of Leadville, Colorado, had the luxury of taking such grandeur for granted.

"There was no real proof. She had an alibi, of course. They claim she was in church that morning. It was Christmas Day, you see. Frankly, I don't know how she managed to do it. But she did. I know she did."

"But how do you know?" Eden really wanted to ask, Did your husband know? Was he involved somehow? Yet if he had participated in the murder of his lover's husband, why did he not seek to make her his wife? Wouldn't that be the sole point of the grisly exercise?

Ellen did not answer, just continued to study the mountain range, which boasted the highest peaks in Colorado.

"Since your husband was in the employ of the Ridenour family, I assume you knew them intimately?" Eden coaxed.

"Hardly!"

The woman turned and opened the door of the orphanage so quickly, Eden grabbed the handrail of the frail stairs for support.

She followed Mrs. Landry back into the busy nursery and knew that the "friendly" chat was over for the day.

Nineteen

"I think I've found Sadie Branch," Bella announced the following morning. She stood on the porch of the Black Lace House from which Christopher Ridenour had emerged only minutes before.

She must have been watching for him to leave, Eden deduced, and wished the girl did not take such reckless chances.

"Why do you 'think' you've found her?" she said as she ushered the young woman into the house quickly before her presence could come to the attention of the neighborhood.

"I found Mr. Sparks," Bella said with a sly smile.

"Who is Mr.—oh, the *parrot?*"

Bella nodded.

Eden sighed with relief that Sadie Branch might still be alive and well. She had tormented herself wondering if Lucinda's former maid lay at the bottom of an abandoned mine shaft or something. She was convinced the mysterious servant knew some dangerous secrets about the Black Lace House and its inhabitants, secrets worth large sums of money.

She had lain awake listening to Christopher Ridenour's

relentless piano stylings through many long nights, jumping at every discordant note, imagining him to have killed the maid to keep her silent. He seemed like such a kind and guileless young man, yet there had to be a reason he never made eye contact.

What did Sadie Branch know? Who killed her mistress? Who killed her late master? What were the details of Orson Ridenour's relationship to his adopted son who meant so much to him he wanted to disinherit his wife in the boy's favor? What were the limits of that love? Had they strayed into forbidden territory that could not be talked about, that must be kept secret at all costs?

"I talked to every gal I could find on State Street, whoever might have known Sadie," Bella said. "Most are new in town and didn't know her before she got respectable and moved to Third Street."

Eden had now lived in Leadville long enough to understand its most critical geography. An address change of a simple block could mean all the difference between virtue and vice in this strange, high place.

The gulf between State Street—which was actually Second Street in the municipal numbering system—and Third Street, the site of the Ridenour mansion, was far wider than the few hundred feet that physically separated them. It might as well have been divided by the Pacific Ocean, so different were its respective shores.

"Where is she then?" Eden said.

"I think she's staying with a girl who lives in a room over the Columbia Beer Hall. The girl wouldn't admit it, but I've got a strong suspicion."

"Why?"

"This girl had a parrot and I don't think it belonged to her."

"Was it Mr. Sparks?"

"Looked just like the bird in that slutty painting of Lucy Ridenour. I suppose one parrot could look like another, but how many people in Leadville own birds from the Amazon?"

"Before this goes further, I think we both need to talk to Kit."

Eden and Bella drove out of town together in Eden's hired rig. The girl seemed oddly despondent at the prospect of seeing Kit.

"Are you all right, Bella?" she asked when she heard the young woman sniffle.

"Why doesn't he love me?"

"He always talks about you in the friendliest way."

"That's just it. He wants to be *friends*. We were once lovers. Now we're just friends. That's about the worst thing that can happen to love."

"I'm not certain that's true," Eden said as she struggled to keep her team on the right path through the heavily treed wilderness. She did not want to have to explain to anyone why she might have broken an axle so far from town.

"To think we went quits over him *wanting* to marry me."

"Kit actually proposed marriage?"

"Don't look so surprised."

"Oh, I didn't mean that the way it came out." Eden felt terrible that she had inadvertently hurt the girl's feelings. "I was just surprised that Kit would think himself in a position to offer marriage to you, or anyone else, for that matter. I mean, he doesn't have a steady job to support a wife and family."

"He didn't propose for the right reasons, if you must know." Bella looked more miserable than ever. "I let him, well . . . move in with me and he thought we'd better get married."

"Oh. That reaction runs in the Randall family, I believe." She had experienced an identical scenario with a certain uncle of Kit's. Randall men seemed to feel an immediate imperative to marry the women they bedded and did not care to have their overtures rebuffed.

"I tried to make him understand my views on marriage. I even gave him a copy of Annie Besant's essays on marriage. Have you read those?"

"No, sorry."

"He wouldn't even look at them." She sighed, then shook her head. "I don't understand it. He was perfectly happy living with that slut, Lucy Ridenour, without the benefit of marriage."

"I think the difference between the two situations is obvious, Bella. He didn't *love* Mrs. Ridenour. And I frankly doubt she loved him."

She seemed only partially mollified by this observation. "I love him so much it hurts."

"Have you ever told him?"

"Well, not exactly. The minute you tell someone you're gone on them, they turn you into their slave. They take your love and crack it over your head like a whip and use it to make you behave."

"I've never thought of Kit as that sort. Though many men are, that's true. Many women as well." She was thinking of Lucinda Ridenour when she said this. Though she had never met the living woman, the image she had left behind was that of a master manipulator who used her beauty and sensuality to control the men in her life.

"It wouldn't matter even if I did tell him. It's not like he'd ever go to India with me."

"India? That sounds ambitious."

"It's terribly important, but Kit thinks it's silly. Madame Blavatsky's gone to Bombay to seek enlightenment and I want to go there too. The rate I'm moving, though, I'll never get out of Leadville. It costs so much to live here that I never get ahead no matter how hard I work."

"Could I offer some advice?"

Bella turned a wary eye on her, but waited.

"You need a higher social level of clientele for your occult work, people who can pay top dollar. Not these rough types you meet in saloons."

The girl shook her head. "The so-called gentlefolk with money shun me like a leper. You won't see one of them so much as tip their hat to me on the sidewalk. Fine ladies—they cross the street to avoid making eye contact."

"Bella, you need a new look. To appeal to these people, you have got to look like them, dress like them, even talk like them. Then they will accept you as one of their own and pay you what you deserve for your psychic gifts."

"I don't want to be one of *them*," she said with a voice rich in scorn. She implied she felt herself above them, not below.

"You don't have to *be* one of them, just make them comfortable enough to do business with you. It's called fashioning yourself for the marketplace, and everyone in commerce has to do it to some degree."

"I don't know, maybe." Bella began to smile. "Kit said you were a grand gal. He was right."

"A 'grand gal'? Hmmm . . . I've been called a lot of things in my life, but that's the topper. I think I like it."

———

Kit laughed out loud when they told him about the parrot. "'Time flies?' That's him, all right. That's old Sparky. That was the only thing the stupid bird knew how to say."

"Why would Sadie Branch have Lucinda's pet bird?" said Bella.

He shrugged. "She always liked him. Maybe she thought Chris would kill him after his mother was gone. Chris hated that bird. It would make a racket and never shut up. He was always threatening to wring its neck and eat it for supper. He was just teasing his mother, of course. He would never do such a thing. I can't see him hurting anything she loved."

"When we find her," said Eden, "I'm going to ask her first what she knows about the death of Mr. Ridenour."

"Why would she know about that?" Bella said.

"I got a chance to browse the family bank account of the Ridenours. Her weekly wages increased tenfold after his death."

Kit and Bella exchanged startled glances at this revelation.

Eden continued. "Jacob Landry's wife is convinced Lucinda killed Orson Ridenour."

"But Lucinda was thoroughly questioned about the death

of old Orson," said Kit. "I read about it in the back issues of the newspaper. She and Chris went to church that morning. Everybody saw them."

"Bet the sight of her in church sent the congregation into shock," said Bella.

Kit grinned at the girl. "You're such a cat."

"Meow."

"Let's stay on the subject here," said Eden. She caught sight of the two young people holding hands on the cot where they sat in the little tent.

"Why does Mrs. Landry think that Lucinda did the old man in?" asked Kit. "Was Landry in on it with Lucinda?"

"I think Landry had a reason to believe Lucinda did it," said Eden as she thought out loud. "Maybe he even knew it for a fact, but . . ."

"But what?" said the young couple almost in unison.

"Maybe it scared him. Perhaps the reality of just how far Lucinda would go to get what she wanted scared Jacob Landry right back into the arms of his wife. Of course, with the Eye Dazzler money, one could simply hire an assassin. Sadie Branch, perhaps?"

"Sadie's a drunk. And too addle-brained to trust, I'd think. Still . . . who knows?" said Kit.

"What about Chris?" said Bella. "Why doesn't anyone suspect him of old Ridenour's murder, if that's what it was."

"Chris worshiped his stepfather," Kit explained. "Sadie Branch told me he was so broke up by his death that Lucinda made a doctor come all the way from Denver to see him. She caught him trying to cut his own wrists."

"If he keeps practicing, he may get it right someday," said Bella.

Kit looked confused by this remark.

"He tried to hang himself the other night," said Eden.

"Je-sus," he said. "Why would he do such a thing? I mean, losing your mother is a sad thing and all, but . . . it happens to just about everybody."

"You and I lost our mothers and we survived," Bella said to Kit.

"You told her your mother was dead?" Eden asked in shock.

Kit shrugged. "She might as well be."

Bella refused to let go of the subject of Ridenour's suicide attempt and said to Kit, "Were you and Chris pretty good friends?"

"I don't know. He used to follow me around like a puppy. It could get to be annoying. His mother was always making me take him places. He didn't seem to have any friends of his own and wouldn't go out by himself. He used to get so happy when I invited him out with me, it was kind of pathetic. We'd go to music halls and theatricals. Lucy always wanted me to take him to places with dancing girls. You know, catch a bit of stocking. But that sort of thing just used to embarrass him."

"Let's find Sadie Branch," said Eden.

"Take me with you," said Kit.

"Don't be silly," was her answer. "You're in no condition—"

"I'm better every day. You said so yourself. I don't even need a cane anymore."

"We can't risk you being seen in town. You're still the prime suspect. They'll arrest you the minute you're recognized."

"But I'm wearing this beard now. I look completely different, don't I?"

Both women scrutinized him critically, but were not persuaded.

"I think you have to take me," he continued as he began to smile in his devilish old way. "Which of you ladies can recognize Sadie Branch?"

Twenty

Ellen Landry sat in the dark of her own porch, twisting the tail ends of her shawl in her lap. Hers was the only dark house on the street. Jacob forbade her to light a lamp at the door because the men who had come to meet with him needed the cover of darkness.

Her stomach churned with the thought of those union leaders in her home. That she would see a day when men would visit her house and need to hide from the light was something she never imagined.

They had been meeting for more than an hour. She could hear the low drone of their voices inside, but could not discern their conversation.

At just after eleven, the two men emerged from the house and spoke on the step, oblivious to Ellen's presence in the far corner of the porch.

"What do you think?" asked the taller man, whose name was Bender.

The other man sighed. "Don't know. I thought he was a sensible sort. But after tonight, I don't know. Do you think he'd been drinking?"

"He didn't smell of it. He seemed so regular most of the time, but then those comments on 'a new Noah's flood' washing away sin? What was all that about?"

· "Beats the hell out of me. He's obviously under a lot of strain in addition to the strike itself. He's still a suspect in that Ridenour woman's murder. Do you think he could have done it? We really hardly know the gent."

"I don't know, but what do you think about his idea?"

"It's bold," said the shorter man. "Attention grabbing, to be sure."

"But doesn't it go a bit *too* far?" worried Bender. "What in God's name will we do if they call our bluff?"

A well-lighted carriage ambled down Sixth Street and cast its light upon Ellen Landry, revealing her quiet presence to the men.

"Oh, good evening, madam," said a chagrined Mr. Bender. "We didn't see you sitting there. Please forgive us. We won't trouble you further tonight."

They hurried off down the street.

Jacob Landry joined his wife on the porch as soon as the two union men departed. He leaned against the railing to face her.

Not enough light shone from the house to make him more than a silhouette to her, but she could tell he was worried, even disturbed, by the uneven sound of his breathing.

"I'll have to leave you alone tonight, Nell. I have important work to do."

"Since when has it ever bothered you to leave me alone at night?"

"Will you never cease to throw that up in my face? It's been over for more than a year and a half. You swore you could forgive and forget. Did you lie?"

"No, no, I'm sorry. But why must you leave now? I'm afraid to be alone with all the trouble."

236

"Everything is spinning out of control. Ridenour's scabs are scheduled to go into the mine tomorrow, but not if we can stop them. To make matters worse, they say that the governor will declare martial law, that he's already sent troops from Denver."

"Oh, dear Lord." She wrung her hands, on the verge of tears.

"Actually, I'll have to go into hiding for a spell. One of my men has a brother on the police force. There's a rumor that this *Committee of Public Safety*"—he spoke the group's name with contempt—"has decreed that all the strike leaders should be locked up or run out of town."

Ellen squelched a small moan at this revelation.

"I have some plans and I've got to put them into action before midnight." He turned to leave the porch, swinging his jacket over his shoulder.

She stood up in alarm. "What sort of plans?"

The dim light from inside the house fell across his face and she could see he wore the oddest smile.

"Read the headline in tomorrow's paper."

———

Bella and Eden, with Kit hidden under a blanket behind them, reached the edge of town and left the rig at the Sixth Street livery. They walked through the town uneasily, ducking into shadows whenever possible. Kit pulled his wide-brimmed hat down low and turned his collar high.

They fought their way among the sidewalk throngs as usual. Leadville seemed to have no quiet times of day. Crowds could be found on the street at any hour. Even Sunday morning was not safe. Eden found these multitudes exciting at first. The hustle-bustle reminded her of the war years in the nation's capital where she had served as a nurse.

She had been twenty then and more tolerant of inconvenience. The constant jostling and bumping and foot trampling grew wearisome quickly now that she was almost in sight of her fortieth year.

They negotiated infamous State Street, lit up bright as day by gaslights every dozen yards. Girls in upper story windows over the saloons called out enticements to potential male customers below. Music blared from the various dance halls and theaters. A juggler tossed knives in the air before a laughing circle of spectators.

The heady excitement of these streets made Eden see what attracted someone as high-spirited as Kit. Bella seemed at home here as well. She led the way with an imperious tilt to her pointed chin. Her long, slender neck transported her above the fray with a hint of elegance.

They reached the Columbia Beer Hall and gazed up at the window on the side of the building. The light shone against its shade, but no shadows moved behind it.

Bella marched up the side stairs and rapped on the door while Eden and Kit stood below watching her. No one answered, so Bella returned to the street.

"I wonder if she's in there?" Eden said.

"Only one way to find out." Bella disappeared into the alleyway behind the saloon.

Before Eden and Kit could follow her she came running out of the alley shouting, "Fire, Fire!"

"You didn't need to set fire to the place," Eden shouted.

"Just an old barrel filled with trash. Don't worry." Bella planted herself at the bottom of the stairs.

Soon people began screaming and running. Miners poured out of the Columbia's front and back doors, beer mugs still in hand. Poker players carried their cards out with them and attempted to continue their game in the street even as the fire bell clanged in the distance.

In the smoky darkness the door of the second floor apartment opened and a small woman, her head covered by a fringed shawl, emerged and glanced about anxiously.

"Is that her?" Eden said as she dodged several men running past her.

They all squinted in the awkward light.

"Yep," said Kit.

Bella, meantime, blocked Sadie Branch's path down the stairs.

"Get out of my way," said the small woman as her shawl slipped from her head and revealed that she carried the parrot, Mr. Sparks. She held fast to the bird's feet as the frightened creature began to flap its colorful wings.

Kit stepped up behind Bella on the stairs.

"Mr. Kit?" said the former maid. "Why aren't you in jail? Stay away from me! I don't want no trouble from you."

Bella backed Sadie up the stairs, with Kit and Eden close behind.

"Get out of my way, you crazy fools! This building's burning down."

"No, it's not," said Bella. "We want to talk to you. Now get back on in there."

Eden was impressed with Bella's no-nonsense handling

of the scene and quickly followed the young people up the stairs and into the rooms of Sadie Branch.

"You sure we're not gonna burn?" said the maid.

"Positive," Bella said. "Now let's talk."

Eden studied the middle-aged woman, wondering how much trust she could place in anything the former prostitute would say. Her caramel-colored skin tones hinted at a mixture of many races, Caucasian and Negro to be sure, but the high cheekbones suggested some Indian blood as well. Her bright, dark eyes darted constantly from face to face, birdlike and wary.

"Don't have nothin' to say. Now leave me be. I don't intend on bein' his next."

"I'm not going to do anything to you, you sorry piece of trash!" said Kit.

"You're one to be callin' names," said the woman.

"What's that supposed to mean?"

"Both of you, calm down," said Eden. She placed herself physically between Kit and the woman. "Mrs. Branch, would you feel more comfortable talking to me, if the others left the room?"

"Sure, fine," said the maid.

Bella was quick to see Eden's point and ushered the sullen Kit out of the small living quarters and onto the staircase outside.

When the two women were left alone, Sadie Branch relaxed a little. "So who are you, honey? I never seen you around before."

"I'm Kit's aunt."

"That boy got himself in a world of trouble," said Sadie Branch in an almost conversational tone, as one concerned woman to another.

"What do you mean?" Eden sat down and adopted a serious and sympathetic air, hoping to encourage the maid to speak as candidly as possible, despite the fact they had only just met. "Kit's always been a good boy."

"He may of started out good, but virtue don't last long in the Black Lace House."

"I know that his association to Mrs. Ridenour was not . . . appropriate, but I don't believe he would do anything violent."

"I never thought he had a mean bone in him. I'll agree to that. But after the argument they had that morning and what she was up to . . . I suppose nobody could blame him."

"What are you talking about?"

"Nothin'." Sadie turned her attention to Mr. Sparks who now sat on a makeshift perch on the sidearm of an oil lamp.

"I need to know, Mrs. Branch. Please talk to me frankly. I'll see that no harm comes to you. I promise."

Sadie looked over her shoulder at Eden. Her dark face wore a curious smile. "Information like that costs money."

Eden inwardly boiled. Sadie Branch, the professional blackmailer. She should have guessed this demand.

"How much do you want?"

"Probably more'n you've got. Information is expensive. Now Mr. Christopher . . . he could afford it."

"Are you blackmailing Mr. Ridenour?"

Sadie tilted her chin in a challenging way. "Did *he* tell you that?"

So that's why she's still in town. She decided to replace one blackmail victim with another. The Ridenour family was certainly the best thing to ever happen to this woman, Eden surmised.

"Is your knowledge really so valuable? I wouldn't want to waste my money."

She shrugged. "That's a risk you'll have to take."

"Maybe you'd prefer me to summon the police and let you explain to them why Lucinda Ridenour started paying you one hundred dollars a week after the death of her husband."

The maid dropped her smug assurance. "I didn't do nothing wrong."

"Then I'm sure you won't mind talking to the Leadville police."

"We don't need to talk to them."

"Why was she paying you? Did you kill Orson Ridenour?"

"Of course not! I just did her a favor and she was grateful. That's all."

"What sort of favor?"

She drew an uneasy sigh. "Just introduced her to a fella I met on State Street. She wanted to meet somebody down on their luck who'd be willing to do anything for a little quick cash."

"A hired killer?"

"I didn't think she had *that* in mind. Lord, I thought she had wanted some back alley lovin'. She wasn't getting any from the old man, that's for sure. And she and her honey-boy Jake had parted company."

"Who was this man?"

Sadie shook her head with a casual laugh. "You won't find him. He's long gone. Doubt I even knew his real name."

"What did you think when you heard that Orson Ridenour had been shot to death?"

She chuckled. "I didn't never believe he shot *himself*. That's the sure-as-the-world truth, honey. But I never said a thing. Never asked a single question. 'Sides, she had a good reason for doing what she did, if you ask me. After what he did to that boy of hers. Not that she didn't know it was goin' on since the first."

"Mr. Ridenour and Christopher? What do you mean exactly? What was the nature of their relationship?"

"If I have to tell you, you probably wouldn't understand it. Nice ladies like yourself don't have a reason to know—"

"Don't be too sure of that, Mrs. Branch. Do you believe Mrs. Ridenour killed her husband because of his relationship with her son?"

"Not really. That's the reason *you or me* woulda done the deed. No, she wanted her precious Jakie. And the money, too. Couldn't have both unless the old man was dead."

"Do you have any proof of this?"

The woman shrugged. "Just what I heard and what I know in my soul. See, Mr. Landry tried and tried to get her to run away with him. She wouldn't do it, though. She didn't want to give up the Eye Dazzler money. That hurt him real bad. I heard 'em arguin' about it, shoutin', carryin' on. About made the windows rattle. Then he stomps out and says she don't love him and he never wants to see her again. Well, that put her in a state."

Eden digested all this information about the notorious

Lucinda. Her solution was to kill her husband, inherit the Eye Dazzler riches, and then live happily ever after with Jacob Landry. Only it did not work out that way.

"She must have been disappointed with the outcome. About Landry not cooperating."

"I think she scared him off. And then there was her problems with the boy."

"What sort of problems?"

"He was so sorrowful over the old man's passing that he didn't want to go on."

So perhaps Christopher was not a victim of an older man's lust, but a willing participant. "He loved his stepfather?"

"Oh, yeah. As strange as it sounds, his mother marrying that rascal was probably the kindest thing she ever done for Mr. Christopher. Old Ridenour was the only person on the face of the earth who ever cared a whit for him and that's God's own truth. He saw to it that boy didn't know an ungranted wish. Lord, how he spoiled him. Still, it wasn't natural, was it? Given what he expected from the poor child in return."

Sadie Branch heaved a long, theatrical sigh. "I reckon we're all whores at some price, ain't we?"

Twenty-one

"I am quite certain she is blackmailing Christopher Ridenour," Eden told Kit and Bella as the three stood in the darkness of the alley behind the Columbia.

"About what?" Kit asked, noticeably disturbed by this possibility.

"I couldn't get her to come out and admit it. Anyway, I asked her if she remembered seeing anyone leaving the Ridenour house the day of the murder. She said no, but she admitted she was so upset by finding Lucinda's body, she had trouble thinking about anything clearly."

"Sometimes people can remember more with the help of magnetism," said Bella. Neither of her listeners knew what she was talking about, so she explained. "You put them in a trance state where their everyday minds can't be so cautious and careful about their memories. It's called magnetic sleep. They're very relaxed, almost like they're asleep only you can talk to them."

"Let's do it," said Kit.

"I want you out of town," Eden said to him. "The longer you stay here, the more danger you'll be recognized and arrested. If you're truly well enough to travel, you should leave Leadville."

"She's right," said Bella.

"No. I won't go. I want to know the truth. Even . . . even if the news isn't good."

Bella and Eden exchanged glances in the shadowy light slanting in from the street. They both knew he still had awful doubts tormenting him about his own innocence.

The same worry clutched the two women who cared about him. They, too, wanted desperately to clear his name, yet even more to clear his conscience.

The decision was made. They marched back up the stairs to the apartment hiding Sadie Branch. With more threats of alerting the police to her activities the morning of Orson Ridenour's mysterious death, Sadie reluctantly consented to further questioning with the help of "magnetic sleep."

Eden and Kit left the room to allow Bella to begin the process. She did not have an easy time getting Sadie to relax, but with enough whiskey, the woman eventually dropped her resistance. Her eyes slowly closed and her jaw went slack. Her mouth hung open slightly and a thread of saliva tracked from the sagging corner of it.

Bella invited the other two back in and began the questioning.

"Sadie, do you remember the day you found Lucinda's body?" Bella asked in a soft and almost seductive tone.

"Yes," said Sadie.

"Where were you that afternoon?"

"Shopping. Well, supposed to be shopping. Supposed to get lace, but I ran into an old friend and we had us a ginger beer. Time got away from me. I had to hurry home, snuck in the kitchen door. Had to start dinner. Damned cook quit."

"When did you find your mistress?"

"Went to ask her how many was coming to supper.

Didn't know if Mr. Kit was gone for good. I went to the front parlor and . . . and . . ."

The woman stirred uncomfortably. She was obviously upset about the memory of finding Lucinda's bloody corpse.

"Sadie, think about coming home that afternoon. Did you see anyone leaving the house?"

"No."

"Did you see anyone on the street?"

"Just one lady."

Both Eden and Kit moved forward at this.

"Can you describe her, Sadie?"

"Tall."

"What else?"

"Don't know. Wore a long, dark veil."

This was not unexpected. Many ladies wore veils with their hats to protect their complexions against the damaging high country sun.

"Try hard to see this woman in your mind."

"Couldn't get a look at her. She was moving too fast. She about knocked me down getting past."

Kit and Eden both took some hope from this revelation.

"Do you remember anything else about her?" said Bella.

"Something shiny."

"What was shiny? Jewelry?"

"Something shiny."

They all frowned at this enigmatic remark. No amount of further questioning drew anything more from the woman, and the three left her apartment to walk the less populated streets of Leadville to ponder what little new information they had garnered.

"A tall woman wearing a veil," Bella said. "That doesn't help us much."

Eden did not point out that Bella fit the description; another more unusual theory actually seemed to her more likely. What if the "woman" was actually a man in disguise?

"I'm going back to the Ridenour house tonight," she said. "I want to talk to Christopher."

"Do you really think that's a good idea?" said Bella.

"He said I could stay on until I found other lodgings. It should be the safest place in town. The bodyguards are still there, you know. Kit, you must go back to the woods."

"Sure," he said, surprising both women with his cooperation.

As soon as he and Bella parted from Eden, Kit revealed his true plan. "Let's go back to your room."

"But Mrs. Murdoch told you—"

"I want you to magnetize me. If you can make Sadie Branch remember Lucinda's last day, you can do the same for me."

"I don't know, Kit, honey."

"I've got to find out, Bella. I've got to know the truth. Not being sure is killing me. And I swear to you, if we find out the worst, I'll go turn myself in."

They returned to the boardinghouse and sat cross-legged on Bella's bed, facing each other. She drew from her bag of tricks a many-faceted glass ball suspended on a silver chain. The candles she had lit about the room caught the glittering crystal and cast rainbow-hued designs on the walls in dancing patterns.

She twisted the chain between her fingers to spin the bright globe and told him to look at nothing else as she chanted a strange rhythmic poem in a language he had never heard before.

"Bella?"

"What? You're supposed to be concentrating."

"Don't let me drool like Sadie did. That's disgusting."

She was forced to chuckle. "It happens to everybody in this state. They get so relaxed, they forget to swallow their own spit."

Kit made a repulsed face, so Bella knew he was too pre-occupied with worldly concerns to succumb to her magnetism. With misgivings, she suggested adding absinthe to the evening.

He had promised her he would steer clear of the stuff, given what had happened the last time he had indulged, but there was no retreating from his resolve to end the mystery of Lucinda Ridenour's last day.

Bella watched as he performed the ritual of the infamous Green Fairy. He placed a slotted spoon with a sugar cube over a pilsner-shaped absinthe glass. He poured the green liquid through the sugar and the spoon, followed by the ice water until all the sugar was dissolved. He drank the over-powering anise-flavored beverage as quickly as he could manage.

"Another," Bella decreed.

"If you insist," said Kit, "though a second glass of absinthe is usually a mistake."

He started the process over again. He had not downed but half the second glass before the room began to spin. His eyeballs felt like they floated in their sockets.

Bella once again held up the glittering crystal before his swimming eyes. He thought it was the most beautiful sight he had ever beheld. Before he could remark on this, though, he had succumbed to her spell.

———

"Kit, do you hear me?"

He nodded slowly.

"I want you to think about the day after you moved out of the Black Lace House. Do you see it in your mind?"

"Sort of."

"Why not clearly?"

"Drunk."

"Where are you?" she said.

"My room. Boardinghouse on Oak."

"Where else did you go that day?"

"Stayed in bed until she threw me out."

Bella grew worried. "Who threw you out?"

"Landlady." Kit almost seemed to snicker despite what Bella deemed a fairly deep trance. "Mean old biddy. Caught me drinking. Against house rules."

"What time of day is it?"

"Late. Getting dark already. Went to see Bella. Hoped she hadn't forgotten me. Hoped she would take me in."

She smiled with relief. "And you didn't go anywhere else that day? Think hard, now."

"Dear Bella. Thank God for her."

She wanted to kiss him at this point. She knew he could not have killed his former mistress. She could have ended it there, brought him out of the trance and shared the happy news . . . but she did not.

250

She couldn't resist the urge to learn what really happened on his last night with the Ridenours. What had her vision meant? What unspeakable acts had transpired?

She pressed on with her questions, leading him through that earlier evening of absinthe indulgence that ended with him in Lucinda's bed. Then the questions and answers took a more ominous turn: She entered his dream world.

———

"What do you see now?"

"A beach. The day of the big Latin exam. We skipped out right afterwards and decided we'd earned a holiday. I stole a bottle of whiskey from under old Father Logan's bed. We took a train to Virginia and walked to the beach.

"The day was so warm for October. Or maybe the whiskey was just making me warm. I decided to go bathing and pulled off my clothes.

"Ian thought I was crazy, but I just laughed and threw my underwear in his face, then ran straight for the breakers. I shouted over my shoulder, 'Come on, you coward!' "

———

Greene carried Kit's clothes to a secluded spot beneath the overhang of a grassy bluff. He continued to nurse the bottle of whiskey while trying to follow Kit's curly black mop of hair as it bobbed in and out of the foamy surf. Eventually, he was forced to rest his spinning head against the back wall of the overhang. He closed his eyes in a whiskey-soaked doze.

A spray of water flung in his face woke him with a start. A grinning, naked bather stood before him. "You missed all the fun, Greene Bean."

"Put your clothes on. You must be freezing."

"Can't—until I'm dry. Why don't you build a fire?"

"You're handy at giving orders." Greene pretended to complain, but got up and gathered driftwood nonetheless. He glanced back. "You could help, you know."

Kit hugged his knees to his chest and shook his head. He took a swig from the whiskey bottle, but there was not much left.

Greene got a small fire going and then pulled a surprise from his knapsack. Ears of popcorn. Both boys skewered the dried ears on the ends of their pocketknives and roasted the corn over the flames until the multicolored kernels began to pop.

After they had eaten what little corn remained unburnt, they both settled against the back wall of their secluded retreat and waited for the sea breezes to clear their drunken heads.

"The last time I was here, I was nine years old," Kit said.

"With your family?"

"Yeah, we had all come to see my uncle Brad before he left with General Custer for the frontier." The entire Randall family had gathered at the seaside. Uncle Brad was about to depart for his new assignment in the west.

"General Custer is a great man," said Ian. "Not many have his mettle. I heard he was going to lead another great campaign against the hostiles soon."

"My uncle had some kind of falling out with him years ago. He never talked much about it. That beach holiday . . . I remember it so well. He taught me to swim that day."

Kit was completely dry now, but in no hurry to get dressed. He preferred to pretend he was stranded on a

South Sea island. He remembered how scared he had been of the ocean years ago when the first wave to hit him had knocked him off his feet. He panicked and was certain he would die until he found his uncle's strong arm encircling his chest and pulling his head out of the water.

Going to be all right? said Uncle Brad.

He clung to his uncle's neck for dear life and wrapped his legs around his waist. Brad held him fast until he stopped trembling. Then he carried him into deeper water until they were submerged to their necks.

His uncle taught him to hold his breath as each wave hit them. Finally he was able to smile when the breakers came and Brad said, *See, they can't hurt us.*

He hugged Brad with delight and kissed his cheek.

His uncle did not look pleased by this.

You're too old to kiss boys, Kit. You have to save your kisses for the girls now.

Do you like kissing Miss Markham? Kit asked, referring to Amanda, the young woman Brad was engaged to marry.

Of course, I do. Once we're married, I'll do a great deal more than kiss her.

They had both laughed at this, though at the time nine-year-old Kit had no idea what his uncle was talking about. Now he sat on the same beach seven years later and chuckled at his own innocence. He felt giddy and aroused by his indecent thoughts. He turned to Greene and impulsively kissed him on the cheek.

"Stop that." The boy blushed and tucked his blond hair behind his ears. He pushed Kit away when he tried for another kiss. "Are you mad? Someone will see us."

"There's nobody around for miles. Come on."

Ian giggled drunkenly. He soon returned the kisses and more. His hand wandered down into Kit's lap.

"You're always telling me it's a terrible sin to spill my seed on the ground," Kit said, laughing in surprise. "And here you are *helping* me do it."

"You won't spill it on the ground today," said Greene with a new boldness, born from the whiskey bottle.

Kit had no idea what he meant but sat tense with anticipation as Greene kissed his neck, his chest, his belly. Then his lips traveled farther south. Kit flinched at the novel sensation of that warm tongue licking him, licking the swollen length of him. He began to breathe hard. The feelings were so intense, he didn't know if he could stand them. The ocean roared in his ears.

He laced his trembling fingers through his friend's long blond hair as he realized what would happen next.

"Oh, my God!" Kit shouted to Bella, as he emerged from the trance with a vengeance. He gulped air as he tried to calm himself. Oh, my god, he thought, in the dream . . . I was remembering Ian! Not Chris. At least, maybe not Chris. He took some queasy solace from this, though he still longed to solve the mystery of that night. Lucinda had shown no doubts about what had gone on.

Are you upset about what happened last night . . . or that you enjoyed it?

Would he ever know the truth for certain? He was more confused than ever.

"Bella, what did I say just now?"

"You didn't kill her, honey. Isn't that wonderful? Now

you can rest easy." She tried to throw her arms around him, but he could not settle down. She had never experienced a magnetism subject react so strongly that they pulled themselves out of a deep trance spontaneously.

"What else did I tell you?"

"Nothing important." She did not wish to admit she had been prying into the most intimate corners of his life. "Let's catch some sleep. Dawn will be here before we know it."

He agreed to lie down with her on the unmade bed, but found sleep impossible. He heard Bella's soft breathing and knew she had dropped off. He sat up and tried to quiet the hurricane in his head.

That day with Ian, what they had done together, the memory of it mortified him still. He had been so ashamed afterward. For the first time in his life, he felt like he had really, truly . . . *sinned*. He and Ian did not talk all the way home on the train. At least, *Kit* didn't talk. He could not face his friend after that. He started avoiding him. Ian was mad and hurt. He knew it, but he just could not help it.

He decided to move out of the dorm so he didn't have to share a bed with Ian anymore. He asked his aunt Jennetta if he could live with her. She said yes, if he would agree to do some chores and help around the house. She and her husband and young family lived only a three-mile walk from the campus. On rainy days, he could take an omnibus.

Ian had entered the dorm room and caught him packing his belongings that last day.

———

"What are you doing? Where are you going?" Ian said.

"I'm moving in with my aunt." Kit did not look up as he

spoke. "It'll be cheaper. My family doesn't have a lot of money like yours does."

"You can't go!"

"Well, I am."

"No, no, please. Why are you leaving? Is it because of me?"

"Of course not," he lied. "I need to save money."

"If you need money, I'll get a loan from my father."

"That's not necessary. Let go of my arm." Kit closed his trunk and snapped the metal fasteners. He grabbed one of the leather handles and lugged it off the bed. Greene blocked his path to the door.

"You wanted me do it and now you hate me for it!"

"Stop saying that. Move away from the door."

"I just did it to make you happy, to make you like me. And you enjoyed it. You can't say you didn't."

Kit let out an angry sigh. "I suppose I did. That was obvious enough. But that doesn't make me proud of it."

"You can't leave me. For God's sake, Kit."

Kit tried to push him aside but the boy would not yield an inch.

Greene's belligerent, outraged tone turned whining. "I can't live without you. You're everything to me. You're the reason I wake up each morning. Please don't go. Please, I'm begging you."

"You'll be just fine. We both will. Now move."

"I'll kill myself if you leave me. I swear it."

Kit had had enough. He grabbed the boy, whose face now ran with tears, and flung him around sideways. Greene crashed back into the end of one of the bunkbeds and fell to the floor.

"You've ruined my life, Kit Randall! I *will* kill myself. Don't think I won't."

"Go right ahead." Kit walked out.

———

That was a Friday, Kit remembered. When he came to class on Monday, they called him into the dean's office. They wanted to know if he had heard from Greene. He'd gone missing since Friday afternoon.

Kit did not tell them he had received a note from Greene, delivered in the evening mail to his aunt's house where he was living now. The message did not seem like a suicide note, at least not to Kit's sixteen-year-old view of the world. It had just contained a lot of rambling thoughts on how he, Kit, should have been a better friend and so forth and wondering if Kit really deserved the great and abiding affection he, Ian, felt for him.

Kit had gone back to the dorm on Saturday, looking for his friend. He wanted to apologize for shoving him. He felt guilty for that now that he had cooled off. Ian was such a harmless soul. How could he stay angry at him? But he had not found him. He assumed he must have gone home to Baltimore for the weekend as he often did. Greene's family was well-to-do and the cost of train tickets was never a concern for him.

Kit missed his companionship with Ian already, but made up his mind not to return to residence in the dorm. He knew what would happen if he and Ian continued to share a bed. Even as he cursed himself for the sins they had committed on the beach, he longed for them to happen again.

He decided he was morally weak and that the only way he could avoid vice was to avoid the temptation of vice. Ian would just have to accept this.

Kit fainted dead away when they told him they found Greene's body in the river. He whacked his head on the edge of a table and woke up in the school infirmary three hours later with a big lump on his head. He could hardly remember a thing that had happened the whole week before. Until now.

——

Kit had fallen asleep in Bella's bed at some point because the morning sun peeking around the shade of her window woke him. He eased out of bed so as not to disturb her. Someone always had a pot of coffee on the stove down in Pris Hart's kitchen any time after dawn, so he decided to wander down there.

He did not want to sit on the bed to don his boots for fear of waking her, so he struggled to balance and pull them on as he leaned against the wall.

A bright ray of sunlight caught a facet of the crystal ball she had used to magnetize him and the bright flash made him blink.

Something shiny.

Oh, God, no. Not Bella. Not his darling Bella. She couldn't have. She was tall and she often wore the crystal around her neck like a necklace.

And Bella owned a knife. She said she used it in rituals. She had a special name for it, but he couldn't remember it. He used to tell her to carry it in her shoulder bag for protection on the rowdy streets of Leadville. She always refused, saying the knife for only for special, magical purposes. Had she used it to stab her rival in the throat? Did she want him back that bad?

He looked at Bella's sleeping form and thought his heart would break. He paced about the room, running his hands through his hair. Tears sprung to his eyes and he did not think he could bear the truth. He never realized before that terrible moment just how much he still loved her.

She had done this horrible thing because of him. Why did he keep inspiring terrible acts in all those who loved him?

First Ian, now Bella. He must have been born with some kind of curse on him. Everyone who loved him ended up doing something unspeakable. Suicide, murder . . . was there no limit to what he inspired in others?

What to do next?

He would hide her crime. That was it. She was probably out of her head when she did it. She was not responsible for her actions and should not be punished. He would get her out of town somehow. But he needed money.

His brain raced with possibilities. There was a petty cash box at the office of the Eye Dazzler. One night when he and Christopher had gone out on the town and run out of spending money, Chris had slipped into the mine headquarters office to replenish their supply. He had not brought his door key, but there was a broken lock on one of the windows in the back. It would be simple.

He wondered who would be up at the mine since the strike closed it. How many picketers? How many armed guards? He wished he had read more newspaper stories about the strike to know what to expect.

The only thing he knew for sure was that they had to leave town—for Bella's sake.

Twenty-two

Eden was awakened to the longest day of 1880 by a loud banging on the front door of the Black Lace House. She pulled a summer shawl over her nightdress and cautiously peeked out her door. She heard Christopher's steps rushing down the stairs and followed him.

"I'll answer it," he said. He hurried to the door unshaven and collarless. He yanked his suspenders over his shoulders and tried to quiet his riotously curly ginger hair, which, free from the confining clove-scented hair oil, formed a wild wreath about his face.

Eden could see through the etched glass of the double doors that a group of well-dressed men stood on the porch, though one of the guards, Marco, physically prevented them from standing too close.

"Ridenour, have you seen it?" shouted George Hauser through the glass.

Christopher opened the big doors and a half dozen men rushed in, Hauser shoving a newspaper into the young mine owner's hands. His worried expression twisted into a look of horror when he read the headline:

MINERS THREATEN TO BLOW UP DAZZLER

He stumbled backward into his dining room and sat down at the table to spread the paper before him. Eden leaned close to read over his shoulder as the men milled about and spoke in terse grumbles.

The newspaper printed an open letter from the union to all the mine owners in the district.

To all concerned:

Be advised that a bomb will be detonated in one of the shafts of the Eye Dazzler Mine today if scab workers are placed in service. Tell the governor that all the militias he can send will not stop it.

The giant powder has been carefully concealed, so look for it at your peril! One of your scabs is actually a union man and will know how to explode the bomb at no risk to himself.

Men will die today if the mine owners' consortium does not agree to come to the bargaining table by noon. The blood of those men will be on your hands! Subsequent bombs will be placed in other mines if the destruction of the Eye Dazzler is not grave enough to capture the attention of the men in charge.

"Do you think it's a bluff?" said Hauser. "The entrances to the Dazzler have been guarded since the strike began. Right, my boy?"

"Yes," said Ridenour. He brightened for a moment, then slapped his hand on the table with a loud moan. "There's an old adit on the far side of the hill. We abandoned it two or three years ago. We just use it for ventilation now. It's been boarded up, but I never thought to post a guard."

"How many know about this opening?" said Hauser.

"Jacob Landry, most certainly."

All the men joined in his lament as they discussed it among themselves.

"Excuse me," Eden said. "But what is an 'adit'?"

Several of the mine owners frowned at her, whom they understood to be a mere servant, for daring to intrude upon their conversation.

Ridenour looked up. "An adit is a horizontal entrance into a mine. As opposed to a shaft, which is vertical and you have to be lowered into it with a hoist of some sort."

She nodded her understanding.

"They're obviously getting desperate," said a portly and prosperous-looking man. "The local police escorted two of those out-of-town union organizers to the city limits this morning before dawn and told them they'd be tossed in jail if they dared to show their faces again. Knocked 'em around a bit, too, just to make sure they got the point."

"But Jacob Landry wasn't with them?" said Christopher.

The man shook his head with a frown. "Just McCoy and Bender."

"What's the status of the governor's men?" the young man continued.

Eden was amazed at how quick Ridenour was to understand and evaluate a complex situation. Kit's assessment of his one-time friend was accurate. He may have been inexperienced, but he was highly intelligent.

"The last word we had was that they left Denver yesterday," said one of the men. "Pitkin has already declared martial law. His cavalry should arrive here sometime today."

"We have to intercept them, don't we?" Ridenour said, his voice growing steadily more anxious. "I think a military presence will only escalate the violence."

"Someone needs to teach those union hooligans a lesson," a third man chimed in.

"Why must they do it at the expense of *my* mine?"

———

Kit made his way to the Eye Dazzler using the least traveled route he could find. It lay no more than a five-minute walk from Bella's boardinghouse. He still limped a bit. He did not know if he could run, should the situation demand it, but he hoped for the best.

He pulled his hat down low and prayed no one would recognize him. Surely his newly grown beard offered some disguise, though Sadie Branch had experienced no difficulty recognizing him.

To his surprise, a huge number of men seemed to be milling about the closed mine. He had expected to see a line of picketers, plus armed guards keeping them at bay, but nothing of this magnitude. Perhaps the Dazzler was scheduled to reopen with scab labor and the union was there to stop it. Violence of some kind seemed to be brewing from the tension in the air.

He began to regret his decision to turn thief. He had no taste for such adventure, but reminded himself he had to help Bella, no matter what.

He managed to reach the back of the main office building undetected, then counted the row of windows that lay just above ground level. They led to a semiunderground floor beneath the main office structure. Once inside, he would be able go upstairs and enter the anteroom of Orson Ridenour's old office. The petty cash box was hidden in plain sight on a ledge above a coat closet. Not very secure, yet the unknowing thief would never think to look for it there and would waste precious time prying open locked drawers and cabinets.

The fourth window from the left was the one with the broken lock. He recalled that for certain. He backed his way toward the side of the building, constantly looking around. No one seemed to be paying any attention to him. In fact, everybody seemed wildly distracted by something, judging from the excited way they all talked together.

Fortunately, the main action lay at the hoist works of the Eye Dazzler on the other side of the office building. He sidled up close to the wall and nudged his boot against the window.

He breathed a sigh of relief when it yielded to the pressure of his heel, but then it made an annoyingly loud creak. Had anyone noticed it but him? No faces turned in his direction. He next heard a shout rise up from the crowd, "Ridenour's here!"

Why was Chris at the mine today? According to the newspaper accounts, he had been avoiding the Eye Dazzler throughout the strike because he feared for his life. This was just the reporters' speculation, of course. Chris never talked to the press.

Kit dropped down to his knees, still facing out from the building, and began to edge his boots down into the window as slowly as possible so as not to create another loud squeak.

He had worked half his body into the low rectangle of the window when rough hands grabbed his ankles and jerked him into the basement of the Eye Dazzler offices. He landed with a crash on the stone floor atop a heap of three large men, one of whom he recognized as Carlos, a Ridenour bodyguard.

The men laid hands on him from all directions and dragged him up the stairs to the main floor and then out into the bright light of the summer solstice morning.

An enormous crowd had formed. What the devil was going on? He saw Christopher Ridenour talking with a grave face to none other than Jake Landry.

Their conversation was interrupted by the arrival of Kit and his captors. Both men looked shocked when they recognized him and rushed over.

"Well, well," said Landry with a theatrical flourish, "damn me if it isn't the murderer of Lucinda Ridenour in the flesh."

Sorel Weston approached. "We've been looking for this rascal for nearly a month. I'll thank you boys now to turn him over to my custody."

"Kit, what are you doing here?" said Ridenour.

"Don't waste the taxpayers' money on a long, drawn-out trial," said Landry. "Let's take care of the matter here and now, Westy."

"Don't be ridiculous," said Christopher. "We came here to discuss this strike today. Let the sheriff handle a criminal matter. I demand that you tell me if there's really a bomb planted in the Dazzler."

"I'd think you, of all people, would be interested in punishing the man who killed your mother," said Landry.

"I didn't do it," shouted Kit.

"The hell you didn't," said Landry. He slapped Kit across the face so hard, the young man lost his footing and the two men who now held his arms fast nearly dropped him.

"Stop that," Ridenour shouted as he lunged toward Kit in an effort to protect him.

\ Several of Landry's strikers used the ill-timed moment to grab Christopher away from his ever-present bodyguards. One of them pulled a revolver and held it to the young mine owner's temple. All of the bodyguards raised open hands and backed away until the pistol was lowered.

The slim mountain air hung tense with the stand-off. Landry's strikers were easily the majority by a factor of ten and knew that they were now firmly in control.

Jacob Landry began to smile. "We came here to settle our labor differences, but it's yielded an unexpected benefit for the cause of justice, gentlemen. One issue on which we all can agree: It's a lovely day for a hanging. Westy, you're the law here. What do you say?"

Sorel Weston looked around the roiling sea of anxious faces. George Hauser leaned near and whispered into the policeman's ear, "Might diffuse the situation long enough for the governor's men to arrive, Weston."

The policeman nodded. He said to Landry, "I can't participate, but I can't stop you either." He raised his palms upward. "I'm outnumbered."

Twenty-three

Eden had not joined Christopher Ridenour on his trip to the Eye Dazzler though she thought to end up there eventually. She wanted to find out what became of Kit and Bella after she parted from them the night before.

She did not trust the manner in which Kit so readily agreed to go back to the woods. That was not Kit at all. She merely hoped Bella would exercise some judgment in the matter.

She checked at the livery on Sixth and Poplar and discovered the bad news she had been expecting. The rig was never removed from the stable last night, nor any horses rented to a young couple fitting Bella and Kit's description.

She next headed for Bella Valentine's lodgings, but on the way found a little boy on the sidewalk crying. She recognized him from the orphanage as the child who had bitten her.

"Hello there," she said in a soft voice, trying not to startle the youngster, but also staying clear of biting range.

She noted with a smile that he had just recently gotten a haircut. His carefully trimmed hairline displayed a half inch of white flesh on his tanned little neck. "What are you doing out here all by yourself?"

He looked up with a sniffle and did not immediately

recognize her. "I ran away, but I'm lost. I don't know where to go."

"Well, let me walk you home again. I know where you live." She reluctantly offered the boy her hand.

"That place ain't my home." He pushed out his bottom lip.

She handed him a handkerchief, but he did not seem to know what to do with it, so she wiped his nose for him. "I know it's not your home, honey, but it will have to do for a while."

He reluctantly allowed her to take his hand and they continued on toward the orphan's home. When they turned the corner, they saw Ellen Landry rushing toward them.

"Broderick! Oh, thank heaven!"

The two women greeted each other with happy smiles and Eden returned the boy. Just as she was about to speak, a bright flashing light caught her eye. She blinked to realize that Ellen's hair-cutting scissors, sheathed in their filigreed chatelaine, had caught the morning sun.

Something shiny.

"What's the matter, Mrs. Murdoch?" Ellen asked, still flushed and breathless from her sprint down the street. Her tightly corseted midriff combined with the thin air of ten thousand feet left little available oxygen for exertion.

"I . . . I'm in a hurry. Cannot chat, I'm afraid. I'm so glad to have helped."

"I can't thank you enough."

"Please don't mention it," said Eden, breathing hard her-self as she backed away from Mrs. Landry and the little boy and promptly bumped into several other persons traversing the busy sidewalk. She begged their indulgence and disappeared into the crowd.

Eden raced to Bella Valentine's lodgings.

"Excuse me," she called to a frowsy older woman fanning herself on the porch. "Which room is Bella Valentine's?"

"Upstairs, third door to the right, but I don't think the girl is up yet."

Eden dashed up the stairs and rapped on Bella's door. She was now as breathless as Ellen Landry had been moments before.

A sleepy-looking Bella Valentine opened the door. Her long hair hung loose about her shoulders and her feet were bare, though she was otherwise fully dressed.

"Where's Kit?" Eden said.

"I'd like to know that myself. He must have left before I got up this morning, the damned fool."

Eden entered the little bedroom.

"Where is he? We've got to find him."

"Eden, I've got the most wonderful news—Kit did *not* kill Lucinda. I know it for a fact."

"Why do you know this?"

"I magnetized him last night. I got him to remember the whole day of the murder and he never went anywhere near the Black Lace House."

"That's wonderful, but we've got to find him immediately. All hell has broken loose in this town. The miners claim they've planted a bomb in the Eye Dazzler mine and the governor's militia is set to arrive at any moment."

Bella gasped and her brows shot up, but with delight, not shock. "It's traditional to celebrate the solstice with fire-works, but a bomb? Good gracious. That's exciting."

"With all due respect, Bella, I don't think that's the proper attitude. Anyway, I believe I know who did kill Lucinda, but I don't know how to prove it."

"Do tell!"

"Mrs. Landry. Jacob's wife."

"Oh, that's just silly. Why would you think that?" She slipped into her sandals and tried to get a brush through her tangled hair.

"I'll explain later. Come on. First let's find Kit." She grabbed the girl's wrist and the pair was out the door and on the chase.

The streets of Leadville, chaotic as always, rumbled with more action than usual today. A wave of bodies seemed to sweep up Chestnut Street toward Carbonate Hill and the headquarters of the Eye Dazzler.

"Why is everyone headed up to the mine?" Bella said. "I'd think that would be the last place they'd want to go, given the headlines."

Before she could get an answer a man next to her shouted over her head to a friend: "They've found him!"

"Found who?" his friend called back.

"The man who killed Mrs. Ridenour. They're gonna lynch him in front of the Eye Dazzler. Come on, let's hurry! Don't want to miss this."

Bella grabbed the man's coat sleeve as he moved away. They were all propelled through the crowd as though caught in a rushing mountain stream.

"Who?" she cried. "Who are they going to lynch?"

"That kid who was living with the hussy."

"Oh, no! Eden, what are we going to do?"

Eden thought quickly and grabbed Bella's arms. "I'll go up to the Dazzler and stall them if it's not already too late. You go get Mrs. Landry and bring her to the mine. Do or say whatever you have to but get her there quickly!"

Bella nodded and ran off toward the orphan's asylum as fast as her flapping sandals would let her.

Eden doubled her own pace, pushing and shoving her way in the moving human mass up Carbonate Hill to the mining district. She could hear shouting in the distance that grew louder with each step she managed to take.

She had never bothered to visit the hill that had made Leadville famous. She did not care for the sight. The road, trod all day by mules and burros carrying their heavy loads, was lined with the stinking carcasses of the animals who had died on the job and were carelessly abandoned along-side the path to rot away in the summer sun now that the long snows of winter had melted.

She arrived at the main shaft of the Eye Dazzler, not a very impressive-looking place for all its grand reputation. Mining was a grim occupation, despite its feverish promise of instant wealth.

As her eyes searched for Kit she began to identify the various factions present. The strikers had formed a human barricade to prevent the scab workers from entering the four mine shafts that led to the labyrinthine depths of the Eye Dazzler. The main shaft had a huge steam-driven hoist over its entrance. The three auxiliary shafts had old-fashioned mule-driven whims. They lowered and raised large ore buckets which could carry two men at a time.

She could not guess the number of men present, but there had to be more than a thousand. The strikebreakers, she counted only a few dozen, stood by looking nervous, but resolute. They did not have the manpower to physically challenge the union men. They could only wait for the state militia to arrive and escort them to work.

The mine owners and their representatives stood by at a more cautious distance. The so-called Committee of Public Safety did not look as confident as they had the night they organized in the Ridenour parlor.

Standing on tiptoe to see above the heads of the men around her, Eden caught a shocking glimpse of Kit Randall physically restrained by two large men on either side of him. They stood beneath the massive headframe which held the sheave wheel of the hoist.

One of the men next to her joked that the headframe would earn its nickname this day.

"What nickname?" she asked.

"Why 'gallows frame,' of course. Everybody knows that," the man said with a laugh.

Eden felt a sick twisting in her stomach. The wooden headframe did resemble a gallows. She worked her way to the front of the crowd where Kit—feisty as always—shouted oaths at his captors, even as others in the group tossed a rope over one of the armatures of the headframe.

Eden saw Jacob Landry directing the action. On the sidelines, burly men held a struggling Christopher Ridenour. He shouted at Landry, though Eden could not make out his words over the general din of the excited crowd.

Two groups of men now argued back and forth. There seemed to be some controversy over Landry's decision to lynch Kit. Was it a carryover of the strife between the striking miners and the scabs Christopher had hired?

"Mr. Landry, I need to talk to you," Eden shouted when she reached the heart of the fray.

"Who the hell are you?" said Landry.

"Kit Randall is my nephew and he's not guilty. Where are the police?"

"Right here," said Sorel Weston, stepping forward.

"This is not legal!" she said. "How can you allow this?"

"We've been looking for this scalawag since the day of the murder," said Weston. "I just wish I'd arrested him the day before when the woman filed a complaint against him."

"Mr. Landry, listen to me," said Eden. "Before you do this, I suggest you talk to your *wife*."

This comment stopped Landry cold. Everyone watched his reaction with curiosity.

"Talk to your wife, Mr. Landry. I bet you suspect the same thing I do."

"Ig—ignore her," said Landry, though he was obviously bothered by Eden's reference.

"What does she know?" Weston asked the man.

"Nothing," said Landry. "Let's get on with it."

"No, I beg you all," she continued. "Let Ellen Landry come forward and see if she will watch an innocent man hang for a crime he did not commit."

"What do you know about all this, lady?" said Weston. "I thought you were the housekeeper in the Ridenour mansion. Were you even living in Leadville at the time of the murder?"

"No, but Lucinda Ridenour's maid, Sadie Branch, was

here and she saw a woman leaving the house that afternoon. A tall woman wearing a veil."

"So what?" said Landry. "Lots of people fit that description."

"The woman also wore a shiny object at her waist."

Landry's dark eyes widened at this reference.

Eden continued her theory. "She carries a pair of hair-cutting scissors. Long, thin, pointed barber shears."

"This woman is babbling," said the increasingly agitated husband.

"My mother was stabbed with a long, thin blade," said the restrained Christopher Ridenour. "The doctor's report confirmed it. A long pair of barber shears could have made such a wound."

"You're right about that," Sorel Weston said. "No harm in asking a few questions."

This brought a mixed reaction from the crowd, but there seemed to be enough controversy among them on what to do next that the lynching might be postponed a moment.

"Please, he's right, there is no harm," she said, appealing to all the men present, though she thought few were as interested in seeing justice done as watching the lurid spectacle of a man dying before their eyes.

"Like it or not, Jake, your wife had a motive and we all know it," said Weston.

Eden held her breath and hoped. The policeman actually seemed intrigued by her theory. Perhaps he was not as corrupt as she had originally thought. Weston conversed with several of his police cohorts as well as some mine owners and union men. They all talked, shook their heads at various moments.

George Hauser stepped over to Weston once again to

remind him: "The more we stall for time, the more chance the governor's men can get here."

"Eden, you should leave here!" Kit pleaded. "This is only going to get worse!"

She rushed to his side.

"I'm not going to leave you."

"That Landry's totally crazy!" Kit said. "He's out of his mind, babbling half the time."

"Shut up, Randall!" said Landry, who stepped up closer. "Move away, Mrs. Whoever-you-are, before you get hurt. If you're telling lies about my wife, so help me God, I'll—" He raised the butt end of his rifle as though to threaten her with a blow, but several other men latched onto his arms to hold him still. He shook them off and lowered his weapon, though he still glared a burning hole in Eden. The man's eyes radiated a dark, terrible passion.

An ominous murmur rolled through the crowd as they parted for the arrival of two women rushing up Carbonate Hill.

Bella maneuvered the anguished Ellen Landry into the epicenter of the chaos and then released her.

"But . . . but I don't understand," said Ellen Landry to Bella. "You told me my husband had been shot. You said he was dying."

Bella shrugged. "I lied."

Eden confronted the woman and pointed to Kit. "Look into the face of that young man, Mrs. Landry. These men plan to hang him for killing Mrs. Ridenour."

Ellen would not raise her eyes. "I'm sure he's quite guilty."

"Mrs. Ridenour's maid saw you on her street the very afternoon of her murder."

Landry stepped nearer. "Is it true? Did you go there, Nell?"

"Of course not." She finally looked up at her husband. "I don't drink tea with harlots!"

"You damned—" Jacob Landry raised his hand to strike his wife, but several men intervened once again.

"How dare you curse at me? Your own wife—a fact you so conveniently forgot on so many occasions." Her eyes filled with angry tears.

"Did you do it? Tell me, damn you!" The man's face contorted with growing outrage.

The crowd stood by silent and gaping. Eden did not imagine that so many people could be so hushed. She seemed to hear the beating of her own heart in the unnatural stillness.

"You were gone that afternoon," he said to his wife as if they were alone in their own parlor. "You told me you were working at the orphans' home."

"Hold on, now," said Weston. "You both swore you were together in your own house all that afternoon. I called on the orphan asylum to check out the story and they said Mrs. Landry hadn't been there all day."

This revelation caused the crowd to break their unholy quiet.

Ellen Landry glanced around with real fear in her once haughty eyes.

Landry seemed in the grips of the appalling realization. He stared at his wife in horror and whispered, "How could you? How could you?"

Eden looked to Kit, who watched the dire proceedings with all the rest. She caught his eye and they exchanged amazed and confounded looks.

"I didn't do it. I swear it, Jacob!"

"You're a damned poor liar, Nell!"

He lunged at his wife once again, but was still restrained by his own cohorts. No one knew what to make of the extraordinary turn of events.

"It wasn't my fault," Ellen cried. "I went there to help you. I went there for *your* sake. To beg her to reconsider and give you your job back. I humbled myself before that monster. And she laughed at me. She taunted me! Saying things about you, about me. How she could give you children and I could not!" Her words were halted by a great shuddering of her body as tears now flooded her eyes. She wiped her face with her sleeve. "I couldn't help myself. I know God will forgive me. She was a murderer herself, after all. You said so! You told me so, Jacob."

"What the hell does she mean, Jake?" said Sorel Weston.

Eden looked over to Christopher Ridenour, wondering if he had guessed what they were talking about. He seemed as confused as the rest of the crowd.

Landry looked strangely calm, a change that gave his terrified wife no comfort. "Let me take her home."

"I don't think so," said Weston. He stepped forward, but before he could take any further action, a rumble of hoofbeats could be heard from the road into town. The human sea that filled Chestnut Street parted once again as a bugle blast echoed back and forth among the far walls of the surrounding hills.

"The militia!" shouted the strikers and the scabs in a single cry.

A fully uniformed and armed cavalry unit rode in at full gallop, firing their guns in the air. The assemblage at the mine dissolved in chaos, scattering in all directions like cockroaches exposed to a sudden light.

Eden got shoved to the ground in the melee. She had no idea how many men stumbled over her as she cowered and covered her face, the only part of her she was able to successfully protect. She was kicked and stepped upon countless times by the fleeing crowd.

She heard rifle shots, men shouting, women screaming. Her mind traveled back to the horror of the Washita so many years ago. The day she met Brad Randall. Again her nostrils filled with the acrid smell of gun smoke and the burnt flesh it rendered.

The frantic exodus finally ceased and she dared to raise her head. In the smoky, groaning aftermath, she saw that most of the crowd had dispersed. Various cavalrymen held some strikers at bay with their surrendered hands over their heads.

The bodies of several men lay strewn about. She saw a young girl throw herself on top of the corpse of a slain young striker. George Hauser knelt over the girl and tried to pry her away, but she would not stop screaming over the young man's body.

The girl must have been Hauser's daughter, by the familiar way he talked to her. Perhaps this was the wayward daughter Kit described who had once flirted with him. Could it be possible she had fallen in love with one of the strikers? An ill-fated match if ever there was one.

Many more strikers lay wounded and she knew she would soon have to put her nursing skills to use. First, though, she wanted to find out what had become of Kit.

"Eden! Over here," called Bella.

Kit sat on the ground with his arms around Bella.

Eden rushed over and kissed his sweaty forehead as he grinned at her.

Christopher Ridenour approached somewhat timidly. "Are you all right, Kit?"

"Yeah, I guess so," he said without emotion.

Sorel Weston stomped over to their group. "What the devil became of him?"

"Who?" said Eden.

"Landry. There's no trace of him. Look what he did before leaving, though."

He led them all, including Christopher, to the spot where Ellen Landry lay dead, staring heavenward, her neck twisted at an obscene angle. A single tear still hung upon her tormented cheek.

"Sweet Jesus," Kit whispered as Bella pressed her face against his shoulder.

"A sick and evil man," Ridenour muttered as he stared at the woman's body. "How could my mother have loved him? I blame him for my mother's death as much as her."

He then looked over to one of the older shafts of the mine. The bucket had been lowered. The hoist mules still walked their circle of burden on the whim, though the hoist operator was nowhere to be seen.

"God help us all," he said. "Landry's gone down into the Dazzler."

Twenty-four

"You've got to go down there, sergeant," said Ridenour. "He's placed a bomb in the mine, or so he claims. He's going to destroy the Eye Dazzler."

Weston did not look enthused about undertaking such a risky mission. "He could have been bluffing about that bomb."

"He obviously killed his wife. Aren't you bound to go after him for that reason alone? Even if you don't care what happens to my mine?"

Kit watched in amazement at the strident and unexpectedly commanding tone in Christopher's voice. He no longer sounded like a boy content to hover on the periphery of, first, his imperious mother, then his blustering banker.

"I can't ask my men to go down in there to possible death. Some of 'em are family men. We'd all blow to kingdom come if there's a bomb."

"Then I'll go myself," said Ridenour, towering over the much smaller Weston. "And damn you for the coward that you are!"

He turned in a slow circle and pleaded to the small crowd still remaining. "Will no one go with me?"

A shuffling silence was the only reply.

"Give me a gun, at least," he said to Weston. When the

policeman handed him his pistol, he called to a nearby miner he recognized. "Jennings, can you operate the hoist?"

"Yes, Mr. Ridenour."

Eden, Kit, and Bella watched as Christopher climbed into the shaft cage and motioned for it to be lowered into the depths of his mine.

Eden felt a chill as she saw the young man's terrified but determined face haltingly disappear down into the shaft. He hung on to each side of the apparatus and looked for all the world like a condemned man. His mournful gaze seemed fixed on Kit Randall.

Once he was gone, Kit wandered over to the hoist and looked down as it lowered its cargo long out of sight.

He uttered a disgusted, but resolute groan. "Oh, hell, I'll go, too."

"No, Kit," cried Bella. She tightened her grip on his arm. "Don't do it."

"Please don't, Kit," Eden said, fearing for him as though he were her flesh-and-blood nephew as well as a friend, even though she wished with all her heart that someone had stepped forward to accompany Christopher Ridenour.

"Kit, for the love of Jesus," Bella said. "What do you care what happens to the Eye Dazzler . . . or to Chris, for that matter?"

"What are friends for?" said Kit with such a strangely malevolent sarcasm that both women exchanged frightened looks.

Weston found him a revolver and the women clung to him as they waited through the long ten minutes it took the cageway to return to the surface.

"Which level did he go to?" Kit asked the man operating the hoist.

"Level nine."

"Is that where the pumps are?"

"Yeah," said the man, "but you can also reach them from level eight. That might be quicker." He gave Kit some terse directions on the alternative route to the hydraulic pumps that involved going down from the boiler room.

Bella and Eden wept with fear as they watched Kit disappear down the shaft.

"Come on, Bella, let's go cover up Mrs. Landry," she said.

They found a piece of canvas and shrouded the woman's face with it. Bella stared at the body of Ellen Landry for a long time.

"I feel like I caused all this," she said. "I cast a spell that day, hoping something bad would happen to Lucy Ridenour. Not death, though. I swear it. I had more in mind her getting fat or a big wart on her nose or something."

Eden placed a comforting hand on the girl's shoulder. She did not believe Bella was in any way responsible for Lucinda Ridenour's demise, but if she said this, she feared Bella would take it as an insult to her occult "powers." She decided to remain diplomatically silent.

―――

Kit passed by the first of the nine levels of the mine and was stunned by the complexity of the workings. He had only been in the mine once before and had not paid much attention, since Chris had led the way. A man could wander through this maze for days and never be found. He could think only of Dante's nine levels of Hell as he pondered the impossibility of finding Christopher, much less Landry.

In between each level, he was swallowed up by a darkness so profound he could not tell if his eyes were open or shut. He thought about the mules that pulled the ore carts, how they eventually went blind from living out their lives in the dark.

No wonder they fought like demons when they were loaded into the shaft cage to be lowered into the mine. Did they somehow know that only their death would return them to the surface of the world?

His anxiety increased with every foot the cage dropped. Finally it jerked to a stop at level eight. He was more than seven hundred feet below ground.

He climbed to the edge of the shaft, trying hard to avoid looking into its gaping maw. When he planted his feet on firm ground, he breathed a small sigh of relief. He grabbed a couple of candles and several matches from a large supply keg and stowed them in his jacket pocket.

He stumbled along the rocky drifts which were lit only by candles sitting in wrought iron sconces wedged into small crevices. The lights were placed just far enough apart that there existed a patch of darkness in between each which caused another moment of blindness. Chris had told him that they did not use oil lamps in the mines because the oil represented too great a fire hazard.

Kit secretly assumed they just wanted to save money any way they could. It seemed clear to him that the mine owners showed about as much compassion for the comfort and safety of their workers as the miners showed those poor mules. They were a cheap commodity easily replaced. Best not to consider that they might have feelings, much less souls.

The rough-chiseled rock floor with its ore cart rails set upon round timbers was too uneven to permit him to travel any faster than a swift walk. Even at that pace, he still managed to stumble occasionally.

The rhythmic wheezing and clanking of the hydraulic pumps was the only noise he could hear in the otherwise silent catacomb. How different from the day he had last visited when the walls had rung with the deafening thunder of the widow-maker drills. Simple conversation had been rendered impossible by the din in the working levels of the Eye Dazzler, which remained a constant fifty-five degrees, summer and winter.

Kit sweated despite the chill. The walls seeped moisture as though they were perspiring too. The reek of feces and urine from both men and mules mixed with the sour smell of the molding timber frames to create a nauseating stench to Kit's unprepared nostrils.

He could not imagine working in this terrible place. Not for any sum of money. No wonder the miners balked at three dollars a day even though this was more than three times the national average for laborers in other types of work.

Kit then heard the murmur of human voices. He must be nearing the pump works.

"Landry?" Christopher shouted down a stone corridor somewhere beneath Kit's feet.

"Keep your distance, Ridenour! I'll blow us both sky high if you come in here."

"Jacob, why do you want to do this?" Christopher called.

His voice echoed in the large chamber where Jacob Landry must be.

Kit scrambled down the dim corridor, certain he would reach them any minute.

"Go to hell! The Eye Dazzler Mine closes forever today. If you don't want to die, I suggest you get out fast."

"If the mine closes, you're hurting the miners as much as me. Perhaps them more. I don't understand."

"The Eye Dazzler money has a curse on it. It's tainted everything it's touched. Corruption and compromise. Total and complete. A cleansing is needed. A new flood, a new Noah's flood."

Landry spoke in a feverish tempo to no one but himself, it seemed. "Wash clean the corruption . . . the degeneracy, the mad call of the blood, robbing you of dignity . . ."

Reasoning with him is a waste of time, thought Kit. At last, some machinery came into view that must be the boilers the hoistman had described.

Kit came to an opening which was connected to the room below by a metal ladder built into the wall. He peered down into the large room and saw that the former superintendent was now perched on top of the main cylinder of the huge pumping machinery about twenty feet away. He appeared to be placing something behind the flywheel.

Christopher appeared in the entrance to the pump room. He raised his revolver with a shaky hand.

"Get out of here," Landry shouted. "I've got giant." He held up a rolled stick of nitroglycerin.

"Leave this place, Jacob, and I'll say I never saw you. We both know there's a back way out. I doubt the police do, though."

"No!"

"But it's your only chance. If they catch you, they'll hang you for murdering your wife."

Sweat poured off Landry's distraught face. "If you fire that gun, this whole place will blow. I have no way of knowing if the nitro is up to temperature."

Nitroglycerin's freezing point was a mere 52 degrees. When in its solid, frozen form it managed to be even more unstable than in its liquid incarnation. The slightest bump could potentially ignite it.

"If you destroy those pumps, I'm ruined anyway, Jacob."

"Hold it right there, Landry," Kit shouted down from the boiler room.

When Landry looked up to see Kit Randall silhouetted in the opening above, his face twisted with an unholy anger. He pulled the stick of giant that he had been laboring to place in the main cog of the flywheel and raised it to throw at his former rival for Lucinda Ridenour's affections.

"Run, Kit!" shouted Christopher as he pulled the trigger of his gun.

He would never know whether the bullet found its target. He started to run the instant Chris fired, but the stick of giant powder hit the floor of the pump room a few seconds later with the expected result.

The earth quaked in a quarter-mile radius of the Eye Dazzler. Bella and Eden rushed to the main shaft and hugged each other in dread as a dense cloud of dust and smoke rose from the opening. The Leadville fire bells rang out in the distance.

"I want to go down there," said Bella.

Eden agreed, but the other men around, miners all, blocked their attempt.

"No women allowed," said a burly young man with a long black beard.

"It's bad luck, ladies," said another miner, a more amiable sort. "No females are ever allowed in mines."

The two women looked at each other in stunned disbelief.

"That's ridiculous," said Eden. "The place has already blown up. What else can happen?"

Several nearby men chuckled at this, but no one would dare to break the taboo. They physically barred both women from going down into the mine, though several men were brave enough to do it themselves and promised to report as quickly as possible.

"Hold both my hands," said Bella to Eden.

She did as she asked and watched the girl close her eyes and breathe deeply. "Think about Kit. Imagine his face in your mind."

Eden did so, seeing in her imagination a smiling, happy young man with deep dimples and curly dark hair and a flirtatious remark for every occasion, the old Kit she had once known, not the tormented young man she had seen since coming to Leadville.

Bella squeezed her hands tighter, then relaxed. She opened her eyes with a relieved smile. "He's alive. I know it."

———

When Kit recovered consciousness he seemed to remember flying through the air and slamming straight into a rock wall. He could not see in the darkness, but he knew he was not trapped in any way. The air was filled with rock dust, smoke, and silica. He coughed and choked on it. He tasted the salty metallic blood gushing from his nose. He felt a trickle of warm fluid on his neck and realized his ears were bleeding, too.

The force of the explosion had snuffed out all the candles in the corridors. He pulled himself into a sitting position to try to recover from his dizziness. Though he ached in many places, some new injuries, some old, he realized he was still in one piece.

The Eye Dazzler pumps were not, however. He heard the dripping of icy water already filtering into the mine.

He located the candles in his jacket pocket and struck a match. The flare blinded him for an instant, but soon his eyes readjusted. He lit the candle and wedged it into a rock crevice while he tied his handkerchief across his nose and mouth to filter the thick air so that he did not choke to death.

He retraced his steps to the opening above the pump room and realized he must have been thrown ten yards at least. He held his candle out and tried to cast some light below. The room was too large and the flame too small to distinguish much in the smoking ruins. It looked as though the far wall of the room had received the worst of the blast, which was probably why he was still alive.

He climbed down the metal ladder carefully into the room below. When he reached the bottom he began to crawl on his hands and knees over the wreckage of the pump works. He placed his hand and knee holds gingerly, afraid the destroyed metal might give way underneath him at any moment.

"Kit? Are you all right?" came Christopher Ridenour's voice from somewhere in the blackness.

Kit's ears did not seem to work right. He felt as though his head was sealed in a bottle.

"I'm okay, I think. How about you?"

"One of my legs is trapped under some rocks."

"I'm going to try and find you, Chris. Keep talking. Loudly."

"I'm sorry about this, Kit," came Ridenour's voice in the echoing distance.

"Don't worry about it, but I've got to tell you, Chris, you're not much of a gunslinger."

He heard Christopher's coughing laugh and soon found him in the smoky gloom. He sat in a pile of rubble at an odd angle and was almost waist-deep in water. One foot was wedged under several large rocks. Kit could not understand why he just sat there, making no effort to free himself.

Kit rushed over and began to push the rocks and debris away.

"Forget it," said the trapped boy. "Just save yourself. Get out while you can. There's no telling how much of the sub-structure has been destabilized. There could be a full collapse at any time."

"Don't be stupid. I'm not leaving here without you." The cold, dank-smelling water stiffened his hands as he worked to free Christopher's foot.

"I'm serious, Kit. Just leave. There's nothing for me to go back to up there."

"Did you get hit in the head as well? You're talking like an idiot. Now snap out of it and help me. Jesus, this water is cold as hell."

"All the lower shafts will be under water soon. All the producing shafts."

"I'm not interested in discussing mining at the moment. Now come on." He began to yank at the boy's foot, which caused Christopher to wince in pain. The flood waters were rising far more quickly than Kit imagined they could. No wonder the health of the pumps had constantly worried the Ridenours. Jake Landry had known exactly how to wreak the most havoc with the least work.

"The only thing I would regret is dying before I got a chance to explain about that night."

Kit paused to stare at him in the flickering candlelight.

"You must put your mind at rest. Nothing happened that night, Kit. It was all quite innocent. I swear to you with my dying breath."

You lying son of a bitch, Kit thought with sudden anger. "If that's true, why did the pillow next to me reek of *your* hair oil the next day?"

Christopher sighed. "I carried you up to bed after you passed out in the second parlor. I made the mistake of mentioning to Mother how beautiful you looked when you were asleep. Like a statue of Apollo we saw in the British Museum. She started teasing me. She told me to kiss you good night. She was fond of plaguing me about my feelings for you. She could be cruel at times. But we were both just being silly that night. Pure nonsense. So I did it."

"Did what?"

"Kissed you. And then she said, 'Kiss him again, you know you want to.' And she was right. I'm sorry. I know it was wrong. I'd give anything to take it back."

"What *else* did you do?"

"Mother told me to stay with you. You were hallucinating wildly at times and someone needed to look after you. You know my mother never cared to play the nurse. I held you until we both fell asleep. When I woke up you were sleeping peacefully, so I returned to my own room for the rest of the night."

"That's *all*?"

"I think my mother assumed more happened. But it didn't. I swear to you. I would never have done anything indecent. I'm not a rapist, for heaven sake."

Kit did not know what to make of this so he continued his work to free Ridenour's trapped foot. "I don't want to talk about that night ever again. Just shut up and help me."

"No, just leave me here. I'm ruined, Kit. I don't want to go on."

"Stop saying that."

"You don't know what my life is like. What if you had to live forever in a kind of Hell in which you dreaded to look anyone in the eye for fear they'd catch a glimpse of your soul and know your secrets? That was Orson Ridenour's true legacy to me."

"Look, stop talking this self-pitying horseshit. You don't know what the future holds."

"I'm afraid I can guess."

He stubbornly sat in the rising waters, still refusing to help Kit free him.

"I know someone who thinks she can tell the future, but who really wants to know it in advance?" said Kit. He

291

worked at one large boulder, but every time he moved it an inch, two more stones replaced it. "None of us knows what tomorrow holds and none of us needs to. That's what makes it wonderful. The surprises, damn it. The *not-knowing*."

"The 'not-knowing'?"

"Yeah, sure. Aren't you curious what might be waiting for you up there?" Since Christopher would not pull his own foot out, Kit grabbed his knee and began to yank on it with all his strength.

"Ouch! You're ripping my foot off."

"The future could be marvelous," Kit continued, ignoring Ridenour's yelps. "Something you never even dreamed about. You wouldn't want to miss it, would you?"

One final yank extracted the young man's foot from his boot and sock as well as the rubble. Kit held the bloody, mangled foot above the icy waters and they both examined it in the flickering light. It still seemed to be in one piece, at least.

Christopher looked up at Kit and tried to smile through his pain. "Always the optimist. No wonder you love to gamble. The High Life Club grew rich off men like you."

"You mean *fools* like me."

They both managed to laugh at this as Kit pulled him to a standing position and they began their halting, staggering climb back to the surface.

"Kit? Do you have any notion what Mrs. Landry meant when she called my mother a murderer?"

Kit did not know what to say. He hated to tell him the truth. Fortunately, he was saved from deciding to answer by the clanking of the hoist in action. The first group of rescuers was about to arrive.

They loaded Christopher into the shaft cage and raised him back up the shaft so that he could be transported to the hospital.

Twenty-five

Three days after martial law was declared in Leadville, the striking miners voted to return to work under their former terms. The owners had won.

The Eye Dazzler miners had no place to return to—all the producing shafts were now filled with water—and so applied for jobs at the other mines in the district. Life slowly returned to normal, which was for Leadville noisy, rollicking chaos.

The city fathers were happy that they could greet former president Ulysses S. Grant at their gleaming new train station without worry of labor unrest.

Bella convinced her friend Etta to double up with another girl at the boardinghouse so Eden could have a room to stay in until Brad returned.

No one wanted to go near the Black Lace House, though Eden wondered how Christopher was doing. She and Kit saw him once on Harrison Street. He walked on crutches and was surrounded by George Hauser's wife and three daughters. They all carried packages from a shopping expedition of some sort. The girls fussed about him and he looked to be bashfully enjoying all the attention.

The day finally came for the arrival of the first train. Former President Grant, on the initial leg of a round-the-world trip, would be the first to step off onto the Leadville platform, but a wire from Denver that morning alerted Eden and Kit to an even more significant passenger, at least from their perspective: Brad Randall.

He hinted in his wire that he brought two pieces of wondrous news, one he revealed—that his son had made a full recovery—the other he kept secret. Eden was beside herself with excitement. Though Kit tried to mask his feelings, she could tell he was eager to see Brad, too.

She worried about this reunion in that she had never told Kit that she had informed Brad about his still mysterious night with Christopher Ridenour. Brad's last letter had been the most scathing of all. He had said, among other things, "If he were mine to disown, I would do so."

The train was supposed to reach the station at around eight in the evening. Eden and Kit, along with several thousand Leadvilleites and the ever-present brass bands, thronged Harrison Street on the way north to the new Denver and Rio Grande rail station on Poplar. Magnificent archways spanned the entrances to State Street and Third Street with patriotic decorations. Every single storefront was likewise decorated with banners, ribbons, welcoming signs, and streamers.

A large podium was constructed in front of the Clarendon Hotel to hold the numerous speakers. Two of the private cavalries rode in full parade dress up and down the thoroughfare with their gleaming sabers out for occasional brandishing. The Tabor hose cart outfitted with their bright blue shirts and white ties competed for attention with the Bush hose cart members who sported white flannel shirts edged in blue.

Eden wondered if this was what Washington City had been like in the celebrations held after the end of the Civil War. She walked along with Kit and Bella, ignoring the occasional stare or remark from someone who recognized them as having been involved in the Ridenour unpleasantness.

The carnival atmosphere was intoxicating, though most men around them also relied upon the more traditional sources of inebriation.

"You'd think he was still president," said Kit, shouting to be heard above the noise and the music.

"You'd think it was the Second Coming," said Bella.

"I met Lincoln once," Eden said with blushing pride.

"You're kidding us," said Kit with a grin.

"It's perfectly true. The sad thing was I didn't realize it was him until it was too late."

"How could that be?" Bella said.

"I worked as a nurse in a hospital in Washington City during the war. One night I stayed late and had to walk home by myself in the dark. A tall man crossed the street and asked politely why a young woman such as myself was walking alone so late at night. When I told him of my nursing work, he called to a soldier nearby and told the man to escort me home. I said it wasn't necessary, but he insisted. Then he left with a group of men. As we walked off, my escort began to chuckle and asked if I knew the man we had just spoken to. I said 'no' but he seemed very nice, though a little bit bossy. The soldier laughed out loud and said, 'You just spouted off to the president of the United States, girl!' "

They laughed as they joined some five thousand other

Leadville citizens at the train station and waited for the grand arrival. Eight o'clock came and went. The crowds grew restless as the evening dragged on. And they waxed drunker and more unruly. The police force had its hands full.

The sky darkened and a full moon rose above the mountains. Bonfires were lit at various locations.

"See there, pagan priestess," said Kit as he squeezed Bella's arm. "You got your wish for bonfires, just a couple of weeks late."

Bella leaned around him to tell Eden, "You celebrate Litha with bonfires, though I doubt any of these fools know it."

"That's the summer solstice," Kit said to his almost-aunt. He turned to Bella. "See, I'm learning."

"Very good," she said, already planning to ply him later that night with the traditional and reputedly aphrodisiacal Litha beverage, strawberry wine. She had made the magical and delightful-tasting elixir the summer before and let it cure all this time for just the right moment.

"Uncle Brad told me you two had planned on a June twenty-first wedding date. Since you missed that, do you suppose you'll do it soon? Tomorrow maybe?"

Eden smiled nervously. Brad had made no mention of the impending wedding in his recent letters. A fact which concerned her more than she cared to admit. "I don't really know."

Two long hours of standing in the noise and jumble of the crowd gave Bella a headache. She decided to forego the big arrival and tried to talk Kit into going back to the boardinghouse with her but did not succeed. He was determined to see his uncle, so she left, disappointed and cranky.

The historic train whistle sounded just after ten, and a great cheer rose up from the weary crowd. The former President and his wife emerged from his Pullman car and were greeted on the platform by numerous dignitaries, including Mayor Humphreys, Lieutenant Governor Tabor, and the leader of the Union Veterans Association. Speeches were made, each punctuated by a number from the band, and all the while the rest of the passengers were made to wait on the halted train.

Finally, the presidential entourage was loaded into gaily decorated carriages and borne on to the grandstand in front of the Clarendon and an exhausted-looking Brad Randall emerged from a first-class car. Eden ran to him and stood on tiptoe to kiss him. Then she looked around in confusion.

"Where's Hadley?"

"Still in Washington City. Staying with my sister."

"But—"

"We're returning there immediately. I'll explain everything as soon as we can sit down. You'll be thrilled, darling."

Eden tried to smile, but could not quite sort out this imperious behavior on the part of the man she was planning to give her future to. How could he make such momentous plans without consulting her?

"Where are we staying tonight?" Brad said.

"We're staying at Miss Valentine's boardinghouse. One of her friends has vacated a room for us."

He looked horrified and bent down to whisper in her ear, "You can't be serious. I don't care to sleep in a brothel!"

"You'll be fine. We don't have another choice. There are no rooms in this town. It's not a brothel, really. Just a rooming house with 'relaxed' standards. Anyway, it's just for one night."

Kit stepped up to join their conversation after hanging back at a discreet distance to afford them the courtesy of a private greeting.

"What are you two whispering about?" he said. "And hello to you, too, Uncle."

"Hello, Kit," Randall said in a tone as dry and dead as the air inside a tomb.

The younger man noticed this, but said nothing.

Brad announced that he was starving, despite the hour, so they arranged for his luggage to be sent on to Pris Hart's boardinghouse and adjourned to the nearest all-night restaurant, of which there were many in Leadville.

As the dinner was set before them, Brad delivered his big announcement: He had an exciting new job offer on the table.

"It's called the Smithsonian Institution. I don't think it was in existence when you lived in Washington during the war years, Eden."

"It's a great place," said Kit.

Brad continued as though his nephew had not spoken, "They are opening a new wing dedicated to the American Indian and the director wants me to be the head of the project. I'll have complete control and a more than adequate budget. They have had their eye on me ever since I left the

Bureau, but did not know how to approach me. They assumed I was staying in the west."

"I guess I assumed you were staying in the west as well," said Eden.

"But you've lived in Washington before. You'll love it. And I know a wonderful school for Hadley. And I've rented a house for us to live in. It's terribly small, but it will do until we can locate something more suitable. B.J. will be able to stay with us on weekends."

She tried to smile as he continued his enthusiastic narrative. She watched Kit's reaction. They were not an hour into the meal before it became clear that Brad was directing all his comments to her as though his nephew were not at the table. She would have to talk to Kit.

———

"You told him what?" Kit ran his hands through his hair in a despairing gesture.

"I'm sorry, Kit. It seemed like a small thing. Just a kiss. If I had guessed his reaction, I would have been much more discreet. He's liberal-minded on so many issues, I just assumed—"

"Oh, God."

"Such a little thing. Just a kiss."

Kit smiled mirthlessly at a sudden memory. *You're too old to kiss boys.*

"I'm so sorry. I just never—"

"How did *you* find out?"

Eden's mind scrambled with confusion and despair. She could not bear to make any more trouble for Kit. If she unwittingly ruined his promising relationship with Bella, she would feel even more miserable. Since the girl had not yet mentioned the matter, maybe this small deception could continue.

"Christopher told me himself," she lied. "The night he tried to hang himself. He confessed it all."

"Does Bella know, too?"

"No." Lies upon lies. She felt her cheeks burn with guilt.

"You're sure about this? You're sure she doesn't know?"

"Pretty sure." Eden felt horrible. She wanted to hide. At least they were leaving the following afternoon, though she was furious with Brad for making such major plans without consulting her. She had little desire to return to the east. She had been born there but was now irrevocably a creature of the west. She would never fit in.

"Well, we're off, I guess," said Brad, as they supervised the luggage being loaded onto the train. The air was chilly, but the noonday sun could burn the skin. He pulled the brim of his hat lower to shield his eyes from the glare.

"What about your wedding?" Kit said. "Your divorce is final now. Right?"

Eden drew a breath and held it as she glanced from one man to the other.

Brad seemed capable of looking anywhere in the world but his nephew's face. "We'll see to that when we reach Washington City."

Kit smiled uncertainly. "But I thought you wanted me to stand up with you."

Eden's heart sank.

"Don't worry about that, nephew. Jennetta and Bob will be able witnesses. It's not important."

She knew it was important to Kit when she saw a crest-fallen look sweep across his face.

"I need to see to some matters," Eden said. She left the platform to allow her future husband and his nephew some privacy.

"Why are you angry at me?" said Kit the moment they were alone.

"I'm not angry at you."

"Then why don't you want me to be your best man?"

"Kit, just let this go."

"I want to know."

"I'm quite certain you already have a good idea."

"Is it because of what she told you? Because I can explain that."

"There's no explanation necessary. In any case, I don't want to talk about it. Especially not here in this public place."

"But it's nothing," Kit said, losing his temper.

Brad moved in closer to speak in grinding whispers. "*Nothing*? Indecent familiarities with another *man*? That's nothing? What's next? Fornication with animals?"

"Oh, for the love of Jesus!" Kit spat out, borrowing Bella's favorite oath.

"Lower your voice, for heaven's sake. People are staring."

"I can explain, Uncle Brad."

Randall shook his head, not wanting a fight, not even wanting a discussion. "I've got to go now. The train—"

"That's it? That's the end?"

Brad sighed and looked off into the distance. "I don't feel the same about you. I can't help it. I'm sorry. Good-bye."

———

Eden wept as she hugged Kit one last time before boarding the train. Brad was already on his way to find their seats. She glanced up at the big, brass clock on the side of the depot. For fourteen years she had lived with only the sun for a timepiece. She somehow resented the tyranny of clocks, always pushing, pushing.

"You're going to be happy in Washington, Eden. I'm sure of it."

"I wish *I* were sure," she said. "To think that I used to live among the Indians and now I will look at what's left of them in a display case."

"Welcome to the future," he said and they both smiled at his sarcasm.

"I'm so sorry, Kit, about the way things are between you and your uncle. I'll talk to him. I'll make things right, some-how." She laid her head on his shoulder for a moment. He smelled of sandalwood and this made her smile. She would miss Bella, too.

Kit shook his head in a casual way and flashed his old charming, if battle-weary, grin. "Don't worry about it."

———

He spent the next two weeks looking for a job. He tried banks, insurance companies, smelters' and graders' offices. All seemed to have openings—until he applied. During the interviews, they suddenly found themselves at full staff despite their HELP WANTED signs in the front windows. His

Georgetown education could not displace the newspaper stories about his tenancy in the Black Lace House.

"You don't need to work," Bella said in an effort to console him. "I'm making plenty for both of us."

"This isn't the first time I've let a woman keep me and we all know how well that turned out before."

"This isn't Third Street."

Bella was doing exceedingly well. The *Leadville Herald* had published a lengthy interview with her after the riot at the Eye Dazzler. She hinted heavily that her psychic abilities led to the solving of Lucinda Ridenour's murder.

Elegant carriages now made their way up Chestnut Street to Pris Hart's ramshackle boarding house and engraved cards with invitations to Bella were left on the table in the front hall.

"Spirit parties" had become the after-dinner rage among Leadville's elite. "Tarot teas," hosted by the city's most fashionable matrons, filled Bella's afternoons.

She was about to wear out her one nice dress, the lavender taffeta. She had completely abandoned her more bohemian garb except when she was out with Kit. She had even given up her signature topknot for a stylish upsweep.

She attended so many elaborate meals in her honor, she was beginning to put on weight. Not that her tall, slender frame was ill-used by the extra curves. Kit could only smile at her blossoming beauty.

He continued to live with her and did not broach the topic of marriage. He still felt odd and upset about it and she sensed this. She mentioned once in passing something about how she might consider entering into a "handfasting," whatever that was. She seemed to feel this might be a symbolic, but nonlegal, bond that contained elements of compromise. He didn't pursue it. He just figured she would eventually get pregnant and then he'd see where she really stood on the marriage question.

"You won't believe who I met with the other afternoon," she said, then answered her own question. "George Hauser."

"What the devil did he want?" said Kit. "I thought his future was pretty bright."

"He's got a world of family trouble brewing. That oldest daughter of his is a handful. I solved all his problems for him and a few other people's at the same time. I don't know how this town ever got along without me."

"Bella Valentine saves the world!"

She playfully punched him in the shoulder.

"So how did you work this magic?"

"Can't tell," she said. "All my consultations are confidential. Like a priest or a doctor. Read today's paper, though. There was an interesting announcement."

"Where are you off to tonight?" He helped her lace her much-hated corset. That she was willing to don one for the sake of fashion spoke loudly of her new commitment to her career among the gentry of Leadville society.

"Tabor's. He's throwing a dinner for his wife's birthday." She glanced over her shoulder with a smirk. "Wonder if that tart, Baby Doe, is on the guest list?"

Elizabeth McCourt Doe, known to her friends and enemies alike as "Baby," was Leadville's newest gossip target. The pretty divorcée with golden curls had caught the eye of Colorado's lieutenant governor.

"You know, I'm good at lacing corsets," he said as he wrapped his arms around her now-tiny waist to tie the laces in front. He lightly kissed her neck. "Maybe I could get work as a lady's maid."

"I meet plenty of ladies who'd rather have you *un*lacing them. But forget it. You're mine, remember?"

"Yes, ma'am."

"Remind me again about the forks. It's always so confusing."

"Work from the outside *in*. If there's a fork up above the plate, save it for the dessert. And if it's some funny-looking little tiny thing, it's probably for seafood."

"Thanks." She gave him a quick kiss before she hurried out the door. He followed her to the porch and watched the gilded Tabor carriage with its uniformed driver bear her away into the chilly summer night.

He ambled down to Harrison Street, making the usual rounds. He picked up a discarded newspaper to read whatever startling announcement Bella had teasingly referred to.

He stood under the yellow light of a gas street lamp and scanned the small print of the *Herald*.

"I'll be damned," he exclaimed when his eyes fastened on the headline: EYE DAZZLER TO REOPEN WITH NEW INVESTMENT FROM MINERAL BANK.

The story described how George Hauser was to be made a partner in the Eye Dazzler in return for a large investment in the mine. Christopher Ridenour was to remain chief operating officer and head of all accounting functions. A new superintendent was being brought in from California.

Ridenour was quoted as being "delighted" with the arrangement and promised that the Dazzler would reopen by the fall. Kit could not figure out Bella's role in all this. How did George Hauser's family problems lead to a partnership with Ridenour when he could have easily fore-closed on the Dazzler and gotten it in the bankruptcy pro-ceedings? This did not make sense.

Upon turning the corner of State Street, Kit noticed that the High Life Club was dark. He walked past its once-dazzling twin bay windows and saw a FOR SALE sign posted in one of them. The sign directed interested parties to inquire at the Mineral Bank. This would be in keeping with Hauser's game plan. He would not want to sully his flaw-lessly moral reputation by owning as tawdry a business as the High Life.

Kit's gaze floated above the sign and he caught his own reflection in the dark glass. The bright lights of State Street illuminated him just enough to make his image visible, if distorted and ghoulish.

And over his shoulder was another familiar face: Ian Greene. His reflection was so faint he could almost be mis-taken for a smear on the window pane. Thoughts about Christopher never failed to summon the ghost of Ian Greene. Would he never rest in peace?

Twenty-six

Kit banged the big door knocker of the Black Lace House, though no light shone from the windows. That no servants were at home made him wonder if Chris's money woes were actually worse than the cheery article in the *Herald* intimated. He sat down on the porch in the shadows of the street lamp and waited.

If the Eye Dazzler was to reopen, he was going to use any means necessary to get a job there, perhaps as Christopher's assistant. Chris would have no reason to hold his sordid reputation against him, as other potential employers had, by God. He made up his mind he would do anything to get the job. Anything. Even resort to hints of blackmail if he had to. The Ridenour family owed him something for all he had been made to suffer. Right?

His conscience pinched at him. He was no Sadie Branch. He could not take advantage of Christopher like that. He already loathed himself enough. No need to add to the remorse that freighted his soul.

He began to sweat and rocked back and forth on the porch chair. His mouth felt dry and he had almost decided to leave when he saw a tall figure turn the corner of Third Street.

Christopher walked at a fair clip using only a cane now.

He jumped when he saw Kit's shape in the porch shadows. "Who's there? I have a gun!"

"Since when did you start carrying a gun?" Kit struck a match to light the doorway.

A smile of relief washed over Ridenour's face. He held his heart in a theatrical gesture. "You nearly scared the life out of me."

"I just came to see how you were doing."

"It's nice of you to come. I haven't seen you since the day we climbed out of the mine together and they carried me off to the hospital. I had hoped you might visit, but—please, come in. Let me pour you a drink."

Kit followed him into the parlor. He sat down in a formal way, as though it were the first time he had ever visited this house, while Ridenour lit several lamps. Chris hobbled around on his still-bandaged and splinted ankle, but seemed to be able to place some weight on it.

"How's the foot?"

"Better every day, though they were forced to amputate two of my toes. At least I'm finally free of those stupid crutches. Is brandy all right? It's all I have." Christopher glanced up with an apologetic smile, then turned his eyes down again, just like he always used to. Ever the downcast red-gold lashes.

"That's fine." Kit took the snifter and gulped down the fiery contents without a pause.

Neither man seemed able to start the conversation. Finally, Christopher said, "Where have you been keeping yourself?"

"Staying with a friend. Her name's Bella." He stood up and paced around the room, pausing to pour another glass of brandy. "I think you know her."

"Bella Valentine? The girl who reads tarot cards and talks to the dead?"

"Yeah, she's a good friend."

The young man looked worried. "Kit, what on earth possessed you to tell her about you and me, about that night?"

"I never told her anything. How could I have? I didn't know myself. Why do you think she knows about that?"

"During a séance she fell into a trance and described the scene as though she had witnessed it. I was mortified."

Kit groaned. So she had seen it in a vision. Maybe she did have clairvoyant powers after all. She probably knew about Ian Greene too.

But if she knew these things about him, why hadn't she started to shun him like his uncle had? Oh well, it didn't make any difference. He couldn't face her now. He could not bear to live with her knowing what she knew of his indiscretions.

His future looked about as bright and cheery as the trim on the Black Lace House. He breathed the uneasy freedom of someone who had nothing left to lose.

"You do believe me about that night, don't you?" said Ridenour.

"I don't know."

"It's *important* that you do. For my sake *and* yours. For the sake of our *reputations*. Once I'm married, I can't afford a scandal like that."

"You really think you'll get married some day?"

Christopher drew an uneasy breath. "I'm getting married a week from Saturday."

"What?"

"I dined at her house tonight with her and her parents."

"Who in the world—?"

"Miss Georgina Hauser."

"Old Hauser's daughter? I thought she had a beau."

" 'Had' is correct. He was killed in that riot at the Eye Dazzler."

"She sure changes directions quick."

"It's not really funny. There's a problem, you see. She's expecting a baby."

"So now she's a fiancé short?"

"Not anymore." Christopher grinned in a bashful way. "Her father approached me the other day and offered to invest a hundred thousand dollars in the Eye Dazzler to get it open again, if . . . I would consent to marry her and save the family from disgrace."

Kit curbed the urge to groan. "Old Man Hauser's buying a son-in-law for a hundred thousand dollars?"

"That's a vulgar way to put it, but yes, essentially." He seemed to hear his friend's silent groan and felt compelled to add, "I don't mind. And it's not just the money. The Hausers are well respected in this town. They move in the highest circles. They've always enjoyed a spotless reputation—well, until this girl's misadventure came to light, of course. But still, some of that respectability is bound to wash over onto me. Don't you think? And then *I'll* be respectable too. Received in the finest houses. Not an outcast anymore."

"You never even liked George Hauser. You didn't trust him, remember?"

"Maybe I was wrong about him." The young man's voice began to gallop with enthusiasm. "He took me to lunch at the Argot Club. Orson Ridenour never got an invitation to dine there. And he was richer than half its members. George says he'll sponsor me for membership. Imagine that."

"But *marriage*, Chris. Think about it. It's not just a business deal."

"I need that money, Kit. I don't have a choice. I'm mortgaged to the eyeballs. Without Hauser's investment, I'd lose the Dazzler. Not to mention this house and everything else I own. Everything my mother worked so hard to give me. All the wonderful gifts Orson gave me. I won't let that happen. I won't be poor again, not ever."

"But—"

"You don't know what it's like to be poor, so don't make judgments about me."

Kit's eyes widened to see his formerly meek friend display such passion. "My family wasn't rich. We never had any spare money—"

"Did you have to eat the refuse from the alleyways behind restaurants to keep from starving?"

"Well, no."

"Did your mother have to share her bed with the landlord because it was either that or eviction?"

"All right. *Je*-sus! You've made your point." Kit dismounted from his moral high horse and hung his head.

"What does this Georgina say to it all? Is it going to be like a real marriage? Is she going to live with you and everything?"

"I don't know, really. I suppose it will all work out somehow. I spoke with her tonight and she's quite agreeable. Obviously, it's not a love match for either of us. We barely know each other. Whenever she came to dinner here, she spent all her time talking to you. Remember?"

Kit nodded. He ached a little at his friend's effort to joke about something so serious.

"She's still grieving for her fiancé, of course, but she told me she was grateful for my offer of help. She called me her salvation, in fact. I pity her the awful circumstance she finds herself in. My own mother was once in that situation and she used to say people can be awfully cruel."

"Well, good for you, I guess. You're a prince."

"Why can't you just be happy for me?"

"Don't be so defensive. I guess if you're happy, that's all that matters."

"Remember what you told me that day in the mine? That I didn't know what might be waiting for me? That it might be marvelous?" Ridenour smiled luminously. "Think of it— by Christmas I'll be a father. I never imagined that would happen."

"It's not like it's *your* kid."

"Legally, it will be. Oh, you won't believe this: Mr. Hauser gave me a thousand dollars *in cash* tonight as evidence of his good intentions. When I left, he handed me an envelope and I though it was just filled with legal papers or something, then I got out under a street lamp and opened it. Ten one hundred dollar bills! I walked all the way home afraid I'd be robbed. That's why I was so startled to see you on the front porch."

Christopher quickly debated something in his mind, then blurted out, "Kit, how much money did you lose at the High Life that night before you came to live with us?"

"Two thousand seven hundred and forty dollars. I remember it well."

"I still feel bad about that."

Kit shrugged. "Spilt milk."

"You know, I'm not even certain that Mother didn't somehow *arrange* for you to lose that money. Those faro dealers are clever. They can manipulate things when they want to. She told me she was going to find a way to induce you to come live with us. She told me that the night before it happened. In a manner of speaking, one could suggest that I *owe* you that money." With a shaky smile, Christopher held out the plump envelope. "Here. Consider this a down payment."

"What?" Kit did not at first understand where Christopher was going with this line of thought.

"I know you must be stretched for cash," Ridenour continued, gaining momentum. "Perhaps if you had some traveling money . . ."

He's trying to get rid of me, Kit realized. He sees me as a potential embarrassment. Or some kind of threat. Or perhaps a temptation.

"And you could take Miss Valentine with you." He leaned a little farther, straining to hand his friend the money without actually getting up and walking on his recovering foot.

Kit shook his head in cynical disbelief as he saw himself rise and reach for it. He could only think: Lucinda was right, I am the biggest whore of all. And an inconvenient whore, at that. He wants me out of town. And Bella, too. My awful reputation might spoil his ambitious climb up the social ladder. Nothing must come between him and the Eye Dazzler riches.

Truly his mother's son.

In leaving the house, Kit caught a glimpse of the second parlor. In it still hung the Eye Dazzler rug, its dancing geometry beckoning, as always, but he left wondering why Orson Ridenour had ever believed it was lucky. If he were Chris, he would burn it.

———

Kit wandered through the tawdry night glamour of Leadville's streets for the last time, ending up at the new railway station. The place was nearly deserted though a few homeless denizens made beds of the wooden benches near the platform. He had no idea when the next train was due or where it was headed. He just knew he would be on it.

He would send Bella a telegram in the morning to let her know he had gone, then he would compose a nice letter on the train to try and smooth it all out with her. That he would write such a letter and leave such a girl pained him too much to think about right now but he knew he had no choice. He had only himself to blame.

He found an empty bench—actually, its occupant had rolled off in his sleep or drunken stupor and now lay beneath it. He stepped over the man's snoring body and made himself comfortable.

———

"Running out on me?"

Kit jerked awake at the sound of that familiar voice. He rubbed his eyes, blinded by the blazing mountain sun as it scalded the white pine train platform with its morning light.

"Bella? How the devil did you know I was here?" Then he slapped his forehead. "Why bother to ask such questions? You'd think I'd have learned by now." He patted the wooden seat next to him and she sat. "I think maybe I should leave. This town's about used up with me, don't you think?" He took a deep breath and decided to add, "Interested in coming along?"

"Depends on where you're headed, I guess."

This flicker of interest gave him courage. "I've got money." He tapped his breast pocket. "One thousand dollars. I counted it twice."

"I'm almost afraid to ask how you came by it."

"As well you should be. Let's just say a debt's been paid and leave it at that."

She gazed off down the street at the mountain range in the distance. The snow-capped summits of Mount Massive and Mount Elbert glistened in the summer sun.

"I suppose you already know who's getting married in a week?" he said.

She pursed her full lips. "The marriage was actually *my* idea. Old Hauser came to me in a state, didn't know what to do. Remember? I told you. The girl was his favorite. He couldn't bear to abandon her, but he couldn't stand the prospect of scandal either. I just made some discreet suggestions, that's all. That a certain young man might be willing to help out for a certain sum of money."

Kit shook his head in amazement. There was no end to her scheming. He had to laugh, but then he sobered. "You know all about the reason I left the Black Lace House, don't you? About that night. About me and Christopher."

"Yes," she said. She looked down at her feet. A long-legged spider made its way across the pine flooring and she reached out to crush it with the toe of her sandal.

Kit now knew Eden had lied to him. He had wondered at the time because of her odd manner, but he was so eager to believe her. He couldn't be mad at her. She was probably just trying to protect him or Bella or simply the future.

"You don't hold it against me?" he said.

"Would I be here if I did?"

"My uncle couldn't get quit of me fast enough after he found out."

"I'm not as judgmental as *some* people." She looked at him archly so there would be no mistaking the fact that by "some" she meant *him,* not his uncle, nor anyone else, for that matter.

He met her eyes. Poetic justice must be sweet. She looked like she'd swallowed a candy store.

"I've changed," he said.

"You're answering a question I never asked, honey."

Neither knew where else to take this uncomfortable conversation, so Bella changed the subject.

"A telegram came for you." She pulled it from her leather shoulder bag.

A quick glance told him it was from *Bradley J. Randall.* A cold stab of tension shot through him. He cleared his throat and read aloud:

JOB OPENING HERE AT SMITHSONIAN [STOP] PERFECT FOR YOU [STOP] LET ME KNOW BY 12TH INSTANT [STOP] HADLEY AND EDEN MISS YOU [STOP]

"My, my," said Bella. "A job in Washington City. I'm impressed. He must not still be mad at you."

"Well, you'll notice only 'Hadley and Eden' miss me. I can see Eden's hand in this. She wants us to reconcile. She thinks she caused the breach, but she's wrong. It's always been there."

"What's your answer going to be?"

"It's a tempting offer, I guess. My uncle obviously thinks I'm still capable of rejoining the world of respectable working dogs like himself. Good job, nice house, flawless reputation, beautiful wife, nine charming children—"

"Nine?" Bella pulled a face of mock-horror.

"—church on Sunday morning to repent the sins of Saturday night, which would only include a few too many glasses at the club or maybe losing too much at cards, but not more than would be prudent."

"Sounds like a perfect life," she said with a counterfeit sigh.

"Yes, it does . . . for somebody."

They sat silently for several seconds, then he gave her a sidelong glance. "Want to go to India?"

The cynical edge to her slender face melted into a look of relieved satisfaction. "I'm already packed."